Someone to Hold

WILD WIDOWS SERIES
BOOK TWO

MARIE FORCE

Someone to Hold
Wild Widows Series, Book 2
By: Marie Force

Published by HTJB, Inc.
Copyright 2022. HTJB, Inc.
Cover Design by Kristina Brinton
Print Layout: E-book Formatting Fairies
ISBN: 978-1952793882

*"To live in this world
you must be able
to do three things:
to love what is mortal;
to hold it
against your bones knowing
your own life depends on it;
and, when the time comes to let it go,
to let it go."*
—Mary Oliver

One

IRIS

There's something to be said for liquid courage. There's also something to be said for knowing my three kids are safe at home with their grandparents, and I'm off duty for the next few days. I haven't often had that kind of freedom since I lost my husband and partner in all things and became a single parent overnight.

As the night around the campfire at Bethany Beach fades into early the next morning, I'm buzzed and fully relaxed for the first time in longer than I can remember. Later, I'll blame the booze, but I'm not so far gone that I don't know exactly what I'm doing when I "accidentally" end up in the wrong bed at two o'clock in the morning.

I could also blame the bathroom that connects our two bedrooms for the "mishap" in an unfamiliar weekend rental house.

The truth of the matter is I want this man, and I suspect he might feel the same way about me, but he'll never do anything about it out of loyalty to his late wife. I understand that kind of loyalty better than most people ever could. I'm extremely loyal to

Mike and the memory of the life we had together. But I'm also a strong believer that life is for the living, and we've both got a whole lot of living left to do.

Starting right now.

I'm one breath shy of full-on hyperventilation when I creep into Gage's room and slide into his bed, completely naked.

My greatest fear is losing one of my closest friends in the "after," as we refer to the period after great loss.

My second greatest fear is that I'll never again take a risk because I'm too afraid of suffering more loss.

Neither of those things can happen. I won't allow it.

I can tell by the change in his breathing that Gage is awake and knows someone got into bed with him.

I hold my breath while I wait to see what he'll do about it.

He turns on the light, temporarily blinding me, which gives me half a second to plan my next move.

I prop myself on my elbows, let the covers slip to my waist and turn toward the light. "What the hell..." I feign shock at seeing him there. "Whoops." I hiccup for effect. "What're you doing in my bed?" To my great disappointment, he's wearing an army-green T-shirt. I was hoping for the bare-chest version, which is quite something. I know this from having seen him swim in my pool.

"Funny," he says, his gaze dropping to my bare breasts. "I was just about to ask you the same thing."

"I guess I took a wrong turn out of the bathroom. Sorry." I start to get out of bed while hoping and praying he'll stop me.

"Iris."

I turn to him, brow raised, breasts bare.

"What're you really doing in here?" His gaze drops again to my breasts, which aren't bad—if I do say so myself—considering they've nursed three babies.

"I told you. Too much wine, followed by a wrong turn out of the bathroom."

He's torn. I can see that in the hungry way he stares at my

breasts and in the fiery look in his gaze when it shifts to my face. "I never imagined you sleeping naked."

"Can't do it at home with three little ones crawling all over me."

He's not exactly kicking me out.

"I, um... I can go. Sorry to bother you."

"Wait."

Best word ever.

"Was there something else?" I ask as innocently as possible, even as my heart pounds and my nipples tingle in a way they haven't in a long time.

"What do you really want?"

I feign confusion, and wish I was filming this performance so I could submit it for awards—and as a training video for other widows trying to jumpstart their love lives. "Uh, well, eight hours of sleep would be cool. That never happens."

"And that's it? That's all you want?"

I stretch out on my side, facing him, head propped on my upturned hand. "Is there something *you* want?"

His face tightens with tension and what might be distress. We can't have that.

"Never mind. Don't answer that. I'll just see you in the morning."

"Don't go."

No, wait, *those* are the best words ever. They're gruffly spoken, as if he's not sure he should've said them. But he doesn't take them back.

I drop down so my head is on the pillow, hands under my cheek. "I'm here."

He releases a short laugh. "Believe me, I know."

"It was an honest mistake."

"Was it, though?"

"What're you accusing me of?" I ask, full of innocence.

He rolls his dark eyes and runs a hand through wavy dark hair. "So many things."

I love that I'm not fooling him at all, but he still doesn't ask me to go. "You want to talk or sleep?"

"Is there a third option?" he asks, shocking me for a second.

"Always."

He tips his head as if considering whether I mean that.

I do. I adore him for so many reasons, and I've had a wicked crush on him for almost as long as I've known him. It's almost two years since he joined the Wild Widows, which was nearly a year after he'd lost his wife and daughters. Hard to believe sometimes the way time goes by after the worst kind of loss. It marches on with no consideration whatsoever for broken hearts or shattered lives.

Gage's loss was worse than most. His wife and twin eight-year-old daughters were killed by a drunk driver. I wonder all the time what he was like before that unimaginable loss. He doesn't smile much, and his arresting face wears the grief he carries with him. It's hard to articulate what I mean by that, but I can *see* his grief whenever I look at him, and that pains me. I'm not sure when his pain became mine, too, but it's been that way for a while.

"If I choose door number three, will it make everything different between us?" he asks.

"It could, but different isn't necessarily bad, is it?"

"I rely on your friendship to get me through the days."

His stark confession touches me deeply.

"Likewise."

"So maybe we shouldn't do anything to screw that up, huh?"

I'm not sure where the courage comes from, because my buzz has worn off, but I slide across the bed so I'm only a few inches from him. "If we both agree not to let it screw up anything, we should be fine, right?"

His hand lands on my shoulder like the hottest of brands.

I shiver under his touch even as I try to project calm coolness.

"I haven't been with anyone since Natasha."

"I know."

"How do you know?"

He never speaks about his personal life in our group meetings, so I don't know anything for certain. It's more of a guess. "I just do. I know you."

"That makes this a bigger deal than it would be otherwise."

"I get it." He and the other Wild Widows know I had sex with a random guy shortly after Mike died so I didn't have to dread the first time with someone else. I regretted it almost immediately, but right now, I'm glad I did it. "We can just sleep together. Nothing has to happen."

His hand slides down my arm to take hold of my hand, which he places on his erection. "You did that."

I lick lips gone dry at realizing he's big all over. "Did I?"

He nods. "What do you plan to do about it?"

"What do you want me to do?"

Shrugging, he says, "Whatever you want."

Gulp. We expected to spend the rest of our lives with other people. No matter how well we know each other—and I know him better than people I've known for decades—it's still strange to be intimate with anyone other than Mike, or for Gage to do this with someone other than Natasha.

I move so I'm on my knees.

He sits up, his back against the headboard.

I consider asking him to kill the light but decide against it as I reach up to caress his face. He's always so serious, so buttoned down, so heartbroken. More than anything, I want to give him some relief from the constant grind of relentless grief.

Something that would've been no big deal back in the day is the biggest of deals as I straddle his lap and lean in to kiss him for the first time. I keep it simple, just lips touching lips, waiting to see if he's with me.

His hands land on my hips to pull me closer as he tips his head to kiss me back.

The second his tongue brushes against mine, I'm sunk.

How many nights have I sat at Wild Widows meetings

5

wondering what it would be like to be with him? How many times have I pondered what he was like before an unspeakable tragedy changed him forever? How many times have I wondered if it would be weird to do this with a friend I met through a group of widows?

Too many to count.

PS, it's not weird. It's hot.

He's like a man unleashed with years of pent-up desire directed entirely at me.

But then it hits me. Is it for me, or is it the end of the dry spell that has him so turned on?

I try to push that thought away to fully enjoy what's happening in the moment, but the question resonates like a bass drum through my head, demanding attention.

"What's wrong?" he asks when he moves from my lips to my neck while cupping my breasts and teasing my nipples.

"Could I ask you something?"

"Sure."

"Is this about me, or would any naked woman have done the trick?"

He goes still.

I instantly regret asking the question, but I still want to know.

"Of course it's about you. Do you think, after everything I've been through, that I could just do *this* with some random woman?"

"I did it with some random guy."

"And there's nothing wrong with that if it's what you needed at the time, but please don't think any warm body would've worked for me, Iris, especially the first time. That's simply not true."

"Oh. Okay. Please continue, then."

He sighs and leans his forehead against mine. "I sort of thought there might be something, you know, between us…"

"You did?"

"I see the way you look at me sometimes, as if you want to do dirty things to me."

I sputter with laughter. "I do not look at you that way!"

"Yes, you do."

Shaking my head, I lean in to kiss him. "You're seeing things."

He squeezes my ass, and just that is all it takes to reignite the fire. "No, I'm not."

"Would you ever have done anything about it?"

"I'm not sure." He continues to run his hands over my back as he studies me in that intense way of his. "I would've been worried about messing up a friendship I rely on."

"That could never happen, Gage. Ever."

"Sure, it can. We all know sex changes things."

"We won't let that happen."

"Do you promise?"

"That'll be an easy promise to keep."

"I'm glad you pretended to get into the wrong bed."

"I didn't pretend! I was genuinely confused."

"Now you're just lying to my face."

GAGE

SHE'S adorable when she lies, but then again, she's adorable all the time. But she's so much more than that. She's one of the best friends I've ever had and a huge reason why I'm still functioning after losing everything that mattered to me.

Have I thought about what it might be like to get naked with her?

Yep. Quite often, in fact, but I sure as hell didn't expect it to happen the way it did. I'm forty-one years old, long past the days when a naked woman showed up in my bed and played it off as an accident. In fact, that scenario has never happened before tonight.

The sexual part of me is waking up from years of dormancy

after losing my love. It reminds me of a limb coming back to life with pins and needles. I haven't wanted anyone else or given much thought to that part of myself until Iris turned up naked in my bed.

I want her, and not just because she's a handy naked body.

I feel safe with her. I love her and she loves me. We take care of each other every day in big ways and small.

Kissing her feels right. Touching her soft skin, having her touch me... It's so good, it makes me feel guilty for wanting someone other than Natasha this much. Everyone in my life has been pushing me for years now to start over with someone new. I'm not sure if Iris is going to be my someone new, but I push past the guilt, determined to make this good for her.

If I stay focused on her, I might be able to get through this without embarrassing myself by breaking down or something equally awful.

I shift us so I'm on top. I kiss her everywhere, making her come twice before it occurs to me that we might need birth control. "I don't have condoms."

"It's okay," she says, sounding breathless from the second orgasm. "I'm on the pill to keep my periods regular."

It goes without saying that widows who've mostly avoided sex since our losses are clean, so I don't bother to broach that subject.

As I have sex with a woman for the first time since I lost my wife, I keep my gaze fixed on Iris's gorgeous face, determined to stay in the present when the past calls to me like a siren. Natasha used to say that life is for the living. That was one of her favorite sayings. I need to believe she meant it and would want me to be happy without her, even if that has seemed impossible at times.

Iris places her hands on my face and kisses me with sweet affection that's exactly what I need. She gets it. She knows this is a big deal for me. Being with her makes it easier than it would've been with anyone else.

I go slow and try not to let this be over before it begins, but control is in short supply when Iris wraps her legs around my hips and moves with me like we've been lovers for longer than ten minutes. Her enthusiasm triggers something in me that's been asleep for years, and I let go of all the worries, fears, sadness, grief and regret.

I give myself permission to take everything she has to give and to fully enjoy it.

Two

IRIS

I wake facedown in Gage's bed, with every muscle in my body on fire with soreness after a night unlike any other.

Four times.

We did it *four times.*

He was like a wild man, unleashed and desperate, and I was right there with him every step of the way.

I feel sick with guilt.

I loved my husband with every part of me. We had great sex. But what I had with Gage goes beyond anything I've experienced with *anyone*.

That's not how it should be.

Mike was the love of my life, the father of my children, the man I wanted to be with forever. I refuse to compare him or our relationship with anyone else. There is no comparison.

I hear a baby crying and wonder how Roni's first night sleeping with Derek went after they got engaged.

And I wonder where Gage has gone or if his world is as rocked by what transpired overnight as mine is.

I get out of bed and wince. Everything hurts. Christ have mercy, the man was relentless.

"Be careful what you wish for, girlfriend," I mutter as I turn the shower in our shared bathroom to the hottest setting. While I wait for the water to heat up, I notice Gage's toothbrush and razor on the sink next to a bag with other items, which makes me realize how long it's been since I shared a bathroom with a man.

Since I shared much of anything with a man.

Judging by the burn between my legs and the aching muscles in every part of my body, I'm desperately out of shape in the sex department despite daily yoga.

Yoga is no match for Gage Collier.

After I'm dressed, I retrieve my phone off the charger in my own bedroom, feeling guilty for not having brought it into Gage's room last night. What if there'd been an emergency at home and I'd been so busy having sex that I missed it?

My mom has sent pictures of the kids having pancakes this morning.

Thankfully, everyone looks happy, and I didn't miss anything important.

I respond to thank her for the pictures and ask her to tell the kids I miss them, but that's a lie. I don't miss them. I spend every waking moment with them or caring for them or thinking of them or doing something for one of them. I'll be right back to that when I get home tomorrow night. Today and tomorrow is all about me, my friends, my needs and my wants. I plan to enjoy every second of it.

Before I venture out to see the others, I take a quick look at Instagram.

Gage's inspirational posts are usually my first stop every morning.

He's posted a photo of the sunrise at Bethany Beach, which means he's been up for hours.

Even after tremendous loss, life can still be beautiful, he wrote. *You never know what's coming right around the next bend, and anything is still possible, even after the worst has happened. It's important that we be open to these experiences when they present themselves to us as a reminder that life goes on, even when you think it won't.*

He included the usual widow hashtags and already has more than a hundred likes and twenty-five comments on his post. He's become required reading in widow circles as he documents his journey and shares insights that resonate with so many.

Today's post is particularly poignant, as I'm certain he's speaking directly to me. At least I'd like to think so.

I need to play this cool and not act like last night was the start of some big romance. It was sex. It was two people who needed a release. Or four of them. That's all it was, and I vow to not make it into something it's not and to keep my promise to him to not let it screw up a friendship we both rely on.

I walk out of the bedroom into the kitchen, where Hallie is overseeing something on the stove, and Adrian is starting another pot of coffee.

"Morning," Hallie says. She's sporting a purple streak in the front of her short blonde hair and looks rested and refreshed. "Coffee?"

"Please, God," I respond.

She laughs and pours me a cup, gesturing to the cream, oat milk, almond milk and every type of real and fake sugar.

"Thanks." I stir in almond milk and Stevia. "Did you sleep well?"

"Like a dead woman. I haven't slept like that in a long time. Since before..."

She means before she lost her wife, Gwen, to suicide.

"I'm so glad you had a restful night."

"How about you?" Hallie asks.

I wonder if my face turns bright red, telling everyone I didn't sleep a wink because I was too busy having sex with Gage. And where is he anyway?

"I slept great. What's for breakfast?"

Hallie insisted on cooking for us this weekend, because, as she said, she used to love to cook and hasn't done it in ages. "French toast casserole with Vermont maple syrup, sausage, bacon and fruit salad."

"Am I drooling?"

Hallie leans in for a closer look. "Not quite, but close."

"Thank you so much for cooking for us."

"I'm so happy to do it. I'd forgotten how much I enjoy it."

"You look happy. It's nice to see."

"It's nice to feel. Been a while for that, too."

Roni is on the sofa, breastfeeding Dylan with a receiving blanket tossed over them. Derek is next to her, checking his phone. The two of them look sleepy and satisfied.

I'm so thrilled that they've found each other and committed to a future together, but I'll confess to being a tiny bit jealous, too. I'm a year and a half ahead of Roni in my widow journey and no closer to figuring out what's next than I was on the day of Mike's plane crash. Since then, my life has been more about survival than planning. I have three grieving kids to care for, a home to manage and a thousand decisions to make every day on my own.

Who the hell has the time to make plans?

Granted, I know how fortunate I am to not have to work on top of everything else. Mike had excellent life insurance that will carry us through until my youngest is in school all day. At that point, I'll have to get a job and start saving for college.

It's daunting. All of it. But I don't need to think about that stuff today or tomorrow, and so I push it all to the back of my mind to focus on my friends and myself and this badly needed break from my usual routine.

"Where's everyone else?"

"They went for a beach walk," Joy said. "Too damned cold for me."

"Me, too." I join Roni and Derek on the sofa and toss a throw blanket over my lap. "I'll burp him if you want to stretch."

"Are you sure?" Roni asks.

"I'd love to. I miss the baby stage. It's all fun and games until they start talking back."

Roni hands Dylan over to me, along with the receiving blanket that I put over my shoulder. "My son will never talk back to me, will you, sweet boy?"

"Haha, you wish," I tell her as she gets up to stretch her arms over her head. "He'll be sassing you long before you're ready for that."

Adrian stokes the fire in the woodstove and then goes outside to get more wood.

"How does he seem to be doing?" I ask the others.

"He's okay," Kinsley said. "The baby is with his sister this weekend, and she's been a big help since his mother-in-law died. But she works full time and has kids of her own, so he's still looking for someone to help him when he's working."

"I told him I'd do it," Wynter says when she plops down in front of the fire. She's the youngest of the Wild Widows, having lost her young husband to bone cancer.

"What did he say?" Joy asks.

"I don't think he took me seriously."

"Did you mean it seriously?" I ask her.

"I did, or I wouldn't have offered."

Wynter's testy retort doesn't bother me. We've learned she's mostly all bark and no bite and is pissed off at the shitty hand she's been dealt. And who can blame her? I can't for the life of me imagine coping with what she has at such a young age. It was rough enough at thirty-three when I had some maturity under my belt.

Nothing can prepare you for this journey, though. That's something we've all learned the hard way.

Adrian comes back in with the wood and stacks it on the hearth. He's tall, Black, muscular and handsome as hell. His wife's death in childbirth followed by his mother-in-law's sudden passing has been devastating, but he seems to be bouncing back somewhat. We were relieved when he decided to come this weekend and that he was able to leave the baby with his sister, so he gets a break that he desperately needs.

I'm dying for another minute alone with Roni, who's become my closest friend in the group, to tell her about what happened with Gage.

"Did you get some sleep?" Roni asks when she sits next to me on the sofa.

With my free hand, I move my coffee away from Roni, who doesn't like the smell of it.

"I did. How about you?"

Roni's cute face flushes with color. "Some."

"I'm going to check on Maeve," Derek says as he puts his phone to his ear and heads for the deck.

"Was it something I said?"

Roni laughs. "He doesn't want to listen to us talk about him."

"I take it things went well?"

"Um, yeah, you could say that."

"And you're okay?"

Gage wasn't the only one in our side-by-side rental houses having sex for the first time after their loss.

"I'm surprisingly okay, but I suppose that's because Derek and I waited until I felt ready. Even though part of me is aching for other reasons. Patrick is very much on my mind, as always."

"I understand. He's part of everything, even your relationship with Derek."

"Yes, he is, and I'm so glad to be with people who understand how strange it all is."

"Thank goodness for the Wild Widows."

"I say that every day."

Hallie, Joy and Kinsley join us on the sofa.

"Are we talking about how Roni feels after having sex with Derek for the first time?" Joy asks, sparking laughter.

"What would we do without you, Joy, to cut through the bullshit?" Hallie asks.

"You'd all be floundering around like fools, wanting to know the deets, but too afraid to ask," Joy says. "That's why you need Mama Joy around. Tell us everything and leave nothing out."

Roni giggles at the intense look Joy gives her. "It was great—and heartbreaking at the same time." She shrugs. "You know what I mean."

"We do." Kinsley lost her husband to pancreatic cancer and is raising their two kids on her own now. "I haven't gotten there yet, but I hope maybe someday I will."

"You will, Kins," I assure her. "Of course you will."

"I'm not sure I want to. The thought of starting over again with someone new is just so... exhausting."

"It is when it's not the right person," Hallie said.

"Have you been holding out on us, girl?" Joy asks.

"No, no," Hallie says, laughing. "I just remember all the dating I did before I met Gwen and how different it was from the start with her."

"I know what you mean," Kinsley says. "It was like that when I met Rory, too. Instantly different."

"Whereas I couldn't stand Mike when I first met him," I confess.

"Seriously?" Hallie asks. "I've never heard you say that before."

"He was an obnoxious jerk. Later, I found out it was because he liked me and was so nervous, he acted like an idiot." I smile as I recall another long-ago beach weekend with friends. "Fortunately, he got it together and showed me his true self before I could run from him screaming."

"That's so sweet," Kinsley says. "That he was so nervous, he lost his shit."

"I found out later that our friends had told him they wanted to fix him up with me, and when he saw me for the first time, he always said he fell instantly in love and then nearly ruined it completely."

"I love that," Roni says with a sigh.

"I was his first real girlfriend," I tell them. "I had to teach him everything. From when to bring flowers to a woman—not only after a fight—to the difference between sex and romance to where the clitoris is located. You name it, I taught him, and he was a very willing student."

The girls lose it laughing at the word *clitoris*, and my heart aches for him as I recall those long-ago days and nights with Mike. He'd had sex before me, but I taught him the difference between basic sex and great sex. However, I've never had as many orgasms in my life as I did last night, but I can't tell them that. I won't tell anyone that. And I'll never tell them about the heart-break Mike later brought to our fledgling marriage when he decided to test his newfound knowledge on someone else. I try not to think about that dark time in our otherwise happy life together, or the excruciating effort it took to put our relationship back together.

"It's a crying shame to put in all that work only to lose him," Joy says with complete seriousness.

That sets us off laughing so hard, we resurface with tears in our eyes.

I wipe away my tears to find Gage has returned and is giving me a curious look. "What'd I miss, ladies?"

"Girl talk," Joy says. "You wouldn't understand."

"That's not true," he says, removing his winter coat, "and you know it."

Hallie gets up to check on breakfast as Derek comes in from the deck.

"Is it safe to return?" he asks.

"They were cackling like hens when I came in," Gage said.

Derek shoots Roni a look. "You'd better not have been talking about me."

"Why?" she asks. "Are you worried what I'd tell them would make them laugh?"

"Burn," Joy whispers, setting off another round of laughter.

I love these people so much.

When Christy and her friend Taylor first approached me about starting a group called the Wild Widows, I assumed that it wouldn't be for me, because there was certainly nothing "wild" about my widowhood except for the unrelenting grief that had me wondering how I'd ever survive the loss of my husband.

Turns out, the Wild Widows were just what I needed, and they continue to be long after Christy, Taylor and I held our first meeting for four young widows. Sadly, the group has grown in number since then as more young widows have reached out to us. Taylor is now remarried and has moved on from the group, but Christy and I have kept it going.

Hallie calls us to breakfast, which is every bit as delicious as I expected it to be.

"Am I allowed to eat the confectionary sugar with a spoon?" Wynter asks.

"Knock yourself out," Hallie says. "I bought it for this breakfast, so the rest is up for grabs."

Wynter scoops up a huge spoonful and pops it in her mouth.

"Ah, youth," Joy says. "I'd be in the hospital if I did that."

"Same," Naomi says, "and I'm not that much older than her." She lost her fiancé, David, to lymphoma two years ago. We had to talk her into coming this weekend, and I'm glad she finally relented. Sometimes she feels like she doesn't belong with us because she and David never got a chance to get married. We tell her she's no different from the rest of us. We're all learning to live without the person we loved the most.

"Don't be jealous, bitches," Wynter says as she loads up a second spoonful. "At least it's not coke."

"That's true," Joy said, "but sugar is every bit as addictive as coke and other drugs."

"Let me have my fun, will you please?" Wynter says.

"Have at it, girlfriend," Hallie says. "But we're allowed to say we told you so when you feel sick later."

"Noted." Wynter fills a third spoonful and shoots us a defiant look before eating it.

"My teeth hurt watching this," Gage says.

"Because your teeth are *old*." Wynter grins at him. "Young teeth don't hurt."

"Now you're just being mean," Gage says.

I want to tell her that if she'd seen him in bed last night, she wouldn't think there was anything old about him.

"Adrian," Joy says, as casual as can be, "Wynter the sugar junkie says she offered to be your nanny. What do you think of that?"

"It's very nice of her, but I'm sure she has better things to do than take care of my son."

"Actually, I don't," Wynter says. "And I wouldn't have offered if I didn't want to take care of Xavier. In case you haven't noticed, I love him, and I'd love to take care of him if it would help you."

I love the way Wynter can shock and surprise us in the span of two minutes. That's her special gift.

"What do you think, Adrian?" Joy asks.

"I'd love to have you help with Xavier, but only if you really want to."

"Duh, I just said I did."

"Then it's settled," Joy says, seeming pleased with herself. She's a bigwig corporate attorney and is good at mediating situations of all kinds.

"Good work, Mama Joy," Kinsley says. "Solver of problems."

"It's what I do all the livelong day," Joy says.

"Has anyone seen Lexi this morning?" Hallie asks.

"Not yet," Naomi says.

Lexi lost her husband Jim to ALS after a four-year battle that devastated her financially as well as emotionally. She said she couldn't afford the weekend away. We told her we didn't mind covering her share, but she hadn't felt right about that. We eventually talked her into coming anyway, but she's been quiet.

"I wish she wouldn't worry about not having the money for this," Adrian says. "Who cares about that? With so many of us chipping in, it hardly cost much of anything."

"We've all told her that," Naomi says. "I hope she can just relax and enjoy the time away."

Hearing about widows like Lexi, who were financially devastated by the loss of their spouses, makes me so thankful for Mike and his insistence on making sure we'd be okay without his income. As a corporate pilot, he had all the insurance he possibly could—and thank God for that. Some of it hasn't paid out yet, as we're still waiting for the accident report from the NTSB, but we have enough to get by, and for that, I'm thankful to him.

Gage and I insist on cleaning up the kitchen and send Hallie on a beach walk with Naomi, Kinsley, Joy, Wynter and Adrian. Roni and Derek took Dylan in for a nap and never came back out, not that we expected them to.

"That breakfast was incredible," Gage said. "I'm stuffed."

"Hallie is in her element cooking."

"She seems to be doing a little better."

I can barely bring myself to look at him without wanting to rip his clothes off and pick up where we left off. "Maybe."

"Iris."

I glance at him. "Yes?"

"What's wrong?"

Three

GAGE

She's barely looked at me since I came back from the beach earlier, and now I'm worried that we made a huge mistake last night, even if it didn't feel like one at the time.

"Nothing's wrong."

"Why won't you look at me, then?"

In a past life, I never would've forced the matter. I would've waited out Natasha while hoping whatever was going on didn't devolve into some big emotional battle. I've had a lot of time to think about why I did that, and the only thing I can come up with is that I was so afraid of making her mad that I didn't engage with her on things I probably should have. I hated when she was unhappy for any reason, especially if I had caused it.

I don't want to be that way anymore, thus my question to Iris.

"I can look at you," she says defiantly, giving me a hard stare. "See?"

"Are you sorry?"

"What? No, I'm sore, not sorry."

"How sore?"

"Not too bad. It's more of an awareness that something transpired than anything overly painful. And not so sore that I wouldn't want to do it again—right now, in fact—if I could."

I look around the empty room. "Why can't we?"

"They won't be out there for long."

"It's nice out today. They may hang for a while."

"So what you're saying..."

I take her hand and give a gentle tug in the direction of our adjoining rooms on the first floor. Derek and Roni have the main suite on the other side of the kitchen.

The door closes behind us with a loud click, followed by a pop as I lock it.

I turn to her, taking a visual inventory of her features. "You look tired."

"Gee, I wonder why?"

Smiling down at her, I touch my lips to hers. "Was it worth losing sleep?"

"You know it was."

I quickly remove her clothes and direct her to the bed, where I arrange her so she's splayed open on the edge of the mattress. Then I drop to my knees and lean in to soothe her soreness with my tongue.

"You didn't tell the girls about this, did you?"

"No," she says, gasping.

"This needs to belong just to us."

"Yes."

I have her on the verge of orgasm when her phone rings.

"I, uh... I have to get that. Might be my mom about the kids."

I pull back to let her up and steady her when her legs wobble under her. She grabs her phone off the bedside table where I only just put it and takes the call.

"Oh, hey." After listening for a second, she frowns. "Didn't you get my text?" And then, "No, I did text you. Hang on." She puts the phone on speaker. "Oh shit. I wrote the text, but never sent it. I'm so sorry, Rob. This is my weekend away with the widows. I told you about that, right?"

I'm so close to her, I can hear the other side of the conversation.

"I don't think you did. I'm at your house now."

"I'm so sorry. The kids are at my mom's. I'm sure they'd love to see you there."

"I'll swing by since I'm in town."

"Okay."

"You sound weird. Are you okay?"

"Yes, I'm good. It's nice to have a weekend away from it all."

"Well, enjoy yourself. I'll see you next weekend and talk to you before then."

"I'm really sorry I never sent that text, Rob."

"Don't be. It's all good."

"Love you."

"You, too."

While she's on the phone, I move to sit on the bed. When she turns to face me, she looks troubled.

I hand her the T-shirt I just took off her, and she puts it on.

"Sorry about that."

"That's Mike's brother, right?"

"Yeah, he comes to see us on Saturdays. Plays with the kids all afternoon. I thought I'd texted him about this weekend... I feel terrible. He drives an hour to come down from Baltimore."

"It's good of him to be there for you and the kids."

She sits next to me on the bed. "He's been a rock from the start. He and Mike were so close."

"I'm glad you've had each other."

"Me, too."

"Why do you seem so unhappy all of a sudden?"

"It's just... what we were doing when he called. I feel unsettled."

"We weren't doing anything wrong." Unless... "You aren't involved with him, are you? With Rob?"

"What? No! He's my brother-in-law. One of my closest friends."

"Would he like it to be more than that?"

"Of course not," she says, but there's no force behind her words.

"Iris."

She looks up at me, her gaze troubled.

"Talk to me."

"I think he'd like it to be more. In fact, I'm almost sure he would."

"But?"

"I love him so much and have relied on him tremendously since we lost Mike. He's been rock solid through it all."

"We're all glad you can rely on him and that your kids have him in their lives. I know how important he is to you."

"It's all so insanely complicated," she says with a deep sigh. "How easy would it be for me to fall into something with a man who loved Mike as much as I did, who already loves my kids and would do anything for me?"

"Very easy."

"Too easy, right?"

"Only you know that."

She's quiet for a long moment before she looks at me again. "As much as I love Rob, and I truly do, I've never been tempted to slide naked into his bed."

I'm far more relieved to hear that than I probably should be. My lips quiver with amusement. "So, you're admitting that was an intentional attack?"

"When did I say that?" she asks, all innocence.

I try to pull off a stern face, but I must fail miserably, because she laughs.

"Do you have regrets in the bright light of day?" she asks.

"None."

"That's good," she says on a sigh of relief. "I'm glad."

Glancing at me again, she says, "Was your Insta post directed at me today?"

"In part. I'm trying harder to embrace gratitude as time marches on, and today, I'm grateful for you and your sexy naked body in my bed last night. And it's funny, because if you'd asked me yesterday if I was ready to have sex with anyone, I would've said no way. But then there you were, and I was suddenly very ready."

"It'd been a while for you. I'm sure any warm, naked, female body could've gotten you ready."

With a finger on her chin, I compel her to look at me. "I told you that's not true. I never could've done that for the first time with someone I didn't already care about."

"So, what happens now?"

"What do you want to have happen?"

"I don't know. What about you?"

"I don't know either. But I do know that what happened last night felt good, and I wouldn't be opposed to more of it."

"I wouldn't either."

"That said... I'm not looking for a relationship beyond the friendship we already have. Even though it's coming up on three years—and how is that possible?—I'm just not *there* yet. I'm not sure I ever will be, if I'm being honest."

"I understand."

"You deserve to find someone who can be there for you and your kids. I don't want to get in the way of that with Rob or anyone else you might be considering for that role."

"I'm not considering anyone for that role. Most of the time, I'm just trying to get through the day."

"I don't know how you do it with three little ones."

"What choice do I have? I have help, thankfully. My parents are great, Rob, Mike's parents, my friends. It's just sometimes... what's ahead stretches out like an eternity with no end in sight. Laney is three and a half, which means I have fifteen years to go before she leaves for college. It's overwhelming to think of it that way."

"I can't imagine how hard it must be. I think about that sometimes, whether I could've done it on my own if Natasha had died in the accident and the girls had lived."

"You could have—and you would have."

"I don't know. Losing the girls was horrible, but losing Natasha was just... That wrecked me."

She curls her hands around my arm and leans her head against my shoulder. "You loved your girls so much. You would've found a way to care for them on your own. They would've helped you cope."

"I suppose."

"You would have, Gage. I know it. As much as single parenthood overwhelms me, it also gets me out of bed in the morning. They need me. I can't afford to wallow in my grief when I've got three hungry kids waiting for me to get my shit together every day. That's how it would've been for you, too."

"You have much more faith in me than I do."

"I know you. I know your heart. I know how much you loved your girls. You would've done whatever you had to for them."

"That's nice of you to say."

"They're not just words. That's how I see you. It's how we all see you."

"And I appreciate that. I really do. It's just that I wonder sometimes how it's possible to still be this much of a mess almost three years later. I thought it would get better. I really did."

"It *has* gotten better. In the time I've known you, I've seen you come back to life. It hasn't happened overnight, but you've done the hard work, and you're still doing it while reaching a hand out to others who've suffered terrible losses with your posts. You have no idea how much your words resonate with so many people."

"That's become a much bigger deal than I ever thought it would when I started posting."

"It's a lifeline to me and so many others. The first thing I do every morning, before I even take care of my kids, is check your Insta."

That surprises me. "Really?"

"Really. You can't possibly know how many times your words have given me the strength to face the day."

"Wow. Thank you. That means a lot coming from you. If you ask me, you're slaying this widow game and giving the rest of us someone to look up to as we fumble through it."

"Don't give me that kind of credit," she says. "I don't deserve it."

"Yes, you do. Maybe you don't see how you're always there for everyone in our group, no matter what might be happening in your own life. If someone is having a rough day, Iris is the first one to step up for them. You give us all summer pool passes and a safe place to hang out when we can't stand our own company any longer. You're like the home base of the Wild Widows, whether you see that or not." I'm horrified when her eyes flood with tears. "What's wrong?"

"Nothing." She dabs at her eyes. "That was just such a lovely thing to say about me."

"It's all true, Iris. You're the heart and soul of this whole thing, and we all know it. That's why I couldn't bear to have what happened last night mess up our friendship."

"It won't. I promise. No matter what, I won't let it."

"I won't either, but I want you to know... It meant a lot to me to be with you that way, that you wanted to be with me that way. All of it."

A smile lights up her pretty brown eyes. "Same."

"We should go back with the others before our simultaneous absence causes a scandal."

"Before we do that, let me just say this." I lean in and kiss her. And because that one feels so good, I do it again.

She looks slightly dazed when I finally pull back from her.

I understand that, because I feel more than a little dazed by how easily we transitioned from friends to lovers.

"You want to go out first?" I ask her. "I need a minute."

She glances at my lap, which doesn't help the situation. "Um, sure."

Nudging her, I say, "Get going."

"I'm going."

As I watch her go, I feel a sense of elation that's so at odds with my usual state of mind that it leaves me staggered. I'm so taken aback to feel something reminiscent of my life "before" that it's like someone has punched me. I sit there for a long time after Iris walks away, long after I need to, reeling from the return of something I would've thought lost forever.

Four

IRIS

It's Sunday lunchtime before I get a minute alone with Roni. "You want to take a walk?" I ask her, giving her a look that I hope conveys my need to talk to her.

"Derek, do you mind listening for Dylan for a few minutes?"

He takes the baby monitor from her. "No problem."

The guys, along with Joy, Lexi and Brielle, are fixated on the TV, where the Commanders are playing the Steelers.

We grab winter coats, hats and scarves, since the temperature has dropped into the forties, and head out, walking onto the beach and down to the water where the sand is packed down and easier to walk on.

I link my arm through hers. "How's the engagement going so far?"

"Couldn't be better."

"We're all so happy for you guys."

"Thanks. We were talking last night about how it's a delicate thing to be overtly happy among our widow friends."

"Don't do that. We all know what you guys endured to get to

this moment. Enjoy every second of it. We also know—all too well—how we have to live every day like it's our last."

"True. We just would hate to be too much, you know?"

"I do, and you're not. If you get there, I'll tell you."

"Thank you. Not just for that... For everything. Seriously, Iris. That day we first spoke, I had no idea what you were introducing me to or how critical this group would become to me surviving Patrick's death. Thank you so, so much."

"Oh, please. Don't thank me. I got a wonderful new friend when you joined us. I should be thanking you."

"It's weird, isn't it? That our closest friends from 'before' aren't so close anymore, but this whole new group of people are like family?"

"Everything is weird in the 'after.' Every single freaking thing."

"Yes, it is. I still feel guilty, you know?"

"For what?"

"For loving Derek as much as I loved Patrick, even if it's a different kind of love. It's a wiser, more mature kind, if that makes sense."

"It does. You've both been through an intensive course at the school of hard knocks. It's made you wiser and more grateful for what you have."

"That's it, exactly. We're not waiting for tragedy to show us how incredibly lucky we are. We're living that every day."

"Speaking of living every day... I did a thing."

She stops walking and turns to face me. "What did you do?"

"I might've pretended to get in the wrong bed—naked—Friday night."

Her mouth drops open. "Whose bed?" Her eyes go wide. "Gage?"

I flash my cheesiest grin. "Maybe?"

"Iris! *And you sat on this all day yesterday?*"

"I couldn't get a minute alone with you."

"You could've texted me!"

Laughing, I say, "I didn't think of that."

"This is huge!"

"Don't make it huge. It's just a thing that happened. Well, last night, too. And a little bit yesterday afternoon."

"Holy. *Shit*. This. Is. *Awesome!*"

"I'm not sure what it is. My head is spinning a bit. He says it's just sex because he's not ready for anything more, but Jesus God above, Roni. It was incredible sex."

She lets out a high-pitched scream that's drowned out by the roar of the surf. "This is the best thing *ever*!"

"You aren't going to make me sorry I told you, are you?"

"Of course not. I'll get it all out while we're on the beach, and when we go back, I'll be the picture of decorum."

I crack up laughing.

The two of us end up holding each other up as we laugh our asses off.

"Ah, it feels good to laugh," I tell her, hooking my arm through hers to walk a little farther down the beach.

"And it feels good to get back in the saddle, too, right?"

"If by 'feels good,' you mean I can barely walk, then yes, it feels good."

"Right there with you, girlfriend. Everything I've got is aching from being back in the saddle, but it's a good kind of ache. The best kind. Even if the other ache is still there."

"Yeah, because God forbid we should get to feel only the joy without the sorrow casting a shadow over everything."

"That's the price we pay for having loved Patrick and Mike the way we did. That we'll suffer over losing them for the rest of our lives."

"I think I'm the one who taught you that."

"Probably, so think of it as a reminder that what you're feeling is totally normal, or totally normal in the new normal."

"I love and hate the new normal equally."

"I do, too. Like, how can I feel this happy about being in love with Derek when Patrick is gone forever? When he'll never get to meet his son?"

"It's unfathomable."

"Yep."

"But wonderful, too. You and Derek are beautiful together, the way he waited for you to be ready... Swoon."

"So much swoon. Sometimes I wonder if Patrick didn't orchestrate our meeting because he wanted someone there for me."

"I wouldn't put it past him from everything you've told me. That man loved you with his whole heart and soul."

"He really did. So, what's going to happen now with Gage?"

"I have no idea. We had a fun weekend, and that might be all it is. He got to break his widow cherry—"

Roni loses it laughing again. "His widow cherry. You're too funny."

"Well, what would you call it?"

"That works for me. I lost mine this weekend, too. Who knew there'd be so much cherry popping when we planned this weekend away?"

"Not me, that's for sure."

"I still can't believe you got in bed with him. That's so ballsy."

"The liquid courage made me do it, even if I'm still pretending to him that it was all a big misunderstanding."

Smiling, she says, "No regrets?"

"None. Not one single regret."

"Good for you."

"Can I say one other thing that makes me feel like a monster?"

"Of course."

"I so do not want to leave here and go back to single parent-hood. I want to stay here forever while my parents raise my kids. I'm a horrible, awful mother."

"No, you're not. You're my Yoda in widowhood and mother-hood. I want to be you when I grow up."

"Oh God, stop. Do not do what I do."

"Sorry, too late. I want Dylan to be just like your wonderful Tyler, the sweetest boy ever."

"He's so sweet and such a huge help to me with the girls. I don't know what I'd do without him, which makes me feel terrible because I rely on my seven-year-old to help me care for my younger kids."

"He's an old soul," Roni says. "He loves taking care of them and watching over them. He takes that very seriously."

"I know, but I still worry that it's too much to put on the shoulders of such a young child."

"Tyler would tell you if it was too much. You'd know. Instead, if you ask me, helping you care for them is his chief purpose in life."

"His daddy would be so proud."

"He sure would. He'd be proud of all of you."

"I think a lot about how Mike talked me into having one more baby when I was content with having one of each. He kept saying, 'We need one more, babe. One more to make us complete.' It breaks my heart that she'll have no memories of him."

"She will, though. She'll know him through you and Rob and the rest of your family and friends. She'll know him, Iris."

"I suppose. Speaking of Rob..."

"What about him?"

"I'm starting to worry that he's going to be a problem."

"How so?"

"It's possible that his weekly visits aren't just about spending time with the kids."

"Ohhhhh. Well. Damn."

"Yeah." We turn around to go back to the house, with the wind now in our faces. "He's been so good to us."

"That doesn't mean you owe him anything more than saying thank you."

"I know, but I really hope it doesn't come to me having to tell him it's not going to happen. I so do not want to have that conversation with him."

"Hopefully, you won't have to."

"He asked if he could stay at my house last night after seeing the kids at my parents' house. I'm worried he's going to be waiting for me when I get home."

"Oy."

"That about sums it up."

GAGE

WE PACK up the two houses, load up the remaining firewood and set out for home shortly after four. I offer Iris a ride home, and she accepts since she came with Joy, who's heading for dinner at her parents' home in Annapolis. Everyone else is in other cars, which leaves us a couple of hours alone together when we're not naked and fucking like rabbits who've been let out of solitary confinement.

That thought draws a grunt of laughter from me.

"What's so funny?"

"I was thinking how we fucked like bunnies who've been let out of solitary."

She groans even as she laughs. "I guess we sort of did."

"Still no regrets?"

"Nope. You?"

"Nope."

"Guilt?" she asks.

"A little, but I'm told that's to be expected."

"That never really goes away. When you're as married as we were, you'll always feel like you're cheating when you're with someone else that way."

"I guess."

"You didn't do anything wrong, Gage. Tell me you know that."

"My head knows that. My heart is another story."

"Tell your heart to get on board the life-goes-on train."

"It's trying. I hear that's a process."

"It's a work in progress forever. No avoiding it." She glances over at me. "Your post today was really special."

I wrote about how a spark of joy snuck into the gloom this weekend and what a shock it was to experience that after so long without it. "I'm glad you liked it."

"I'm glad you felt it. And if I was in any way responsible—"

"You were entirely responsible."

"Oh. Wow. Well, it's great I could do that for you."

"Did I do any of that for you?"

"Absolutely. I enjoyed myself more this weekend than I have since Mike died, and that was mostly thanks to you and our adjoining bedrooms."

Last night, I tiptoed naked into her room and pretended to get into the wrong bed.

"The adjoining rooms were hella convenient, huh?"

"Sure were. I never would've had the guts if I'd had to sneak into your room where someone might've seen me."

"Is that a confession that Friday night's events were intentional?"

"Absolutely not. That was an honest mistake."

"Made while naked."

"These things happen."

I laugh harder than I have in longer than I can remember. She's delightful, sexy, funny, sweet and a wonderful, supportive friend.

"Thanks for getting me over the hump—literally."

"Glad to be of service."

We tease and joke and laugh all the way back to Northern Virginia while singing along to classic rock. It's the most fun I've had since my life fell apart, and as we pull into her subdivision, I tell her so.

"It was fun. Thanks for giving me a ride home."

"Any time."

As I take the turns to her house, I realize the path to her home has become as familiar to me as the roads that lead to my own place. I've felt at home with Iris for much longer than this weekend, which is why it was easier to take the huge step of being intimate with her than it would've been with anyone else.

She groans. "My brother-in-law is still here."

I note the Maryland plates on the dark green Jeep Cherokee in the driveway. "Is that going to be a problem?"

"No. Nothing to worry about. I'm just surprised he's still here this late on a Sunday when he has to work in Baltimore in the morning."

"I'll walk you in."

"You don't have to."

"I'd love to say hi to the kids." When I first met Iris, I resisted becoming friendly with her kids because it was just too painful. But over time, they've grown on me, and now I truly enjoy the time I spend with them.

"Oh, sure. Come on in."

I carry her suitcase for her and follow her into bedlam.

When the kids see her in the foyer, they let out shrieks of excitement that remind me of returning from the only vacation Natasha and I took without the girls, to celebrate our tenth anniversary. The memory of the reception we received upon returning home overtakes me out of nowhere, sucking the air from my lungs.

Thankfully, Iris is thoroughly engaged in the reunion with her kids, so I have a second to recover before she notices something has happened. Grief is so fucked up, coming at me that way when I was having a good day. A good few days, I should say.

The man stretched out on the living room floor eyes me warily.

The brother-in-law, I presume.

"Your folks got invited to dinner with the Millers," Rob says. "I told them I'd hang out until you got home."

"Thank you for that," Iris says.

"Mr. Gage," Tyler says. "Come see my new truck!"

When he takes me by the hand, I let him lead me into a room littered with toys. He releases my hand and bends to pick up the new treasure, thrusting it up at me with a look of excitement and wonder on his cute little face. He has dark hair and big brown eyes. "What do you think?"

"That's a heck of a truck, buddy. Show me what it does."

He gives me a full demonstration of all the features, which include a snap-on plow, a toy helicopter that sits in the bed and lights and buttons that make a wide variety of sounds. "Uncle Rob said he saw one just like it at work last week, right, Uncle Rob?"

"I did," Rob says as he sits up.

Laney launches herself at him, and he catches her with practiced ease, making her giggle in a matter of seconds with kisses to her neck. Her dark hair is a mass of curls, and her face is stained with red, probably from juice.

As I take a seat on an ottoman to further examine the new truck, I experience a sinking sensation. This weekend with Iris was great, but she needs someone like Rob. Her kids already love him, and judging by the way Rob looks at Iris, he loves her. Besides, like I told her, I'm in no way ready for a relationship with anyone, let alone one that would include three small, fatherless children.

I don't have the bandwidth to take on someone else's kids. That much I know for sure, regardless of how sweet Iris's kids are.

Five-year-old Sophia is in tears as she clings to her mother. The poor girl has probably fretted all weekend about her mother's safety, the way kids do when life teaches them that a beloved parent can be ripped from their lives without notice. She's almost five, so she probably has only faint memories of Mike, but she's certainly aware of his loss and how it permeates their daily lives. According to Iris, Sophia is Mike's mini-me right down to her light brown hair and blue eyes.

"Who's hungry for dinner?" Iris asks.

The kids raise their hands.

"I'm thinking pizza," she says. "Who agrees?"

All three kids chime in with agreement.

"Can you stay?" Iris asks Rob and me.

"Love to," Rob says.

"I can't." I hand the truck back to Tyler. "I've got some work to get done before tomorrow."

I say goodbye to the kids and tell them I'll see them soon.

Rob stands to shake my hand. "Good to meet you."

"You, too."

Iris walks me to the door. "Are you sure you can't stay for pizza?"

"I'm sure, but thanks for the invite."

Laney runs after Iris, wrapping her chubby little arms around Iris's leg. "Don't go, Mama!"

"I'm not going, sweet pea. I'm just saying goodbye to Mr. Gage."

Laney continues to cling to her mom.

"Talk to you soon," I say, uncertain of how to end this weekend that went in directions I never saw coming when I left home on Friday, especially with an audience looking on.

"Yes, for sure." She picks up Laney, who lays her head on her mother's shoulder and eyes me with trepidation, as if she's afraid I might take off with her mom.

"Be good for Mama," I say to the little girl, who gives me a faint smile.

Five

GAGE

I head out into the cold, aware of Iris watching me as I go. She stands in the doorway to wave me off as I drive away. What the hell is wrong with me that I feel so gutted to be going home alone? So we had sex. Big deal.

Except...

It was a big deal. I felt part of something special with her, something I haven't been part of in years, and I liked how that felt. Even when we were surrounded by our friends, we were still caught up in the thing only we knew about. Well, I'm sure Iris told Roni, because those two tell each other everything.

I don't mind if Roni knows what happened with Iris. I'm confident she won't tell anyone else, except for Derek, and that's fine, too.

Honestly, I wouldn't care if all the Wild Widows knew that Iris and I got busy at the beach, but I'm not going to be the one to tell them. That's another oddity that comes with widow life. Something that would've been totally private in the past is now picked apart for meaning and significance by the other widows in your life.

We talk about *everything*, even things that should probably be kept to ourselves. I've often wondered why it took widowhood for me—and others—to become so open about our feelings. Natasha used to accuse me of being remote and closed off emotionally at times. If she could see me now, she'd never recognize the man I've become without her.

And yes, it pains me to realize she had to die for me to become the man she hoped I'd be. Don't get me wrong, we were solid, and she'd say so, too. Her complaint was about my moodiness, and how I'd withdraw into myself for days on end. In hindsight, I don't even recall why I did that. It seems so stupid to me now, but then again, I didn't know then that our time together would end far too soon.

Thirty minutes after leaving Iris's house, I pull into the driveway of the craftsman-style house I bought a year after I lost Natasha and the girls. I still own the house we lived in together, but it's rented to another family now. I did the requisite year of no big decisions, and the minute that was up, my first impulse was to get the hell out of the house where I could see them everywhere I looked. It was a good move. Holding on to the place where we were a family while not having to live there anymore made it bearable to leave.

I've been lucky to own a successful cybersecurity business that didn't crash and burn while I was out of my mind with grief, which is thanks to the amazing team that supports me. They kept things going when I couldn't function for months after the crash that stole my family from me. Even now, I'm not back to working at the same level I was before, because I can't make myself care the way I used to.

I care just enough to stay in business. I delegate a thousand times more than I used to. I don't live to work anymore, which is another painful lesson I've learned after losing everything that truly mattered to me.

I've received multiple offers for my company, and lately, I've started to pay more attention to them. I'm still not sure I want to let it go, but the thought of being free from that grind appeals to me more than it should. Reviewing the latest offer is on my agenda for tonight. My CFO tells me it's a good one, the best yet, and I should consider it.

In my new home, I have one photo of Nat and the girls on display. It sits on my dresser, where I see it every morning and every evening and at times in between when I seek out the reminder that they were once the center of my universe.

The girls, Ivy and Hazel, were about six in the photo, their blonde curls the same exact color as their mother's hair. Nat and I used to joke that there wasn't an ounce of me in either of them. Except, as they got older, I started to see more of myself in them, especially in Ivy's love of watching baseball games with me—and her desire to play the game—and Hazel's affinity for learning how to use the computer.

I'm left now to wonder where those interests were leading. Would I be coaching Ivy's softball team or teaching Hazel how to code?

Standing before the photo of them, I run my finger over Nat's gorgeous, smiling face. "I'm sorry," I whisper. "I hope you know I never would've been with someone else if you were still here."

If she were here, Nat would tell me to knock it off and quit feeling guilty when I didn't do anything wrong. She was the most practical, keep-it-real person I've ever known, and she had no patience for bullshit or manufactured drama, as she liked to call it.

The path my fingertip cuts through the dust on the photo makes me feel guilty, too.

I grab the frame and take it into the kitchen to clean the glass with Windex, wiping it until the glass and silver frame are shiny again before returning it to my dresser. For the millionth time since I lost them, I wish for a handbook on how I'm supposed to do life without them. After being at Iris's chaotic house, the quiet in mine is surreal.

Nat and I used to long for quiet with two crazy girls underfoot. They kept us hopping from sunup to sundown every day of their too-brief lives. I recall weekend deals with Nat in which we'd each take a morning to let the other sleep in. Inevitably, our rest was disturbed by the crying, screaming and laughter of the two little girls who ran our lives. Now I can sleep in any time I want, but years later, it still seems weird to not be abruptly awakened every morning.

After I unpack and throw in a load of laundry that smells of woodsmoke, I sit down at my desk and check my email for the first time in days. I respond to several inquiries from my team and review reports they've submitted on current projects. Finally, I check the email account that's devoted to new business and find ten inquiries from potential new customers. I pass them on to one of my assistants to deal with.

Back in the day, I took on every customer who wanted my services. Now we triage new clients to ensure we're a good fit before we even reply to their inquiry. We have more work than we can handle, so we rarely take on new clients. In this interconnected world, our services are in greater demand than ever, so I can afford to be choosy.

After the work email is attended to, I open my Instagram account. I think this is the area of my new life that would surprise Nat the most. That I share my innermost thoughts on widow life online every day and have a huge following hanging on my every word is a shock to me, but she'd be floored. I used to grumble to her about privacy when people would tell me they loved a family photo she posted. Airing out our life online ran counter to everything I preach in my work about less being more in the internet age.

Now I post every day and have more than one hundred thousand followers waiting on my insight. Some tell me they live for it, depend upon it and draw immeasurable comfort from knowing they're not alone in their losses. It's become far more than I ever expected when I sat down a month after my loss to thank all the people who'd been there for me since it happened and to share a few thoughts on coping with such a huge loss.

I was immediately overwhelmed by responses from other widows, some who'd been at it for years and others who were like me, just starting their journey. I've developed close friendships with many of them and rely on them as much as they do me to get through the days. My connection to Christy began on Insta and led to her inviting me to join the Wild Widows group that she and Iris had founded along with another woman named Taylor, who has since moved on from the group.

The Wild Widows has been my greatest source of support. I love those people like family and am rooting for each of them as they work to put their shattered lives back together. Nat would be amused by my many widow friends because of all the times I grumbled about plans with people I barely knew. She was forever making new friends, and I was happy with the friends we had. She'd think it was hysterical that I've made hundreds of new friends since she and the girls died.

And yes, in thinking about this stuff, I do see there was a lot of grumbling on my part. That's just another thing to add to the list of what I'd change if I had a do-over with her. I wouldn't complain so much about the things she wanted to do. I'd be more accommodating of her friends and her interests, of which there were many. It's funny how you miss things you used to disdain, such as gallery openings and annual opera outings. There was *a lot* of grumbling about the opera, which I despise.

Thinking about that now, what I remember most is Natasha's enraptured expression as she soaked in every precious second of it.

I was a dick about it, and I took something away from her enjoyment of it. I hate myself for that now and hope wherever she is, there's opera on-demand.

I've written a lot about why it is that life has to kick us in the teeth for us to wise up about what's important. I've written about the opera and how much I regret not making a bigger effort to enjoy it simply because she did. That should've been all the incentive I needed, but it wasn't. How I regret that now.

Regret has been a regular theme in my posts, especially the many ways it serves to remind us to give of ourselves to others while we can.

I create a new Insta post and start typing. *I've just spent a weekend away at the beach with some of my closest widow friends and had a great time resting and relaxing with the crew that has become so essential to me. Funny how that happens, huh? The people you were closest to in the BEFORE are still there, still an incredible source of love and support. But it's the people in the AFTER who truly understand the journey the way no one else ever could. I'm eternally thankful for both groups, the before and the after, because there's no way I'd still be here without all of you.*

I post photos from the weekend, add all the usual widow hashtags that connect me to my core audience and post it. A few months ago, I was shocked when a blue checkmark appeared on my account, because I've heard how hard it is to get an Instagram account validated. After the checkmark came endorsement offers, some of which astounded me. If I wanted to, I could probably make being a widowed Instagrammer my full-time job.

I don't want that. A few minutes a day wallowing in my widowhood isn't the same as a full-time job would be. It's enough to live with that reality every day without fully immersing myself in my grief.

Work gives me an escape that I still need, even if it often drives me crazy. I just wish I could find the passion for it that I once had. That, more than anything, has me thinking more about a buyout than I ever have before.

I cook a frozen pizza, because Iris got me thinking about pizza earlier—and yes, I would've liked to have stayed to have it with her and the kids, but not with the brother-in-law giving me the stink eye. I have just enough produce to make a salad to go with it and eat in front of the TV while watching the Patriots play the Ravens. I'm a low-key Ravens fan because I just can't stick with the Washington team that's broken my heart so many times—I'm done with them.

That's another thing I can add to the list of things Natasha would find shocking. I surrendered the season tickets I had for more than twenty years—long before I could afford them—because of the chaos surrounding the Washington team. There was a time when I never missed a home game, no matter what else was going on. Those days are also over.

I want to text Iris, to tell her... What is it I want to tell her? That this weekend meant a lot to me? It did, but if I tell her that, will she read too much into it? What if the BIL is still there and sees the text? What's the deal with him anyway?

"That's none of your business," I say as I shut off the TV at eleven and head to bed. I'm working in the office tomorrow and have back-to-back meetings, which means I need to get some sleep.

I never took a sleeping pill in my life before the accident. Now I require them if I want to have any prayer of sleeping. In bed, I'm awake for a long time, thinking about the weekend and the two nights I spent with Iris. I pick over every detail of what we did, arousing myself to the point of pain as I relive it. I forgot what it was like to connect with another human being like that, and now that I've had a taste of what it's like with her, I want more.

IRIS

MY KIDS ARE OVERTIRED, overstimulated and overwrought from being without me for three days and two nights. It's a difficult few hours after Rob leaves as I march them through baths, pajamas, stories and bedtimes that they resist. They want to have a campout in my room, which was something we did for months after Mike died. But since it took me months to undo that habit, I'm not giving in on that.

By eight thirty, everyone is tucked into their own bed with orders to stay put or else.

I'm exhausted from tending to their every need on my own. I'd give anything to close my eyes and be back at the beach, where no one was clinging to me, asking me to cut their food or wipe their butt.

It's all me, all the time, and sometimes I hate Mike for dying and leaving me to do this on my own. Which is completely unfair because there was nothing Mike wanted more than to raise our kids and be there for every bump, scrape, growing pain and bedtime ordeal. There's no way he would've ever left me to do this on my own. That's something I'm as sure of as I am that tomorrow will dawn far too soon, and the needs of three young children will once again exhaust me.

After they're in bed, I usually catch up on laundry, put away the toy bomb, clean up the kitchen, catch up on my email and social media and have a glass of wine in front of the TV before going to bed. Tonight, I'm straight to bed. As I plug my phone into the charger, I glance at my texts. I'll never admit, even to myself, that I'm hoping Gage has texted me.

But there's nothing from him.

So I check his Instagram and see the post he made about the weekend. This time, there are no subliminal messages to be found in his always-poignant words, and I'm disappointed by that.

"Knock it off. He told you he's not ready for a relationship."

I respond to the text from my mom asking if I had a nice weekend. *It was great! So much fun. Thank you for having the kids. Hope they didn't run you guys ragged.*

They were wonderful, as always. We love every minute we get to spend with them. Dad and I were saying you need to get away more often so the kids are used to being without you occasionally.

I wouldn't be opposed to that. I just don't want to impose. They are a LOT, especially on the weekends with all the sports and stuff.

We love it. Please don't think a thing of asking us to take them.

We say all the time that we don't know how you do it all on your own.

It's not so bad. A lot of people have it worse. At least I don't have to work right now.

True, but being a full-time mom to three little ones is no small thing. Take full advantage of us. We want to help.

Thank you. I know I say it all the time, but I never would've gotten through this without you guys.

We love you. We love the kids. We're happy to help.

Love you, too. Talk to you tomorrow.

Sleep well.

I got so lucky in the parent department. I always knew that, but since Mike died, I've realized it a million times over. I see some of my widow friends struggling so much without the safety net under them that I took for granted until it became my lifeline. My mother and beloved stepfather were always just there, like furniture in a well-loved living room. I loved them and enjoyed being with them, but I never fully appreciated the way they'd sacrifice anything to be there for me and my siblings until I lost Mike and needed them more than I ever had before.

I've gotten accustomed to going to bed alone, although that was one of the toughest challenges at first. For six months after Mike's accident, I had kids in my bed or slept in the old recliner in his office that he insisted on bringing into married life from his bachelor pad. I hated that chair until it provided me comfort that I couldn't get anywhere else. The last place on earth I wanted to be in those first dreadful months was in the bed I'd once shared with him.

I'd settle into our bed with the kids, wait for them to fall asleep and then bail out to Mike's office to sleep in the ratty old chair I never gave a second glance to—except to complain about how hideous it was—before he was gone.

Part of me wants to sleep in the recliner tonight because being alone in bed again, after two nights wrapped up in Gage, makes me feel lonelier than I've been since disaster first struck.

It's irritating how two nights with him makes me lonely for him when it took me so freaking long to get used to sleeping alone. I'll admit that I hadn't considered that possible outcome before I snuck into his bed. I certainly didn't expect it to set me back on this painful journey.

I reach for my phone and compose a text to Roni, who's probably having wild sex with her new fiancé. Now that they've crossed that threshold, they've got a lot of time to make up for. I still send the text. *So here's a pleasant thought. Two nights in bed with Gage has set me back to the early days of trying to figure out how to sleep alone.* I add a frown face to help convey my state of mind.

She writes back a few minutes later. *That stinks. Are you ok?*

I'm fine. I just didn't expect that.

You could invite him over...

Just the thought of that lifts my spirits so hard that it hurts when they crash back to earth—and hello, that turn of phrase is not one I want in my vernacular after losing my husband to a plane crash. *He said he doesn't want a "relationship."*

You're already "in a relationship" with him. You have been for a while now.

You know what I mean.

I do, but you've only added another element to something that was already there. It's not like you're starting from scratch with him.

I guess... Anyway, I don't mean to bug you when I'm sure you've got far better things to do now that you're doing the deed with D.

Hahaha, I have to take a night off, or I'm going to need physical therapy.

LOL. I hear you. I was worried Gage might find bats in the tunnel cuz it's been so long.

OMG, stop! LOL

I send her bat emojis and get back laughing emojis.

If you want him, invite him over. I give you permission.

You're a terrible enabler.

I want all my friends to be happy. I'd love to see you two happy together.

It's not like that for us. It was just sex.

Hmmmmmm. If you say so.

He means a lot to me—and he did long before this weekend. If he says he's not ready, then I have to respect that. I'd hate to do anything to mess with the friendship.

I hear you, and I get it. I'm only saying that if you wanted to invite him over, you could.

LOL. The weekend was fun. Ten minutes after I got home, I wanted to turn around and go back. The kids were extra needy.

Aw, they missed you.

They did. And Rob was here when I got home. He took over from my parents.

That was nice of him, right?

He's great with them. They adore him.

But?

I just hope he's not thinking there's going to be something between us. I might be reading it wrong, but there's a vibe...

Yikes. What do you do about that?

I don't know! I rely on him so much, but I don't want him that way, even though I probably should. How simple would that be?

If it ain't there, it ain't there.

WHAAAA, I don't want to have to SAY that to him.

Maybe you don't have to. Just don't do anything to encourage it.

I never have. It's just sort of evolved into a "situation."

I'm sure you'll find a way to handle it that makes sense for you and the kids—and him.

I hope so.

You will, Iris! You're the one we all turn to about stuff like this. You always have the answers.

Everyone else's stuff is easy. Haha, but thanks for the vote of confidence. Go get some sleep. Thanks for being there.

Always. TTYT

I send her a heart and kissy face emojis. I adore her. Since she came into my life last Christmas, she's become one of my closest friends. Watching her and Derek evolve from close friendship to a second chance at love for them both has been so rewarding and life-affirming. They've inspired the rest of us more than they know.

Our Wild Widows group has one rule—prospective members must be open to the possibility of a second chance at love. We don't require people to actively date or anything like that. When Christy, Taylor and I founded the group, we came up with that rule to inspire hope for a future that won't always be as difficult as the present is for so many of us. It's more about the Mary Oliver quote that inspired our name: "Tell me what it is you plan to do with your one wild and precious life." There's no judgment or expectations or anything like that. It's more of a philosophy than a requirement.

A few months after Mike died, my sisters and cousins took me to Portugal for five days, hoping a change of scenery would help. I enjoyed the getaway. And as I sat in the caves and contemplated my life without Mike and what it might look like, I tried to envision a future that wouldn't be shrouded by loss and grief. It was on that trip that I opened my heart to the possibility of someday falling in love again in the far-off future when I was ready for such a thing.

I've been ready for a while now, but I hadn't done anything about that until I slid naked into bed with Gage. While many of my widow friends swear by the online dating apps, I haven't activated accounts on any of them. I'm not sure why, because I'm not at all opposed to meeting someone that way. I've seen it work for lots of friends, before and since I became a widow.

Setting up my accounts was a New Year's resolution, and here it is October, and I've done nothing about it. Instead, I do things like sneak naked into bed with a close friend and think that's going to solve all my problems. Instead, it's created new ones that I don't need. I've got enough on my plate without messing up a friendship that's important to me.

I shut off the light, determined to suck it up and get back to sleeping alone. I refuse to allow any kind of setback after having had a wonderful time with him. I loved having sex with him and wouldn't mind doing it again sometime.

But if that never happens, I'll be fine.

Six

IRIS

My phone rings before my alarm goes off to get Tyler up for school. Who is calling me so freaking early? I grab the phone off my bedside table and answer the call without checking the caller ID.

"Iris? Hey, it's Steve. Did I wake you?"

"Hey, Steve. No, I was up. This is a nice surprise."

Mike's partner in the charter flight business and his wife, Jenny, have been so good to me and the kids since Mike died. He's even insisted on still paying part of Mike's salary.

"Sorry to call out of the blue this way, but I just got home from a trip and found a letter from the NTSB about the crash."

We've been waiting a long time for the results of the investigation.

"What'd it say?"

"Iris..."

"What is it, Steve? You're scaring me."

"They're blaming the crash on pilot error."

"What? That's not possible. Mike was the best pilot in the world. You said that yourself."

"He was, and I can't imagine what they've found to lead to that conclusion. The letter said the report will be issued this week. As soon as I get a copy, I'll let you know."

"I don't know what to do with this. What does it mean?"

"If they make a compelling case, some of the pending insurance payouts might not happen, and we could be looking at lawsuits from the other families."

"Oh my God. Steve..."

"Try not to worry too much about the lawsuits. We've got all the best insurance that would cover any settlements."

"But Mike... His reputation..." Being a pilot wasn't just what he did. It was who he was. This is devastating.

"We knew the turbulence would be a factor," Steve said. "I told you that from the start."

"Yes, but what could he have done about that?"

"Not a damned thing. That kind of turbulence often doesn't come with a warning. I'm sure he did everything he could to get them through it. As soon as I know more, I'll call you."

"Thanks for the heads-up."

"I'm really sorry to have to give you this news."

"It's not your fault."

After we end the call, I feel sick. There's no way Mike could've been at fault for the crash. I simply can't hear that and go on with my life. The shock reminds me of the first days after the accident, like I'm wading naked through hip-deep snow. I'm hot and cold and shaking while trying to decide if I'm going to vomit.

That's where Tyler finds me. His alarm has gone off, and he's gotten himself up and dressed, which is his one job every morning. "You didn't come in," he says.

"Not yet, honey." I force a smile for him and reach for him, enveloping him in a tight hug that has him immediately squirming to break free. I let him go, and he takes his soothing body heat with him. I need to get the girls up and dressed. I need to feed the three of them. I need to function even though I can barely breathe.

I'm in a grief-fueled fog as I go through the routine that's so familiar to me, I could do it in my sleep. I navigate the daily argument with Sophia, who hates to have her hair brushed, and the daily battle with Laney, who can never find anything. Can I send her to preschool in a mismatched pair of shoes? I'm about to when she pops out from under her bed with one of the missing tennis shoes.

They have cereal and juice for breakfast, the girls and I walk Tyler and Sophia to the bus stop at the corner and then return home for the ride to the preschool with Laney. My babies are growing up fast, but even still, every day feels like a year without their dad. I have fantasies about what our life would be like with him here, but I can't allow myself to indulge in them or I set myself back. Today is going to suck badly enough without going there.

I pull up to the circle driveway at the preschool and get out to help the teacher unbuckle Laney's seat, which tends to be difficult to get undone.

My mother can't get over the drive-in drop-off at preschool. She makes jokes about whether you can order a side of fries with your babies.

Thinking about those things keeps my mind off the bombshell from Steve's call. I drive home, trying to keep my shit together so I won't crash the car, but once I'm inside the house, I slide to the floor inside the mudroom and break down into the kind of heartbroken sobs that remind me too much of the raw grief of the first few days after the crash.

I have so much to do. I use these kid-free hours to get *everything* done so I can focus on them when they're home, but I can't move. I can't breathe. I can't think. I can't do anything but cry. Of all the things that might've come from the NTSB report, the one thing I did not expect was that they'd blame Mike.

My phone rings. It'll be my mom. We talk every morning

around this time after I get the kids off to school. She'll worry if I don't answer, so I take the call, trying to hide my current emotional state from her. "Morning."

"What's wrong?"

I laugh even as tears spill down my face. She could hear my distress in one word. "Nothing more than a pending NTSB report that's going to put the blame on Mike for the crash."

"What? No. That's not possible. He was an excellent pilot."

"Yes, he was, but that's what the report will say. Steve got a heads-up."

"I don't know what to say, Iris."

"Neither do I. He said... There could be lawsuits."

"My God. They can sue *you*?"

"I don't know. I'm not sure about anything. Steve said they have insurance. I just don't know."

"Do you want me to come over, sweetheart?"

Monday is her lunch day with her girlfriends. "No, no, that's okay. I'm going to pull myself together and get on with it the way I have all along."

"I'm so sorry that this is happening right when you were starting to get your sparkle back a little. Daddy and I say all the time that we wish there was something more we could do to make this easier for you."

"I wouldn't still be here without you and Dad, so don't worry about what more you can do. You're already doing everything."

"We wish it could be more."

"I appreciate you guys so much. The kids had a great weekend."

"We had fun. It's so quiet here after they leave. We miss them right away."

"When Mike first died, I worried that no one else would ever love them as much as I do, but you guys do, and Mike's family does, too."

"Yes, we do, and they do, too. Those babies have so many

people who love them." After a pause, she adds, "Will you call me if you need me?"

"Always."

"We love you so much."

"Love you, too. I'll be okay. I promise."

"I'll call you later."

"I'll be here."

Long after I end the call with my mom, I sit on the mudroom floor, staring at the wall and trying to get my mind to quit spinning so I can function.

My phone chimes with a text from Steve. *The report is in. Do you want to see it?*

Do I want to see it?

No, I do not.

My phone rings with a call from a news channel in Wisconsin, where the crash occurred.

I respond to Steve. *No, I don't think I should see it. The media is calling me.*

Don't take those calls. I'm talking to a crisis communication expert about how to deal with this.

The phrase *crisis communication* sends my anxiety through the roof.

I'm trembling so hard, I can barely hold the phone. *What's going to happen?*

I'm not sure. I've never been through something like this. I'll keep you posted if you want me to.

Maybe just the need-to-know stuff.

Understood.

By the time I pull myself off the floor, an hour has gone by. A precious hour that could've been used for laundry, cleaning and many more of the endless chores that make up my days. I also planned to do some work on a business plan I've been developing to provide a wide variety of support services to single parents. It's a lofty idea born of my own circumstances as well as a TikTok following I've stumbled into by posting about the perils of single parenthood. In forming my plan, I've focused on the needs I would've had if I had no support system. I was looking forward to getting back to work on that, but it's not happening today.

In the kitchen, I make a cup of coffee and sit with it at the table, staring out into the backyard, my gaze drawn to the play set Mike and Rob spent an entire weekend assembling. My heart aches for Mike, who took such incredible pride in his work. A finding of fault in an accident would've devastated him.

I get a text from Tracey, the wife of the copilot. *I can't believe this. I'm heartbroken.*

Same. I don't even know what to say.

The families of the other people killed in the crash have become close friends as we supported each other through unimaginable loss. Will they turn away from us now?

My phone rings incessantly with calls from media outlets. Thankfully, the names of the places pop up on my caller ID so I can decline the calls and block the numbers. Do they honestly think I'm going to have something to say to them?

I get a text from Jeanette, the wife of one of the other men who was killed in the crash. *I'm so sorry, Iris. I know this has to be heartbreaking for you, as it is for all of us. Whatever happens next... Please don't take it personally. Be well.*

God, that all but assures they're going to sue the company because of my late husband's negligence. How do I not take that personally? Ugh, I cannot add that to my own agony.

When the doorbell rings, I'm terrified of who and what I might find on my front porch. I go to the door, peek through the glass and am shocked to see Gage. I unlock the door and open it.

He comes in, bringing cold air and the appealing scent that takes me right back to being in his bed. "I saw the news. I figured you might need a friend."

I walk into his outstretched arms and lose it all over again.

"Shhhh." He runs his hand over my back in soothing circles. "What can I do?"

"This helps."

He holds on tighter, and so do I. It means so much to me that he came, knowing I'd be upset and need a friend.

"I feel like I did when it first happened."

"I'm sure. Have you heard any of the details?"

"No, and I don't want to. I'm so afraid of a massive setback. It's taken so much to get this far..."

"I know, and you're right to protect yourself from things you don't need to know." Gage leads me to the sofa, sheds his coat and sits next to me, putting his arm around me and bringing my head to rest on his chest as he runs his hand up and down my arm.

"Mike's partner said there could be lawsuits."

"He had insurance, right?"

"Yes, but... What if they come for me, too? The other people on the plane... Their families have become my friends. And now they might sue me?"

"They won't."

"I don't know... If they feel they have a case, why wouldn't they?"

"Because they know it wasn't your fault, and if they've become your friends, they won't want you and your children to suffer any more than you already have."

"My heart is broken. Someday our children will find out that he was blamed for the accident that took him from us."

"I only know Mike through you, but I believe he did everything he could to try to prevent the accident because you know he wanted to come home to you and the kids. He wanted the others to get home to their families."

"That's all he cared about. He said it all the time—that his only job was to deliver people safely. And he cared so, so much about that. Even with having thousands of hours of flight time, he was still constantly doing continuing ed, training in the simulator, doing everything he could to stay at the top of his game, as he put it. I just can't for the life of me imagine how he could've made a mistake that led to a crash."

"You've said they encountered heavy, clear-air turbulence, right?"

"Yes, that much I already knew." Others on board had sent terrified texts to loved ones about the turbulence.

"Even the best of pilots is still human, Iris, and in a situation like that, there's probably an element of panic, even with all their training."

"Turbulence freaks me out, but it never bothered him. He said it was a normal part of flying."

"But maybe what he encountered that day was unlike anything he'd ever experienced, and perhaps it exceeded all his training."

"I suppose that's possible." Talking to him has calmed me somewhat, and I decide I should tell him so. "It helps me to have you here. Thanks for coming."

"I was in a meeting when I saw something online. I told my colleagues I had to go and jumped in the car."

"Means a lot to me."

"I'm here, Iris. For as long as you need me."

"That's apt to be a while."

"That's fine with me, sweetheart."

GAGE

IT BREAKS me to see her so devastated as she goes through the motions of picking up her kids, getting them snacks and listening to their nonstop chatter about their school days. The Iris I know is a force of nature, able to deal with anything that comes her way or the way of anyone she loves. She's the one we turn to when shit goes sideways in our lives, and I want her to have that same support. Midafternoon, I summon the Wild Widows for an emergency intervention at Iris's house.

Bring food and drink, I tell them, after giving them a quick summary of what's going on.

Wait, Roni says. *Mike was the pilot? My sister said he was a passenger...*

No, he was the chief pilot.

Well, my sister got that wrong. We'll be there after work.

Iris's mom comes by around four and invites the kids to her home for dinner. Before they leave, she summons me to the kitchen. We've gotten to know each other through cookouts, pool parties and other occasions over the last two years.

She's an older version of Iris, with darker brown skin and her daughter's sweet dark eyes that look at me now with affection and concern. "I'm torn about not being here for her," she says softly so she won't be overheard, "but I figured what she needs most is someone to care for the kids. I packed bags for them, and we'll get them to school in the morning and pick them up tomorrow."

"That's exactly what she needs. I'll be here, and the other Wild Widows are coming, too. We'll get her through this."

"She's lucky to have such amazing friends."

"It's not luck. She's an incredible friend to us, always there when we need her. This is the least we can do for her."

She pats my arm affectionately. "Michael took such pride in his work," she says tearfully. "I just can't imagine how the crash could've been his fault."

"As I said to Iris, we can be certain he did everything within his power to prevent it. Even the best of pilots can be outmatched by their circumstances and Mother Nature."

She sighs deeply. "I suppose so. This is going to crush her when she was doing so much better."

"We won't let it crush her. I promise."

"Thank you for being here."

"Of course."

Iris hugs and kisses her babies and sends them off for the night with her mom.

Tyler hangs back after his grandmother walks out with his sisters. "Are you okay, Mommy?"

"I am, honey. Mommy's just having a rough day."

"Because my daddy went to heaven?"

"Yes, sweetie. That never stops being hard."

"I know." He hugs her tightly. "Call me at Grandma's if you need me."

"I'll do that. Love you so much."

"Love you, too. Are you sure you'll be okay if we go?"

"I'm positive. Mr. Gage is here, and my other friends are coming, too."

"I'll make sure your mommy is okay," I tell the cute little guy.

"Thank you," he says with more wisdom and understanding than any seven-year-old should have. He scampers off to join his grandmother and sisters.

I go to the door to make sure he's safely in the car and wave to Iris's mom as they drive off.

Seven

GAGE

"Thank God for parents," Iris says when I return to her.

"For sure." Mine were so devastated to lose Nat and the girls that they weren't much good to me, but that's okay. Plenty of others were there for me, and my parents have rallied as time has gone on, and the shock of the loss has receded somewhat —as much as it ever will.

She looks over at me. "And thank God for wonderful friends who come running."

"I was on my way before I even thought about whether I should intrude."

"You should always intrude."

Her phone rings, and she glances at the caller ID. "It's Rob. I need to take this."

"Do whatever you need to."

"Hey," she says to Rob, instantly tearing up again. "I know. I can't believe it either."

I get up to fetch her a glass of ice water and stand in front of the sink, looking out at the covered pool while she's on the phone with Rob. It bugs me that I'm bugged by her tight bond with her brother-in-law, and I'm self-aware enough to realize how stupid that is. Of course she's close to her late husband's brother. They've been to hell and back together, and naturally, news like they received today would only cement that bond.

But I'm still bugged by it, even if I have no good reason to be.

It's not like she and I are together.

We had sex. A lot of sex. Really good sex. But that doesn't give me a claim on her or anything. I'm the one who said I didn't want that, and nothing has changed.

Except... I'm bugged by the brother-in-law. I take a long drink from the glass I poured for Iris, trying to resolve my own mixed emotions. That's something I never would've done before I was widowed. I spent exactly six seconds a day considering my emotions. Now, like so many other things, monitoring my emotional health is a daily priority.

Today, my emotions where Iris is concerned are all over the place.

I hear her assuring Rob that he doesn't need to come, that she's fine, that she'll call him if she needs anything. After I fill a second glass for her, I bring both with me to the living room, handing one to her.

"Thank you."

"How's he doing?"

"Not great. He left work after he got the news and doesn't know what to do with himself."

"Where are their parents?"

"In Italy on a long-planned vacation they'd already postponed several times because they didn't feel ready to travel yet. Rob has decided not to call them with the news."

"They won't see it somewhere?"

"He doesn't think so. They're mostly off the grid when they travel. They never turn on a TV if they can avoid it."

"It's the right thing to let them enjoy the trip. Telling them now won't change anything, and it'll only upset them."

"That's what we figured."

"Did Mike have other siblings?"

"No, just Rob. They were only a year apart, so they were super close."

"Poor guy. That's got to be so rough."

"I would be a mess if something happened to one of my siblings."

"Me, too."

"It's the craziest thing, isn't it? To have to go on without the people who are most essential to us."

"It's unnatural, even if it's a parent who's supposed to go before you."

"Yes, exactly. And then to have the loss compounded, even years later, by something like the NTSB report... The nightmare never ends."

"No, it doesn't."

"How could Mike have been at fault? He knew what to do in every situation. I would ask him why he still spent all that time doing continuing ed, and he'd say a pilot can never have too much training. It's not fair that he worked so hard only to be blamed for the crash." She wiped away new tears. "I don't know what to *do* with this information."

I don't know what to do with it either, so I put my arm around her and offer what comfort I can. "I wish there was something I could say to make this right for you."

"I'll never believe this was his fault. I don't care what the experts say. Something else must've happened."

"You're allowed to believe anything you want."

"What'll I tell my kids, though? When they're old enough to ask... What'll I tell them?"

"The truth. You tell them what the NTSB said, and then you tell them what you believe to be true, knowing Mike the way you did. You tell them how hard he worked, how invested he was in training and how much he cared about safety. None of this has to change who he was to you and the kids."

When the doorbell rings, I tell her I'll get it.

"Watch out for reporters. I don't want to talk to them."

"I'll get rid of whoever it is."

I open the front door to a man I don't recognize as one of Iris's friends. Not to say I know them all, but I've met a lot of them.

"Hey, I'm Steve Harris. I was Mike's business partner. I'd like to see Iris."

"Let me check with her. Hang on." I don't invite him in to wait in case she's not up for seeing him. "It's Steve Harris."

"Oh, he can come in."

"I'll get him."

After I escort him to the living room and take his coat, I glance at Iris. "You want me to stay?"

"Yes, please." She pats the seat next to her. "Steve, this is my friend Gage Collier."

I shake the guy's hand, even though he gives me an odd look, as if he'd like to know just what kind of friend I am to her. *None of your business, asshole.* I take a seat next to Iris, leaving only an inch or two between us. Let him wonder about that, too.

Am I being ridiculous? Probably, but seeing her so upset has triggered my protective side, which is a revelation of sorts. I haven't stretched my protective muscles since I suddenly lost my family and had no one to protect anymore.

"How're you holding up?" Steve asks when he's seated across from us.

"Oh, just dandy. You?"

"About the same. It's a lot to process."

I want to tell him to get on with his purpose for bothering her at such a difficult time. I hope he's not here to make things worse for her somehow, although how could anything be worse than finding out her husband was responsible for the crash that killed him and five others?

I don't know this guy from Adam, but even I can tell that he's upset about something else besides the NTSB report.

"What's going on, Steve?" Iris asks.

He rubs his hands over his jeans as he seems to struggle to find the words he needs. "I hate to do this to you when you're already upset about the NTSB report."

"Do what?"

I want to throw myself in front of whatever he's about to say, to push him out the front door so he can't upset her any more than she already is.

"A year ago, I received a call from a woman in Denver. She said..."

"What did she say?"

"That she has a five-year-old son with Mike."

Beside me, Iris goes completely still. "That's not possible."

Steve glances at me, as if to ask me to help convince her it's possible. I'm not doing that.

"I... I didn't think so either," he says. "She... she wanted money for the child, and Mike told her to contact me if anything ever happened to him. I told her she was going to have to prove he was Mike's before I'd even speak to her. She..." He swallows hard. "She sent proof of an ongoing affair."

Beside me, Iris begins to tremble violently.

I want to stab him in the fucking heart for doing this to her.

"But she had no way to prove her son was Mike's. The last time you guys were at the house..." He swallows hard. "I kept a bottle Tyler drank from."

Iris gasps.

"I had to know for sure before I told you, Iris. The results came back a week ago, confirming they have the same father."

The news sucks all the air out of the room. I put an arm around her.

She shakes me off and stands. "Thank you for coming by, Steve. You can go now."

"Iris, I'm sorry. I wanted to be sure before I brought this to you."

"Why does she even need to know about this?" I ask him,

outraged that he would blindside her with this when she's already upset enough.

"Because the woman is threatening to sue Mike's estate for child support. I couldn't let that happen without you being aware of what's going on. I tried to deal with this without you. I offered her a settlement. She said it wasn't enough, and now she has this lawyer playing hardball with me, and he's implied that he's coming for you, too, since Mike didn't leave her child anything in his estate."

"I'd like to see the proof of the affair and the DNA testing."

I don't like that idea. "Iris…"

As if I hadn't spoken, she says, "You can send it to my email."

"Are you sure?" Steve asks.

"Very sure. Thank you for coming, but you can go now. You've done your due diligence."

Steve stands. "I'm sorry, Iris. I had no idea this was happening when he was working out there."

"I don't blame you."

The lack of emotion in her voice and expression worries me. The Iris I know and love is always full of fire.

He glances at me and then back at her. "Will you be all right?"

"She'll be fine." I stand to escort him from the room, with a look that leaves him with no doubt that he's not welcome here any longer.

"We'll fight this, Iris. Together."

She nods but has nothing else to say to him as I send him packing.

I really wish murder was legal, although the person I'd like to kill is already dead.

"I'm sorry," Steve says when I walk him out. "I hated having to do this, especially now, but I couldn't let her be served without knowing what's happening."

I don't know what to say, so I say nothing while I wait for him to leave. After he's gone, I close and lock the door as my mind races with concern and anguish for my friend. What do I even say to her after this? What would it be like to find out Nat had been involved with someone else? I simply cannot imagine that.

When I return to the living room, Iris isn't there. I find her in the kitchen, waiting for the kettle to boil. "What can I do?"

Her laugh is brittle. "What can anyone do? Just when I thought this widow thing couldn't get any worse..."

I place my hands on her shoulders.

She stiffens, but I don't remove them. "This is like day one all over again."

"I know, honey."

"If she sues me, will she win?"

"Joy would know." She's an attorney, specializing in family law.

"I don't want people to know this."

"Which is totally understandable, but if there's a lawsuit, you'll have to defend against it."

"I want to go back to the beach, before I knew this stuff."

"I wish we could go back."

"You don't have to stay. I'm sure you have stuff to do."

"I'm not going anywhere, Iris."

"You said you don't want a relationship. I respect that. You're under no obligation."

"I'm not going anywhere."

Because my hands are still on her shoulders, I'm aware of the exact instant when she crumbles. I turn her into my embrace, holding her up as she releases deep, gut-wrenching wails that break my heart. Only my arms around her keep her from falling to the ground. I pick her up and carry her to the sofa, sitting with her on my lap. We're there long enough for daylight to fade into darkness. "Do you want me to tell the others not to come?"

She shakes her head. "They'll find out soon enough."

"But if you need a minute with it first..."

"What will that change?"

"Nothing, I suppose."

"How could he have done this to me again, Gage?"

"Again?"

"It happened once before, the second year we were married. Before kids. He had an affair with a woman he worked with. He swore to me it was a one-time thing, and after intensive therapy, we were able to put our marriage back together. After all that, he did it again."

I hold her closer because I don't know what to say. I hate that he put her through such a thing.

"I've always thought that women who said they didn't know their husbands were cheating had to be naïve. How could you not know? But I didn't, either time, and I'm not naïve."

"No, you're not."

"I didn't know. I had no idea." A sob erupts from her chest. "How could he do this after all the work we put in to repair the damage from the first time? He begged me to take him back and said I was the only woman he would ever love. And then he had a *son* with another woman and kept that from me. That baby would've been born between Tyler and Sophia." She shakes with sobs. "Oh God. I'm going to be sick."

I'm up before she finishes the sentence, rushing her to the bathroom in the hallway, where she's violently ill while I stand by helplessly, wishing I had a magic wand that could make this nightmare go away for her.

The doorbell rings.

I glance at my watch and am shocked to see that it's already after six.

I close the bathroom door to give her privacy and go to admit Derek and Roni, who come in laden with bags.

"We weren't sure anyone was home," Derek says. "The house is dark." He turns on a light in the foyer that has me blinking from the sudden onslaught of light. "Are you guys all right?"

I shake my head. "It's bad, guys."

Tears fill Roni's eyes. "Poor Iris."

She comes out of the bathroom.

Roni goes to her and hugs her. "What can we do?"

"Nothing," Iris says in a dull tone that's so far from her usual exuberance that it immediately alarms our friends. "There's nothing anyone can do."

She trudges into the living room and curls up on the sofa.

"There's more," I tell them, almost as if to explain why Iris is in such bad shape."

The NTSB report was one thing. What she's learned since then makes that look like nothing.

Roni gives me a questioning look, but it's not my story to tell.

I go to sit with Iris while they take the food they brought to the kitchen. "Can I get you anything?" I ask her.

She shakes her head and then reconsiders. "Maybe some Advil. There's some in the cabinet over the dishwasher."

I get up to fetch the pills and bring them back to her. She takes the pills with a sip of water and then hands the glass to me.

Roni and Derek join us in the living room, the four of us existing in awkward silence until the doorbell rings again.

Derek goes to get the door, admitting Lexi, Hallie, Joy and Wynter.

I feel like I did when my family first died, and I had no idea what to do next. I always know what to do. I'm never indecisive. But this... How does one support a friend at a moment such as this?

We gather in the living room.

Iris has her head back against the sofa, her eyes closed, her face red and puffy.

Brielle, Adrian, Kinsley and Naomi are the last to arrive.

Christy said she couldn't make it tonight because her son has a basketball game.

Iris opens her eyes and seems surprised to see everyone.

"What can we do, Iris?" Brielle asks.

"Mike had a five-year-old son with another woman, so unless you can make that go away, there's nothing anyone can do."

Eight

IRIS

I've shocked my friends with the blunt statement. I feel bad about that, but I feel bad about everything. The man I knew and loved for ten years—and forgave after an earlier indiscretion—never stopped lying to me. I have to live the rest of my life knowing I wasn't enough for him. Who knows how many others there were? How will I cope with knowing our family wasn't enough for him? What will I tell my kids?

They have a brother.

For a second, I fear I'm going to be sick again.

Gage hands me the glass of water.

I take a sip, hoping the bile burning in my stomach will stay down.

"How did you hear about that?" Roni says.

I glance at Gage and nod.

He fills them in for me. Thank God for him, because I don't think I could've said it.

"Good Lord," Joy says.

"Don't forget the part about how she might be suing me and Mike's business partner for support of her son, who was born between Tyler and Sophia." I look to Joy. "Can she do that? Can she come for the money he left for me to raise our children?"

"Do we know for sure the child is his?"

Gage tells them about the DNA test that tied him to Tyler, which is further outrage on top of everything else. That Steve would do that without my consent is shocking.

"Hmm," Joy says. "I'd have to do some research about precedents in situations like this."

"I was hoping you'd say it's preposterous that she could sue someone who didn't know she or her son existed until today."

"It's not impossible," Joy says. "People file lawsuits for everything under the sun. But is the estate closed?"

"It is. Has been for a while now."

"Then it would be very difficult for her to stake a claim on it at this point."

My entire body aches the way it did when Mike first died, and I wasn't sure how I'd survive without him. In the time since I lost him, I've slowly, painfully and meticulously put my life—and my children's lives—back together. All that progress has been lost. I'm right back to where I started, mourning the man I loved and the marriage that's been exposed as a fraud.

Somehow, I managed to survive losing Mike, but this... I'm not sure I'll survive learning that he lied to me, cheated on me again and had a child with another woman.

"I need someone to tell me how I'm supposed to deal with this, because I can't fathom how I'll do that."

Gage puts his arm around me.

I force myself to let him comfort me when I don't feel worthy of comfort. Does that make sense? No. I know it doesn't. But that's how I feel. I'm spinning like an out-of-control comet heading for a crash landing that'll break me into a million tiny pieces that'll never be put back together the way they once were. "What'll I tell my kids?"

This group of people, usually so full of wisdom and answers to every dilemma, is completely silent, which proves how surreal this is. There are no answers to my questions that'll satisfy my need to understand the man I was married to. I think of Rob and their parents, how they hold Mike up on a pedestal and how crushing this will be to them.

I can't think about that now, or I'll lose what's left of my mind.

"Is there food?"

"Tons of it," Roni says.

"Let's eat." I'm not sure my stomach will be able to handle food, but I need to do something. "And drink. I need a huge fucking drink."

"I got you, baby," Joy says.

She and I share a love of bourbon, and she makes the best cocktails.

Adrian stops me as everyone else heads for the kitchen. "You would remind me, in a moment like this, that the one thing we've learned is that nothing feels this bad forever."

That is, I realize, exactly what I need to be told in this hellacious moment. "You're right, and that's very true. Thank you for the reminder."

He hugs me. "Still, this sucks gigantic cock."

I wouldn't have expected to laugh just then. "It sure does." Being with people who understand always makes such a huge difference, even when the latest catastrophe isn't something any of us have contended with before. Grief is grief, and now I can add grieving for the marriage I thought I had to my already formidable list.

Joy has a strong drink ready for me that hits my empty stomach with a thud. I'm very careful never to drink too much lest my kids need me, but tonight is an exception to all the rules. I have a second bigger sip of the drink and love the way the bourbon warms me from the inside.

Gage appears at my side with a plate of food and silverware. "Sit and eat."

I want to snap at him to not tell me what to do, but all I see when I look at him is concern and care. So I do what I'm told. The food, the booze, the company... They get me through the night. When I realize the others are much quieter than usual, I encourage them to be themselves and talk freely about other things.

"Please," I tell them, "keep it real and give me something else to think about."

We sit at my dining room table and have a full-on Wild Widows meeting, with everyone contributing something about their latest struggles and challenges. It helps me to immerse myself in their problems, even while my own feel too big to bear.

Christy calls me after her son's game. I put her on speaker so she can participate with the rest of the group.

"Gage, would you mind giving her the CliffsNotes?" I ask.

"Sure." In as few words as possible, he fills her in on what happened today.

"Son of a bitch," Christy says on a hiss.

Back in the earliest days of our losses, she and I vowed to each other that neither of us would ever be alone. In the ensuing years, we've kept that promise while adding a crew of fellow travelers to our group.

"But I'm done talking about it for now," I tell her. "I want to hear everyone else's crap. Adrian, your turn. How're you doing?"

"Eh, okay. Everything is harder since Sadie's mom died, but I'm finding a new routine. I go back to work in three weeks, so that's when things will get interesting."

"Have you lined up childcare?" Roni asks.

"Not yet. I'm still trying to figure that out."

"I told you I'd do it for you," Wynter says.

"And I appreciate that, but he's a lot, and you've got your own life to think about."

"I need a job. You need a nanny. It's a win-win."

Adrian tips his head as he considers her. "You're serious about this?"

"Duh. If I wasn't, I wouldn't have offered. Xavier is adorable. I already love him. I'd take amazing care of him for you."

"Let's talk more tomorrow," Adrian says.

"You know where to find me."

"I think you'd be an awesome nanny, Wynter," I tell her. "My kids adore you."

"I love kids. I always have. My mom says I'm magic with them."

"You are for sure," Roni says. "Dylan and Maeve love you, too."

"Those are my references, by the way," Wynter says to Adrian.

The whole group cracks up, even me, and it feels damned good to laugh. Wynter's blunt humor is just what I need tonight. All of them are just what I need, and I figure I should tell them that.

"You guys... Thank you for this. Truly. I'd be losing it if you all hadn't come to make things better."

"We can't fix the pain of this latest blow, baby," Joy says, "but you won't have to face it alone."

I place my hand on top of hers. "And that makes all the difference."

BY THE TIME everyone leaves around ten, I'm comfortably buzzed and strangely removed from the latest trauma. It almost feels like it happened to one of them rather than me. I'm sure it'll hurt like hell again in the bright light of day, but for right now, I'm relieved to carry on as if I haven't taken another blow that would've leveled a lesser person.

I refuse to be a lesser person. I refuse to backtrack to the early days of my grief when I could barely get out of bed or care for my kids and relied on my parents and siblings for everything. I can't go back there, because dragging myself up and out of that took everything I had. My reserves are tapped out. If I let myself fall that low again, I won't come back from it.

These are the things on my mind as I load the dishwasher while Gage wipes the countertops and the dining room table. He sent the others along, assuring them he'd help me clean up. I heard him tell Roni he wouldn't leave unless he was sure I was all right. It's strange to think that if Mike hadn't died, none of the people who got me through this crisis would've been in my life. I'll never reach a point where I'm "thankful" to have been widowed so young, but I'm eternally grateful for the people I've acquired through my loss.

"What else can I do?" Gage asks when the kitchen is cleaner than it's been in weeks.

"Not a thing. I'm sure you have to work early tomorrow, so you should get home and get some rest."

"I cleared my schedule for the next two days."

I'm shocked. "Why'd you do that?"

"Because I don't want you to be alone with this. You shouldn't be alone with it."

"Can I ask you something?"

"Sure."

"You don't feel... like... responsible for me because of what happened last weekend, do you?"

He recoils from the question. "Fuck no, I don't feel responsible for you. I care about you, and I hate that this shit is happening to someone who doesn't deserve any of it. I can't go home and leave you here alone with it."

"I'm sorry. I didn't mean to make you mad."

"You didn't, but I don't feel responsible for you. I'm here because I want to be. It's that simple."

I go to him, put my arms around his waist and rest my head on his strong, solid chest. "And that complicated."

"It doesn't have to be complicated."

Men are so naïve. Any time sex is involved, it's complicated.

But I'll let him have his illusions. "You can go, Gage. I'll be all right."

His arms encircle me, and I experience a strange feeling of homecoming, which I immediately suppress. He's not my home. I'm more determined than ever after today to be my own home. Look at where putting my faith in a man has gotten me.

I start to back away from him.

He holds on tighter. "Don't push me away, Iris. I want to help."

"You have helped. You've been right here all day, but you can't fix what's wrong here. Only I can do that."

"You don't have to do it alone."

"I know, and I won't do it alone, but I've got nothing to give anyone, even you, right now."

"I'm not asking for anything other than permission to keep you company." He looks down at me, his gaze full of concern and affection. "Can I stay with you tonight?"

I hate that I don't want him to go, that I want him here to keep telling me everything will be okay. But I also appreciate that he wants to be there for me. "Sure."

After checking to make sure the outside lights are off and the doors are locked, I lead him upstairs. "Don't look at the mess in the kids' rooms."

"I'm not looking, and I had kids, remember? I know how messy they are."

"The shock of losing Mike was compounded by the things I learned today, but it has nothing on you losing your wife *and* kids. I feel silly for even being upset about it."

"Don't do that. What happened today was brutal, and you have every right to be upset about it."

"I don't think I would've survived losing my kids, too."

"Yes, you would have, because you have no choice but to carry on, no matter how big the losses are."

"I hope you know how much I admire the way you've carried on and how you help others by sharing your journey."

"It helps me to do that, or I wouldn't do it."

"Don't discount how much your words mean to so many others."

"Why are we making tonight about me? This is about you."

"It's about both of us finding our way through the swamp of loss and looking for meaning in what remains."

"'Meaning in what remains,'" he says. "I like that. Can I use it in a post?"

"Of course."

"I'll give you credit."

"You don't have to."

"Sure I do."

"By the way... Everything in this room is new since Mike died. I completely redecorated." The room has belonged only to me—and my kids, of course—since it was finished.

"Good to know."

He strips down to underwear and points to a doorway. "Bathroom?"

"Yes, and there are new toothbrushes in the cabinet. Make yourself at home."

"Thanks."

For the first time in hours, I glance at my phone. My mom has reported that the kids went to bed easily and were well behaved.

She'd never tell me if they weren't. Usually, I hear about it from them. Like Sophia telling me Tyler was fresh to Grandma or Laney pitched a fit at bedtime. When I ask my mother about those things, she downplays them.

"They were fine," she always says. I get that she's unwilling to add to my burden, and I'm grateful for the instances when she and my dad deal with behavior issues so I don't have to. I deal with plenty of them on my own, which is one of the hardest parts of single parenthood for me—not having another adult in the room to back me up like I did when Mike was here.

I was so caught up with juggling three kids, a house, a

marriage and a few important friendships that I failed to notice that my own husband was leading a double life right under my nose. The company he and Steve founded was offered a big contract with a Denver-based firm that had offices in the DC area as well. For a time, Mike and Steve kept an apartment near the Denver airport to use when they were there for longer stretches. Sometimes, Mike would be there for a week or two at a time. I remember thinking then that single motherhood didn't look good on me—and that was before Laney arrived, the third child Mike convinced me we needed to complete our family.

"What're you thinking about?" Gage asks when he returns from the bathroom and sits next to me on the bed.

"About Mike working in Denver for a week or two at a time, and how, after the gut-wrenching effort we put into repairing our marriage after the first time it happened, it never occurred to me that he'd cheat on me while he was there. Part of me wants to know how it happened, how they met, how long they were together. Was it a one-night thing or a full-on relationship that led to the baby?"

"What difference would knowing those details make at this point?"

"None, I suppose, but I still want to know." I stand and go into the bathroom. When I return a few minutes later, he's gotten into bed.

"I figured that was your side by the well-occupied bedside table."

"You figured right." I've changed into flannel pajama pants and a long-sleeved T-shirt because I can't get warm no matter what I do. When I get in bed, Gage reaches out to me, encouraging me to come to him.

I curl up to him and sigh when he holds me just right.

Nine

IRIS

"You know what makes me almost madder than what Mike did?"

"What's that?"

"Steve having my son's DNA tested without my consent. Who does that?"

"I thought that was very strange, too. I mean, I get that he wanted proof before he brought it to you, but having the DNA tested should've been your call, not his."

"Exactly. I feel so violated by that."

"You should.

"His intentions were good. I believe that. But Jesus..."

"The whole thing is unreal. From start to finish."

"I'm not sure how I'm supposed to feel about any of it. What would you do if you found out that Natasha had kept something like this from you?"

"I don't know."

"Not that she ever would've done that, but I wouldn't have thought Mike would either, especially after how hard he worked to convince me to give him a second chance."

"Why did you? Give him another chance, I mean."

"He was so sorry, so remorseful, willing to take the full blame for it happening. He said he couldn't even explain why it did because he loved me so much. I believed him about that, because whenever he was with me, that was all I felt from him. And I was pregnant with Tyler when it all happened, so leaving him was almost too daunting to consider."

"I get that."

"I loved him, too. So, so much. It nearly broke me when I found out he'd been unfaithful, but I really thought we'd put things back together. What do I know?"

"One of the things we see a lot in widow circles is people putting their late spouses on pedestals, as if we forget the things about them that drove us crazy and only focus on the good things."

"Yes, that's true. We wax poetic about our lost loves without giving a thought to how many times we had to ask them to take the trash out or why they thought they deserved a medal for taking care of their own kids."

"Exactly."

"What did Natasha do that bugged you?"

"She was so messy. I was constantly cleaning up after her. I used to call her Pigpen from Charlie Brown. She had a cloud of mess always surrounding her. And don't get me started on her car. I called it the rolling Superfund site."

That makes me laugh. "My car is pretty bad, too, but I blame the kids for the Goldfish dust ground into the carpet."

"Her car was that way before we had the girls. It only got worse after."

"What else?"

"She couldn't get anything done. She'd start a big project, lose interest and walk away from it to start something else. We would fight about her taking on new stuff before the old stuff was done."

"From the way you talk about her, I can't imagine you fighting with her."

"We used to have rip-roaring, screaming fights on the regular. We tried not to do that in front of the girls, but every so often, it would erupt when they were around. The thing was, though, we got over it just as quickly. I could never manage to stay mad at her, even when I wanted to. Did you fight with Mike?"

"Not really. I've always had a hard time with conflict. I had a screamer for a teacher in first grade, and that gave me so many stomachaches, my parents took me to doctor after doctor until one of them put it together with the teacher. Fighting and conflict make me sick, so I avoid it. With hindsight, that might not have been the best way to run a marriage."

"You didn't do anything wrong, Iris."

"How can you say that knowing what you do about Mike having a whole other family?"

"That failing was on him, not you."

"I must've done something—or not done something—to drive him to it. We had three little kids. I wasn't always the most attentive wife."

"It's not your fault. If he wanted to be with someone else, he should've told you that."

"But he knew how I felt about conflict. Maybe he thought it would be better to keep it from me for that reason—and the kids."

"There's no excuse for him being unfaithful, having a child outside of his marriage and letting you hear about that after he's dead."

"Where do you suppose she's been all this time?"

"Is it possible she didn't know he died?"

"I guess, but I doubt it. The crash was big news here and in Denver. Most of the other passengers were based there."

"Something must've changed for her to have reached out so long after the fact," he says. "Like maybe she was married, too, and that ended, so she's making threats about lawsuits because she needs the money. Or maybe Mike promised to take care of her if anything ever happened, and when that never materialized, she decided to come after it. Could be anything."

"I suppose I'm going to have to talk to her if I want answers to these questions."

"Or you could let the lawyers handle it and stay away from her."

"Her son is my children's half brother."

"They don't need to ever know about him if you don't want them to."

"Mike's family will want to know him. The baby is a connection to him." I take a deep breath and let it out slowly. "The thought of telling people who knew him about this is overwhelming."

"Let Rob tell everyone else who matters. You don't have to be the one who does it."

"This'll change the way people remember him."

"That's also not your fault."

"I've been protective of his reputation and legacy. It was important to me that the kids see him as a man they could look up to and emulate."

"That doesn't have to change. I'm sure you're teaching them that everyone makes mistakes, even parents."

"Were we the mistake, though? Did he love her?"

"I hate that you're torturing yourself with these questions. You know he loved you and the kids."

"I was always so sure he did, even when he screwed up before. Never in my wildest dreams after that first time would I think he'd have had someone else—and a child with her. What rock was I living under that I missed that?"

"The nature of his job meant that he was away from you a lot. He probably took care of things with her when he wasn't here."

"Was he there when the baby was born? Where did I think he was that day?"

"You'll drive yourself crazy with those questions."

"I want the details."

"Let me ask you this—what will it change if you have the details? Mike will still have had an affair and a child with her. Nothing you find out will change that fact of the matter, but the things you learn might hurt you more than you already are."

"That's true." I shift so I can see his face. "What would you do if you were me?"

He gives my face a light caress that I feel everywhere. "I'd probably want all the dirty details, too, even if I knew I was better off not knowing."

"I worry about not being able to care for my children properly. That's always my greatest concern since I became a single parent."

"Then you shouldn't do anything that might make that job more difficult than it already is."

"It's amazing, isn't it, how the most terrible thing to ever happen can get even worse after all this time?"

"You're so much stronger than you were when it first happened. We all are. We got through something we would've thought impossible to survive. We've carried on with all the dignity and grace we could find, and you'll continue to do so even now. I have so much faith in you."

His words stir something in me that has nothing to do with grief or heartache and everything to do with the courage it takes to continue living when your life is upended. I move closer to him and press my lips to his, hoping he'll kiss me back. He does. For a second. And then he stops.

"Iris, honey... You're upset. I don't want to take advantage."

"You're not. You'd be giving me something I want and need tonight. I need to feel like I'm still here, that I'm a survivor and not a victim. I'm all jumbled up, but the only thing I know for certain is I want to feel the way I did this weekend. With you."

"That's not why I stayed... Because I wanted that. Even

though I do." He closes his eyes and takes a breath. "For fuck's sake. I'm making a mess of this."

I start to laugh and can't stop. I laugh so hard, I have tears in my eyes. I laugh until he turns us so he's on top of me, staring down at me with the intense gaze that's intrigued me from the first time I met him. His eyes say so much about who and what he is. And right now, he's as fierce as I've ever seen him, staring down at me with a mixture of annoyance and amusement reflected in his expression.

"Are you finished?" he asks.

That sets me off again.

He kisses me until I quit laughing and start kissing him back.

I curl my arms around his neck and my legs around his hips, pressing my core against his hard length. This is what I need. *He* is what I need. He makes me feel alive in a way I haven't been since tragedy struck.

His hand slides down my back to cup my ass, holding me in place as he rocks against me while never letting up on the tongue-curling kiss.

Yes. Yes. *Yes.*

When he's touching me and kissing me and making me see stars, I have no bandwidth left to think about the latest catastrophes to befall me. There's only space for him and me and us and this. He moves quickly to get rid of our clothes and slides into me, the tight fit demanding my full attention.

Then he dips his head to take my nipple into his mouth, and I nearly come from the combination of that and the pressure from where our bodies are joined.

I cling to him, wanting this feeling to last as long as it possibly can, because only this can block out the darkness and make me forget. My hands coast over his back and down to cup his muscular backside as he pumps into me, reminding me that I'm still very much a woman with so much left to give.

I needed that reminder so badly.

"Look at me," he whispers gruffly.

I open my eyes and blink him into focus, so sexy and handsome and devoted. To have his full attention this way is such a gift.

"You're magnificent, and anyone who didn't realize what he had with you is a goddamned fool."

Nothing he could've said to me would've meant more than that tonight.

We stare into each other's eyes as he reaches between us to tease me into an orgasm that comes from the deepest part of me. The release is a purging of sorts, a letting go of the stress and trauma that's held me in its grip for hours. As I come down from the highest of highs, I expect the gloom to reappear. But it doesn't. I feel too good for gloom.

"I might need a regular dose of your special brand of mind-altering treatment."

His gruff chuckle makes me smile. "Any time, babe."

"You made me feel something other than horrible. I'm incredibly grateful for that."

"Likewise." He kisses my forehead and lips. "I haven't felt this good in a very long time."

"I'm glad. I want that for you."

"I want it for you, too."

"But no relationships."

"Right."

Again, there's a hint of amusement in his eyes as he confirms his earlier position.

It's fine. If all we ever have is this, it's more than enough. Or so I tell myself.

GAGE

SHE SEEMS BETTER in the morning. I'd like to think it was the sex. We did it three times during the night, and while I should be exhausted after barely sleeping, I'm energized and determined to get her through whatever comes her way today.

It's strange to realize that I don't feel guilty anymore about having sex with Iris, probably because we've been friends for years, and I think Natasha would've liked her as much as I do. That helps me to make peace with being intimate with someone who isn't my wife. If I'd been with some random person, I would've been a wreck over it.

"You can go to work, Gage," Iris says over coffee. "I won't fall apart."

"I can work from here, unless you'd rather be alone."

"I like having you here, but I don't want you to miss work."

"I never missed a day of work when Nat and the girls were alive. I barely took vacations, and when I did, I was so distracted, I could hardly enjoy them. I regret that I wasn't more present with them, and I'd like to think I've learned a few things about what's important in life. Work doesn't come first on my list anymore."

"That's a tough lesson to learn."

"It took losing everything that mattered to wake me up to it. I'm not proud of that, even if I'm proud of the company I built from nothing. If it can't function without me occasionally, then it's all for naught."

"I suppose that's true."

"I used to believe it would fall apart if I wasn't hands-on all day every day. After the accident, I found out how truly nonessential I really am when I didn't work for six months."

"You also found out that the amazing team you'd assembled could keep things running."

"Why didn't I realize that before? Why did it take losing Nat and the girls to wake me up?"

"I don't know, and I'm sorry you feel guilty about that."

"I've learned that time with the people we care about is the only thing we have on any given day. Sure, we must work and make a living to support ourselves but letting that become the most important thing in our lives isn't worth it."

"Have you posted about that?"

"Not yet. I haven't wanted to confess to that level of guilt."

"It's a very powerful message that someone out there might need to hear."

"Yeah, I suppose so. I'll think about that. Today, I posted about how you never know what's coming around the next curve in the road and how it's a good idea to appreciate any peace or serenity you can find while you have it."

"Another good message."

"Inspired by what happened to you yesterday."

"I was thinking in the shower, about when Mike was living part-time in Denver, and how many times I planned to visit him there only to have it canceled at the last minute because a 'flight came up.' I'm wondering now if he was lying whenever he told me that or when he couldn't get home from there because of a weather advisory that I never bothered to check, because why would I? If my husband told me he couldn't fly, I believed him."

"You had no reason not to believe him, and I'm sure he wasn't lying every time he told you something like that."

"I'm not a 'blind faith' kind of person. I don't just sign up with a guy and turn things over to him, confident that he'll always do the right thing. I kept a hand in our finances, so I'd know what was going on if I ever needed to. I insisted on all big decisions being made together. I made sure I talked to him every day, even when he was away, so we'd stay connected to each other. I never ended a call without telling him I loved him. I took comfort in that. After. That he knew how much I loved him."

"I have no doubt you were a wonderful wife."

"Then how could this have happened?"

Ten

IRIS

In the bright light of day, I can't avoid it even though I wish I could. I want to know what happened and why.

The phone rings with a call from my mother. "I have to take this."

"Go ahead. I'm going to check my email."

"Hey, Mom. How'd everything go?"

"Totally fine, as always. They're very good for us. How're you doing?"

"I'm okay."

"Daddy and I can't get over Mike being blamed for the accident. He was so diligent and focused on safety."

"Yes, he was." I swallow the surge of nausea that burns my throat at the thought of what else I need to tell her. "So, after you left yesterday, Steve came by. You remember him, right? Mike's business partner?"

"Of course. He must be as upset as you are."

"He is. But he told me something else I didn't know, something that's truly rocked my world."

"What?"

"He said Mike had another child with a woman in Denver."

"No."

"He has proof."

"How does he have proof?"

I tell her about the DNA test.

"He took Tyler's DNA without your consent, and had it compared to this other child? That's outrageous!"

"I agree, and I plan to tell him so, but he wanted to be sure before he told me about it."

"Why did he have to tell you? What good could it possibly do now for you to hear that?"

"She's threatening to sue the company and me for child support."

"Come on! No way. What will you do?"

"Fight it, I suppose," I say, even though the thought of that kind of thing is draining before it even begins. "My friend Joy, who specializes in family law, is doing some research to get a handle on what my liability might be."

"How in the world can you be liable to a woman and child you didn't even know existed before yesterday?"

"I'm not sure. The estate is closed, so the question is whether she can sue me personally."

"Jesus, Mary and Joseph. Right when I think I've heard everything. How could he do such a thing?"

"That's a very good question."

"I'm so sorry, honey. Just when you were starting to get your sparkle back."

I hate the tears I hear in her voice. We've shed enough tears over the last few years. "I'm determined not to let this be a setback, Mom. I'm crushed to learn this about the man I thought I knew, and I'm devastated about the NTSB report, but I can't go back to where I was when I first lost him. I just can't."

Gage gives me two thumbs up when he hears me say that.

I send him a warm smile.

"I'm glad to hear you say that," Mom says. "We never want to see you flattened like that again."

"I'm not going back. I've learned that there's only forward."

"You make me proud every day, Iris, but I'm especially proud today."

"Aw, thanks. You know that means everything to me."

"I'll pick up the kids and have them for another night. Take a minute to deal with all this and don't worry about them. Take care of you."

"I don't deserve you."

"Sure, you do. And you can pay me back when I'm drooling and in diapers a few short years from now."

"Haha, it's going to be more than a few years, and you know I'll always take good care of you, the way you've taken care of me."

"Love you, honey. Call if you need anything."

"I will. And I'll call to say good night to the kids. I'll be back on duty tomorrow."

"Will you tell them?"

"Not now. Maybe later when they're older and more able to handle the implications."

"I agree. They're too young to understand. We'll talk to you later."

I end the call more thankful for my amazing mother than usual, and that's saying something. "Thank goodness for awesome mothers," I say to Gage.

"She's great, and I love how close you two are."

"We've been an unstoppable pair since I was very little, when she took off with me in the middle of the night to escape a violent marriage to my biological father. Her mother never forgave her for marrying Darryl, who's white. My mom says the only thing good that came from him is my gorgeous skin color that's a perfect combination of them both."

"I agree your skin is gorgeous, and I never would've guessed that Jimmy is your stepfather."

"He's wonderful. She met him when I was five, and he's been so good to both of us."

"Do you see Darryl?"

"Sporadically. My mom sued for full custody and won. She allowed only supervised visitation with him, which he rarely requested. The most I've ever heard from him was after Mike died. He said he wanted to be there for me and the kids, and he has been, as much as he's capable of being. But Jimmy is my dad, and he's my kids' grandpa."

"They had more kids together?"

"Three. I call them my first babies. I adore them all. And my mom... She's turned lemons into lemonade. All my life, even to this day, she takes in women who were in domestic violence situations and makes them part of our family. There's probably been a hundred of them over the years."

"Wow, that's incredible."

"She's never forgotten how difficult it was to escape that situation, or how much the kindness of strangers made a difference."

"Is it safe for her to take them in?"

"We've had a few situations over the years, but for the most part, it's fine."

"It's an incredible thing she's doing."

"She'd tell you that after raising her four kids, it's her life's work. She got a master's in social work while we were all still at home and works for two different agencies that serve the DV community—and helps me with the kids any time I need it. She's a wonder woman."

"Like her daughter."

"Oh, please. I aspire to be a fraction of what she is. I've always felt like a slacker next to her."

"What was your career before you had kids?"

"I worked in online marketing for years. I still do some freelance projects in that space, but I've been working on something else recently that I'm excited about."

"What's that?"

"I haven't told anyone."

"Okay, now you have to tell me, or I'll die of curiosity."

"Don't say 'die.' We've had enough of that."

"Then you'd better tell me."

I pick up my phone and find what I want to show him and then hand the phone to him.

"What am I looking at?"

"It's called TikTok." I giggle at his confused expression.

"I think I've heard something about that."

"How can you be so hip to Instagram and know nothing about TikTok?" I ask with amusement.

"I refuse to take on another social media site. It's all I can do to keep up with Insta."

"About a year ago, I started posting videos of single-mom hacks... little things I do to make my life easier as a suddenly single mom to three little kids. It's, um, sort of taken off." I take back the phone and tap some more on the screen before handing it back to him.

His eyes bug out of his head when he sees I have one point two million followers. "Iris! What the hell? You have *more than a million* followers?"

"I know, right? And now I'm getting sponsorship offers every day. It's turned into more than I ever expected, which has me working on a business plan to capitalize on it."

"Why have you never mentioned this to us?"

I shrug. "It was just something I did for fun. I never expected anything to come of it."

"This is incredible. Congratulations."

"Thanks. It's been a fun outlet for when the kids are at school. I can give it an hour a day and still get everything else done."

"And here I thought my hundred thousand followers was impressive."

"It's so impressive. What you're doing is incredibly important. It helps so many people. Mine is just silly mom fun."

"It's not silly. Like who knew that a Bounce sheet in a backpack keeps the funk away?"

I laugh at the way he says that. "Stop. It's got nothing on helping widows survive another day."

"There're a few guys on here who think you're a MILF."

"What?" I take back the phone. "Ew. That's gross. I blocked them."

"With that many followers, you're going to have weirdos in there. You need to be on the lookout for that."

"I barely look at the comments. Who has the time?"

"Iris... Seriously. You can't be too careful in this day and age."

"They have no idea who I really am or where I live or anything about my kids other than that I'm a single mom to three of them. Don't worry."

"They can also see you're sexy as all hell, and that's why you're getting randos making inappropriate comments."

I prop my chin on my upturned hand. "Am I sexy as all hell?"

He rolls his eyes. "As if you didn't already know that."

"I didn't know that until you told me."

"I'm sure Mike told you, too."

"At first, he did. Toward the end, not so much."

"That's a crying shame. He should've been telling you that every day."

"Now I know he was probably saying that to someone else." I stop short, gasping. "What if there was more than one?"

GAGE

"Iris..."

She launches out of her chair and leaves the room, returning with an iPhone that she plugs into a charger on the counter. "I've never looked through his phone, because I didn't think I had any reason to."

"Maybe it's not such a great idea for you to do that now

either." I hate this idea with every fiber of my being. "What difference will it make for you to know?"

"After what I learned yesterday, I'm wondering if I knew my husband at all, or if I knew some version of him that he created for me. Does that make sense?"

"It does, but why can't you hold on to the version of him that you knew and let the rest of it go?"

"Because I want to know. I want to try to understand why he did the things he did. Did his distraction over leading a double life lead to the crash?"

I reach out my hand to her.

She takes hold of it and lets me bring her to sit on my lap.

"I don't want to see you hurt any more than you already have been. All you need to know is that he was unfaithful. You don't need to know the full scope of it. Knowing won't change anything. Like I said before, all that will do is hurt you more than you already are."

"I appreciate where you're coming from, and I agree with what you're saying. It will hurt me more to find out there were others. But I need to know—and I want to know why. I can't have those questions hanging over me for the rest of my life."

With my arms around her, I keep her from getting up. "Iris, please... Last night, you said you're worried about being able to take care of your kids. What if you learn something from looking at his phone that makes it impossible to do that?"

"I'm ready for whatever I might find out. I already know he wasn't the man I thought he was, and in a way, that sort of changes how I think of him. I loved him so much. I did everything I could to make our marriage work. I thought he was doing the same thing. It's crushing to find out otherwise, but I still need the details. I want to understand."

"I don't like it."

"Thank you for caring."

"I do care. So many people care about you. None of us wants to see you hurt any further."

"I'll be all right. I promise." Because I can't stop her, I let her up to retrieve the phone, which comes to life with a beep. "Did you go through Natasha's phone after she died?"

"My sister uploaded the pictures from Nat's phone to the cloud, so I'd have them, but I've never looked at anything else. I just couldn't look at the rest."

"I felt like I'd be invading his privacy or something if I went through his phone, which is silly when you think about it. He's dead. What does he care about his privacy? But I always prided myself on being the kind of wife who didn't pry. Turns out I should've been prying."

"No, you shouldn't have. Living like that is no kind of marriage. You either trust the person you've committed to spend your life with, or you don't."

"I trusted him," she says sadly. "After that first time, he gave me no reason not to, or so I thought. I really believed he'd learned his lesson from nearly losing me the first time."

"Why can't you take what you already know, deal with it to the best of your ability and go forward from here? Knowing the full extent of it is only going to make everything worse." I'm as certain of that as I've ever been of anything.

"It could make things better if I find out why."

"Will it, though? What if you find out he never loved you, or he thought of you and the kids as a terrible burden, or some other awful thing you didn't need to know? Please, Iris. Don't go through his phone. Nothing good will come of that."

She stares at the phone for a long time before she powers it down.

I'm so relieved, I'm nearly faint with it. I'm not sure why I'm so positive that looking at the phone is a bad idea, but I feel it in my bones. "Come here."

She returns to her perch on my lap, and I wrap my arms around her while pressing my lips to her forehead.

"I'm not saying I'll never look, but I hear what you're saying, and you're right. Now is not the time."

"Here's what I know for sure. You had a life with him, a life that you loved and cherished. Those are the memories you need to hold on to now. The rest of it had nothing to do with you."

"Didn't it, though?"

"No, it didn't. It would matter very much if he was still alive. What does it matter now? He's gone, and you're left to finish raising his children alone. Why should you have terrible thoughts in your head about their father while you're doing that? I mean, what we know is awful enough. The dirty details aren't going to make it better."

"Thank you for being the voice of reason."

"I understand the need to know everything that happened. I've been that way as the case against the driver who killed Nat and the girls works its way through court. I'm obsessed. I want every single detail, and some of them made an already unbearable situation a thousand times worse, such as finding out that his friends knew he was loaded and did nothing to stop him from driving. I didn't need to know that."

She rests her head on my shoulder. "No, you didn't."

"That's what I mean... Just when we think something hurts as much as it possibly can, something comes along that makes that pain seem like nothing. You have to protect yourself from that, Iris. You've worked so hard to get where you are now, and you've been such an inspiration to so many people just starting this journey. I don't want to see you set yourself backward by accessing information that won't change anything. Mike will still be dead, and you'll still be here to carry on without him, but with information that'll make your journey more excruciating than it needs to be."

"I hate him a little bit today."

"I don't blame you."

"There was this one time when we were on a family vacation at the beach when he got called to work for something in Denver. I wonder if that's when the baby was born."

"Again, what does it matter? It's in the past. Please don't drive yourself crazy asking questions like that. Having those answers will hurt you more than help you."

"What am I going to do if she sues me?"

"You'll get a lawyer, like Joy, to fight her tooth and nail. I wouldn't want to go up against Joy in a courtroom."

That draws a laugh from her. "Me neither. Girlfriend is fierce."

"She'll make it go away."

"Maybe I need to start accepting some of the sponsorship offers so I'll have extra money to fight a lawsuit."

"Wait to see what happens. She may be advised that there's no point suing you because Mike's estate has already been closed. It has, right?"

"A while ago."

"The time to sue has passed. She might be able to go after some of the insurance money he had through work, but with him being blamed for the crash, that gets trickier, too."

"I'd planned to put the rest of the insurance money away for the kids' college funds, but I probably won't get it now that they're blaming him for the accident."

"You'll have what you need for the kids."

"What does that mean?"

"Just what I said. I don't have kids to put through college anymore. I can help you with that."

"Gage... Stop."

"Stop what?"

"You're not paying for my kids to go to college."

"I can if I want to."

"No, you can't."

"We can have that fight in twelve years."

"We're having it now, and you're not paying."

"My company makes a lot of money. Like, a lot a lot. If your kids need college tuition, they'll have it. End of story."

"You're too kind, but the answer is still no."

"We'll see."

"Gage?"

"Yes?"

"You said you don't want a relationship, right?"

"That's right."

"I'd just like to point out that by running to me in my time of need, by holding me and making love to me all night long, by talking me through the calamity and wanting to pay for my kids to go to college... This is starting to feel like a relationship."

"It's not."

Her body shakes, and for a second, I'm alarmed, until I realize she's laughing. At me. "You think that's funny?"

She nods because she's laughing too hard to speak.

"How dare you laugh at me?" I ask in pretend outrage.

"Can't help it," she says, gasping for air. "You're in a *relationship*," she adds in a singsong voice. "Gage plus Iris, sitting in a tree, K-I-S-S-I-N-G."

The only way to shut her up is to kiss her. I can't be in a relationship with her or her kids, not when I promised myself I'd never again love anything or anyone I can't live without.

Eleven

IRIS

I decide I want to be with my kids. When they're around, I have no time to think about anything but them and their endless wants and needs, their arguments, their sweet commentary and their sweeter love. I text my mom to let her know I'm feeling stronger and will pick them up after school.

Are you sure? I don't mind having them another night.

I'm sure. After being away from them for the weekend and then last night, too, I don't want them to think something is wrong. And when they're around, I don't have time to think.

Understand completely. I made a lasagna for dinner that I'll drop off so you don't have to cook.

I don't deserve you.

Quit saying that. LOL

For the longest time, she thought LOL meant *lots of love.* When I told her it actually means *laugh out loud*, we laughed so hard, we had to hold each other up. So now she says it stands for both. No one has ever loved me the way she does, and I'm thankful for her every day, especially since I lost Mike. She's always been one of my greatest sources of support, but never more so than the last few years.

Without her to help, encourage and support me, I probably would've rolled into a ball after Mike died, when the idea of raising three heartbroken little kids on my own was more than I could bear to contemplate.

"I'm going to pick up my kids," I tell Gage at two forty-five. He's been strangely quiet since I teased him about being in a relationship. "You want to come for the ride?"

"Will it confuse them if I'm around?"

"I don't think so. They know we're friends and are used to seeing you."

"I don't even know what I'm doing here."

"I do," I say with a knowing smile.

"Really, Iris... I probably should just go."

"Don't go unless you really want or need to."

"I don't want to, but..."

I lay my finger over his lips. "Let's spend some time with the kids and talk about the rest of it later."

His entire body goes slack with relief at being given a reprieve.

I love having him around, especially during this latest upheaval, but I'm not sure what I'm dealing with when it comes to his relationship issues. I hope he'll eventually share his thoughts on the matter, because I feel ready for the R-word, and he's my leading—and only—candidate.

And it's not just because we had sex. For the last year or so, any time I pictured myself with someone new, it was his face I saw, and I've only realized that in the last few days.

He gets into the passenger side of my silver Toyota Sienna minivan and puts on his seat belt. "This is fancy."

"No one grows up saying they can't wait to drive a minivan, but I love this one. Although by the time I finish paying for it, it won't be worth a dime with the way my kids treat it."

"Like Nat's rolling Superfund site, and she couldn't even blame the kids. It was like that before them."

"I may borrow that description."

"Feel free. I used to joke that I needed to don a hazmat suit to clean it." After a long pause, he says, "She'd like you."

At a stoplight, I glance over at him, floored by the comment. "You think so?"

"Definitely. She had the same snarky sense of humor you have, and she was funny like you are with the commentary on everything. She had a very small circle of girlfriends because she said women were catty beasts most of the time, and she had no patience for that or mom drama or any of that crap."

"I feel the same way. From everything you've told me about her, I bet we would've been best friends."

"Definitely."

"I try to surround myself with supportive, loving, thoughtful women who raise each other up rather than tear each other down."

"Like I said... She would've liked you."

"That's an amazing compliment, Gage. Thank you."

He shrugs. "It's true."

"Can I ask you something?"

"Sure."

"What's your objection to the R-word?"

He doesn't answer for almost a full minute, as if he needs that long to decide what to say. "I promised myself after I lost Nat and the girls that I'd go forward on my own. It's just easier that way."

"How did you get into the Wild Widows with that philosophy?"

"When Christy said the only rule was being open to a second chance at love, I said, fine, I'm open to it, because I was desperate to meet some people who got it, you know? Even though I agreed to the group's rule, I've planned to stay single."

"I can understand why it's easier that way, but isn't it lonelier, too?"

"It can be, but it's better."

"How so?"

"It just is. It's what works for me."

As I pull up to Laney's preschool, I ponder that reply and grapple with the disappointment that comes with realizing this bond between us will never go beyond friends with benefits. I can live with that if he's still my friend, but as much as I wish it could be more, I won't force myself—or my three young kids—on a man who doesn't want what I do.

Laney is full of delightful chatter and news as always, and as we drive to the elementary school to get her brother and sister, we hear a long story about an exploding juice box that has her laughing so hard, she can barely breathe. She's so damned cute and sweet, and I love her unreasonably, which is such a relief.

For a time after Mike died, I was so overwhelmed by caring for an infant on top of two other children that I resented her. It's not something I'm proud of now—and I've never told another living soul I felt that way about her, even my mother. It was all caught up in my anger at him for dying after talking me into a third child. I don't think about that time very much anymore, but the little girl I once saw as a burden has become my daily ray of sunshine.

Tyler comes bursting out of school and runs for the car, holding a box in his hand that he waves around as he comes toward us. "I won a *Titanic* model today! Can we put it together when we get home? I bet there's a YouTube video on how to do it."

Sophia, my dawdler, gets in the car, buckles in and blows a kiss to Laney, who is always thrilled to see her big sister after a long day apart.

"Mom!" Tyler says as I pull out of the pickup line. "Can we make the model?"

"I'll check after dinner," I tell him.

"I can help," Gage says. "I used to build models all the time."

"Awesome," Tyler says. "We learned all about the *Titanic* today in the library. Did you know it hit an iceberg and *sank*?"

"What's an iceberg?" Sophia asks.

"Duh," Tyler says, "it's a block of ice in the water."

"Be nice, Tyler," I tell him.

"Did people die?" Sophia asks.

"Like fifteen hundred. They froze like Popsicles."

"Tyler!"

Gage shakes with silent laughter, and it's all I can do not to lose it laughing, too. Honestly, the things that come out of Tyler's mouth. And why are they teaching second graders about fifteen hundred people dying on the *Titanic*?

"They weren't like Popsicles," I tell Sophia, concerned that she'll never eat another one.

"What's a Popsicles?" Laney asks.

"Duh," Tyler says.

"We're going to have a conversation about kindness if you keep saying that D-word, young man."

"It's a frozen treat on a stick," Sophia tells her sister. "We had them last summer, and they turned your lips red, remember?"

I catch Laney nodding when I glance in the mirror.

"Did my daddy like Popsicles?" Laney asks.

"He loved orange ones," I tell her. She asks questions about Mike every day. I never know what it's going to be as she builds a profile of the father she never knew. She was a newborn when he died. We have only thirty-two photos of the two of them together that I put into a picture book that she looks at so often, I've had to reprint it twice.

"Mommy, are you going to have more babies?" Sophia asks. "Lauren's mom is having another baby, but she said you can't because we don't have a daddy."

"Jesus," Gage says under his breath.

"I have all the babies I could ever want," I tell her, even as my heart breaks once again.

"I want an orange Popsicles," Laney says. "Like my daddy."

I catch her staring at pictures of Mike all the time, looking for answers to questions she doesn't know how to ask yet. But she will. I worry about all three of them, but her thirst for details about Mike makes me worry about how she'll fill the blank places where he should be.

"Mr. Gage, can you stay for dinner so we can work on the model?" Tyler asks. "Mom, can he stay?"

"Of course he can, if he wants to. Grandma made lasagna."

"Her lasagna is *sick*," Tyler says. "You don't want to miss that."

"I'm sold," Gage says.

"Yes!" Tyler's fist in the air pops into the rearview mirror.

"Homework and chores first," I remind him.

He groans loudly.

"The faster you get your work done, the sooner you can build your model."

"Fine."

"Fine."

We pull into the garage, and Tyler launches out of his booster seat like he's been shot out of a cannon, backpack dragging behind him.

Sophia, the helpful big sister, releases the latch on Laney's seat that confounds most adults and helps her down from the car. They take off inside in hot pursuit of Tyler.

"Holy. *Shit*."

Gage's two-word summary cracks me up. "Just another day in paradise."

"Is every day like that?"

"They went a little easy on me today."

"How do you do it?"

"One minute at a time." I look over at him. "No pressure on dinner and the model. I can help him with it."

He raises a brow, his expression skeptical. "Have you ever built a model?"

"No, but I learn everything I need to know on YouTube."

"It would take you four days of doing nothing but that."

"No way."

"Way. They're crazy complicated, but I've got you covered. I told him I'd help him, and I'd never disappoint him."

"Thank you."

He looks straight ahead, seeming lost in thoughts, or memories maybe. "I'd forgotten."

"What?"

"How intense kids can be. I remember the big things, like how Ivy liked dark chocolate and hated peanut butter, and Hazel would've eaten spaghetti three meals a day if we'd let her. But the questions, the bickering, the sheer insanity of it. I'd forgotten that, and I never wanted to forget any of it."

"Mom! I can't find the trash bags!" Tyler says from the doorway to the garage.

"I'm coming." I look over at Gage, smiling. "Duty calls. I'm sorry if we made you sad."

"It's okay. I enjoyed listening to them. They're delightful."

"They can be."

"They're delightful all the time. I'm sure it must seem hard to believe when you're in the trenches like you are now, but the time will go so quickly. My older sister talks about how she cried her eyes out when she sold her minivan after her youngest went to college. She said she raised her kids in that car, and she grieved that time in her life for a long time, even as she upgraded to a Mercedes two-seater."

I laugh at that last part. "Good for her. And I know it's going to fly by. It already is. I can't believe I'll miss this car someday."

"You'll miss what went on inside this car. I remember Heather telling me to enjoy every ride I gave my kids, because the second they got their licenses, I'd never drive them anywhere again."

"Mom, are you coming?"

"I gotta go," I tell Gage.

"I've got to make a call. I'll be right in."

"Take your time."

As I go inside to supervise snacks, drinks, chores and home-work, I ponder how Gage offered to build the model with Tyler and agreed to stay for dinner. For a man who says he wants to stay removed, he's not doing a very good job of it.

Twelve

GAGE

Before I go inside, I call my older sister.

"Hey," Heather says, "this is a nice surprise. Everything okay?"

"Everything is fine. I was thinking about you and figured I'd give you a call."

"What were you thinking about?"

"Your minivan and how you cried when you sold it."

"I still cry when I see it around town, packed to the gills with kids."

"You're ridiculous."

"I know," she says with a sigh. "I used to do nothing but complain about their never-ending schedules and running a taxi service. Now it's a major event if all five of us are in a car together."

"I remember the complaining."

"I regret that now," she says softly. "More than you know."

The loss of her twin nieces devastated my sister. "It's perfectly normal to feel that way when you're in the heat of battle with your kids. Nat used to complain all the time that their lives were way better than hers."

"I remember that," Heather says with a laugh. "She was so funny with the commentary. I miss that. I miss her. Every day."

"I know. Me, too."

"What brought on memories of me and my minivan?"

"I took a ride with a friend to pick up her kids in her minivan, which looks—and smells—a lot like yours used to."

"Ugh, the smell! It was revolting! Dave used to clean it once a month and joked that he needed antinausea medication ahead of time."

"That sounds about right," I say, amused. "Two little girls made a hellacious mess of Nat's car. She used to say we had to take my car occasionally to keep things fair."

"So, you're riding in a minivan to do a school pickup with a friend? What's up with that?"

"Just what I said. I went for the ride."

"During a workday?"

"I took the day off."

"You took a day off? Are you feeling all right?"

"Haha, very funny."

"I'm serious. You've barely taken a day off since you went back to work."

"My friend, who's also a widow, is having a bit of a crisis."

"What kind of crisis?"

"The kind where the NTSB blames her late husband for the plane crash that killed him and others, and the kind where, on the same day that bombshell lands, she finds out he had a fourth kid with another woman who may want to sue her for child support."

"Damn..."

"Yeah, so I didn't think it was a good idea to leave her alone with that."

"Good call. Are you, you know... involved with her?"

"Kinda?"

"What does that mean, Gage?"

"We spend time together. She's got a lot on her plate with three little kids. The oldest is seven."

"That's a lot on her own, the poor thing. Does she have help?"

"Her parents are nearby and are a great source of support."

"Oh, that's good. And she has you, too."

"We're friends through the Wild Widows."

"Iris, right? You've told me about her before."

"Yes. What have I told you?"

"How much you admire the way she's raising three kids as a single mom while dealing with her grief and theirs."

I don't recall talking to her about Iris. "It's rather impressive."

"Do you like her?"

"Of course I do. I told you. She's my friend."

"Do you like her as more than a friend?"

"No."

"Are you lying?"

"Maybe," I confess with a laugh.

"I had a feeling..."

"I never have been able to lie to you."

"So don't start trying now. What're you going to do about this woman you like as more than a friend?"

"Nothing."

"Why?"

"You know why."

"You're forty-one. You can't honestly expect to spend the rest of your life alone."

"That's the plan."

"It's a terrible plan! I've told you that so many times."

"I know, but that's how it has to be."

"No, that is *not* how it has to be. What happened to Nat and the girls was horrible and tragic and never should've happened. But to refuse to ever care that much about anyone again out of fear of losing them is no way to live."

"It works for me."

"Does it, though?"

It strikes me as funny that Iris asked that exact question earlier.

Tyler comes to the door to the garage to make sure I'm still there. I wave to him and stick up a finger to tell him I'll be there in a minute. I haven't built a model in years, and I'm looking forward to helping him.

"Gage? Does it really work for you?"

"Most of the time."

"I don't know why you insist on limiting yourself this way. It won't bring Nat or the girls back."

"I know that," I snap more harshly than I intended. "I know." I gentle my tone because Heather has been a rock for me through this nightmare and doesn't deserve me snapping at her.

"What's the point, then? Who benefits if you sacrifice yourself this way?"

"It's not a sacrifice. It's a choice."

"It's a bad choice, especially when you have someone right there in front of you who could be so much more than a friend if you'd let her."

"How do you even know that?"

"She has you riding to her kids' school in her minivan. If she didn't have feelings for you, you'd never get anywhere near her kids."

"I'm her friend. We're close because of the widow group."

"That's not all it is, and you can't convince me otherwise."

"I don't want it to be more than that."

"Okay."

"What does that mean?"

"Just what I said. If you insist that you don't want anything more with her, then I can't change your mind. But let me ask you this—if, God forbid, something happened to Iris and her kids tomorrow, would you grieve them?"

"God, yes. Don't even say that."

"Then I hate to tell you, little brother, but you're already in trouble where they're concerned. Allowing it to be even more won't make it any worse than it would've been otherwise if something were to happen, which it won't."

Her observation makes me feel panicky. "You can't know that."

"Do you know anyone else who's lost their spouse and kids in an accident? Because I don't. I don't know of a single other person who's been through what you have, and I have thousands of friends and contacts online. It's not going to happen again. It's safe to care about Iris and her kids."

"No, it isn't." She's made me realize that losing any of them would devastate me, and we're not even involved that way. Or are we? *Son of a bitch...* This is why I've avoided shit like this since I lost Nat and the girls.

"Yes, it is," Heather insists. "It's safe to love and be loved. I promise."

"You can't promise that, Heather. You're not God. You can't protect the people I love."

"No, I can't, and neither can you. There was nothing you wouldn't have done to prevent what happened to Nat and the girls. *Nothing.* Even you couldn't have prevented the accident that took them from us because you weren't there. No one can be everywhere, not even a superman like you."

I've relived that day a thousand times, trying to figure out how I might've changed the outcome. I had a presentation for a huge new client that morning that I'd prepared for over several months. Nat and the girls had gotten up early to make me breakfast, kiss me goodbye and wish me good luck with the pitch. When I left the house that morning, I never imagined I'd just said goodbye to them forever.

And I didn't get the client.

"What're you thinking?"

"About that day, how I was consumed with work while they were being slaughtered by a drunk driver who should've been in jail." The murder of my family was his fifth DUI offense.

"Your work supported your family. You weren't doing anything wrong by focusing on it." She and others have told me that a thousand times since that tragic day but hearing it repeatedly doesn't change the narrative in my mind. "No one can be everywhere," she says again, more softly this time. "Caring about Iris and her kids isn't going to ruin your life a second time."

"You can't know that for certain."

"No, I can't, but what I do know for certain is if you spend the rest of your life alone out of fear of more loss, you'll be compounding the tragedy you've already suffered."

Tyler comes back to the door, his expression achingly hopeful and innocent.

"I need to see a boy named Tyler about a model of the *Titanic*."

"Gage..."

"I heard everything you said, and I'll even admit you're right about everything. I just don't know if I can."

"Try."

"I gotta go."

"Call me tomorrow."

"I will if I can."

"I'll worry if you don't."

"I'm fine. I promise."

"Call me."

"All right. Don't tell Mom any of this. I don't need you guys double-teaming me."

"I won't say anything, but I'm looking forward to meeting Iris and her children."

"That's not going to happen."

"Love you, Gage."

"Love you, too." As I end the call, I realize I've made a huge mistake involving Heather in this situation with Iris. Of course she's going to be on Team Iris, because she's been after me for a long time to get back out there and meet someone new. I've never wanted to. I still don't. But Iris isn't someone new. She's been by my side for a while now and understands my journey better than anyone in my life, other than our widow friends, that is.

If I'm being honest with myself—and what's the point of not being honest—this thing with Iris, while it only recently turned physical, isn't new. It's been happening for quite some time, the connection between us on low boil long before last weekend. I can't deny that as much as I'd like to.

It's not too late for me to take a step back out of self-preservation.

And I might have if Tyler hadn't come to the door a third time to see if I'm coming to work on the model.

I cannot disappoint him.

I won't disappoint him, even if spending more time with Iris and her kids risks things I promised myself would never again be in play.

"Here I come, buddy," I say as I get out of the car.

His little face lights up with such unfettered joy that I feel my heart contract despite my best effort to remain aloof to feelings that could wreck me.

He takes me by the hand and half leads, half drags me into the kitchen, where he's already got the box opened and pieces scattered all over the place. Looks like I got here just in time to prevent a modern *Titanic* disaster.

IRIS

OUR EVENING with the kids is lovely. After we devour my mother's delicious lasagna, Gage and Tyler work for hours on the model, until I insist that Tyler shower and get ready for bed. For a second, I worry my son will have a meltdown, but thankfully, that doesn't materialize. Due to the hard work of the therapist the kids see monthly, Tyler has been doing better about controlling his propensity for tantrums, which became a problem after his father died.

"Can we finish it tomorrow, Mr. Gage?"

"Sure thing."

"Don't do anything without me."

"I never would. I need your help."

Tyler spontaneously hugs him, taking Gage—and me—by surprise. "Thank you so much for helping me. You were right. It would've taken me and Mom four days to do it."

Then he's gone in a flash, rushing by me toward the stairs.

"Use soap *and* shampoo," I yell after him.

"Yeah, yeah," he replies.

"You really gotta tell him that?" Gage asks as he stretches out kinks in his neck from the tedious work of model building.

"I do after I discovered he wasn't using either."

"How did you find out?"

"His hair felt like straw, and he smelled bad. I sat him down, looked him in the eyes and made him confess to showering with no soap because he wanted to get it over with faster. We had to talk about how important it is to keep our bodies clean."

"That's hilarious."

"It was funny, and it made me sad, because that's something Mike should've been teaching him when they showered together. Once when Tyler was little, like maybe three, he and Mike were in the shower together. When they came out, Tyler told me in all seriousness, 'Daddy has a *huge* penis.'"

Gage sputters with laughter. "I bet Mike loved that."

"He mentioned it daily for the rest of his life."

"Of course he did. That's hilarious."

"That's the stuff I want to remember about him, you know?"

"Yeah, and that's why you need to stay off his phone. You can't let the other stuff ruin your good memories of him. What you already know is enough."

"I'm trying to tell myself that, but the temptation to dig for more is pretty strong." Steve said he'd send more info to my email, but I probably ought to avoid that, too.

"What can we do to keep you from giving in to that temptation?"

"Stick around until after the kids are in bed to entertain me?" I ask with a suggestive smile.

He's torn. I can see that as plainly as the nose on his arresting face.

"Only if you want to," I add to give him an out.

"I want to, it's just…"

"Let me get them down, and then we'll talk." I have no fewer than thirty messages from our Wild Widows to return, all of them checking on me after yesterday's drama. But he's the only one I want to talk to tonight.

"Okay."

"Make yourself at home."

Thirteen

RONI

"I'm worried about Iris. She hasn't replied to my texts all day."

Derek is already in bed with a stack of work on his lap that he puts aside when I crawl in next to him, exhausted from another full day as the communications director to the first lady, mom to a four-month-old and stepmother-to-be to a three-year old. Life is busy and full and rewarding, but I'm worried about my sweet friend.

"Did you text Gage?" Derek asks. "He might know how she is."

"True." I fire off a text to Gage. *Just checking on Iris. Have you seen/talked to her? I haven't heard from her, and I'm worried.*

He responds right away. *I've been with her today, and she's doing okay, all things considered. I'm sure you'll hear back from her soon.*

Tell her not to worry about responding. If she's okay, that's all I care about.

I'll tell her you were checking on her.

Thanks!

"Sounds like he's with her now," I tell Derek.

"Good for them." He slips an arm around me and draws me in closer to him. "I'd love to see them get together."

"I would, too. I want everyone to be as happy as we are." Since we got engaged at the beach over the weekend, I've felt a sense of calm come over me—for the most part. For some reason, though, today was a rough day.

"Why the deep sigh when you talk about how happy we are?"

"Can I tell you the truth?"

"I wish you would."

"I had a rough Patrick day today."

"Aw, baby, why didn't you tell me?"

"Didn't get the chance until now."

"All you have to do is text or call me. I want to know if you're having a rough day."

"You're so busy. I'd never want to bother you."

"Please bother me. There's nothing I'd rather do than pop over to the East Wing to see my beautiful fiancée during the workday."

"I should've told you."

"Yes, you should have. What brought this on?"

"I don't know. I hate to think it might've been the engagement triggering something..."

"That was bound to happen for both of us, don't you think? Deciding to remarry is a big deal when you've been through what we have."

"True." Despite my best efforts to hold them back, tears fill my eyes and spill down my cheeks. "I just really miss him." I can't believe I've already lived more than a year without him.

"I know, and that's totally normal."

"How do we know what's totally normal?"

"When you're grieving the loss of the person you loved the most, anything and everything is normal. No one else gets to decide that for you."

"Even your new fiancé?"

"Especially him."

I wipe away tears that continue to flow. "Thank you for understanding."

"I'll always understand this particular pain, Roni. Please don't feel like you have to hide it from me. I'd never want that."

I take a deep breath and try to get my emotions under control. I've been a red-hot mess all day. "I never used to be such a waterworks."

"You have very good reason to be now. Don't apologize for that."

"Will you always be the perfect man for me?"

"I'm going to do my darndest to be everything you want and need, love."

That only makes me cry harder.

Derek holds me through the storm, comforting me with sweet words of love and understanding that soothe my soul. I'll mourn the loss of Patrick and the life we had planned forever, but it helps to be able to share that grief with someone who gets it.

"Sometimes I can't believe the way life marches on like the worst possible thing never happened."

"It's astounding, isn't it?"

"Yeah. Like how dare that happen when I have to live the rest of my life without him?"

"Exactly."

"But then I think about all the amazing gifts that have come from the worst possible loss. Like my new job with Sam, who I never would've met if Patrick hadn't died. Like my new Wild Widows friends, who are some of my favorite people in the world. Like you and Maeve, who I love so, so much. That so much good could've come from such an unspeakable tragedy is also hard to fathom."

"I agree. Maeve and I have been blessed with such incredible support since Vic died. It's been life-affirming. And now there's you and Dylan and our new life together. I feel guilty sometimes for being so happy when Vic is gone forever."

"Grief is the weirdest thing ever."

"Yep."

"But the good news—if there is good news—is that somehow, in the mess known as life, we found each other. Or I should say, you found me, stalked me, freaked me out and then made me fall in love with you and your son."

His recitation of how we met makes me laugh, the way it always does. "I want that in our wedding vows—to love, honor and stalk all the days of our lives."

His low chuckle rumbles through his chest. "For sure."

"I feel so bad for Iris, too. That's another reason I've been a mess all day. I can't imagine what she's dealing with, finding out that Mike had a child with someone else."

"I can't stop thinking about that. It was a little triggering for me after what I learned about Vic after she was gone."

"Oh, jeez, I didn't even consider that."

"I'm fine. Don't worry. It just brings it all back. I worry that maybe there's more that Iris doesn't know."

"God, I hope there isn't."

"Guys either cheat, or they don't," Derek says bluntly. "When they do, my experience is that they go all in."

"Ugh. Poor Iris. She's just the best person ever. She doesn't deserve this."

"No one does, but especially not her."

"I hope she'll be okay."

"She will be. We'll make sure of it."

GAGE

I DON'T KNOW why I'm still here, waiting for Iris to put her kids to bed so we can be together when I told her I don't want what this is turning out to be—a full-on relationship that not only includes the two of us, but her children, too. I'm not so far removed from parenthood that I'm not aware that me becoming involved with her kids is a very big deal and a responsibility that can't be taken lightly.

Despite my best intentions to remain footloose and single, I'm getting involved here. More so by the minute.

I should go.

I'm looking for my coat when my phone rings with a call from a New York number. Since it could be about work, I take the call.

"Mr. Collier?"

"Yes, who's this?"

"This is Sabre Douglas from the Elite Dance Academy in New York City. I have the names of your daughters, Ivy and Hazel, on an old list of dancers interested in performing at the Radio City Christmas show and wondered if they're still dancing? I see they'd be eleven now, so that's just the age we need after a couple of our dancers were forced to drop out. I tried to call Mrs. Collier, but her number isn't in service. Mr. Collier? Are you there?"

I can't breathe or think or do anything other than spin.

"Hello?"

"I, uh, they're no longer dancing."

"Oh, I'm so sorry to hear that. They came so highly recommended. Thank you for letting me know. Have a nice evening."

She's gone before I can tell her to do the same or say any of the things expected by politeness. How is it possible that there are still people out there who don't know? Who haven't heard? What other lists are my daughters on that might someday result in a bomb detonating a fresh wave of grief?

A year or so before they died, Nat, who was a highly accomplished dancer as a younger woman, asked a friend in New York how to get the girls an audition for the Radio City show. It didn't come to anything then, but apparently, they were put on some sort of list for future opportunities. I didn't know that. Nat would have been aware of it, though.

The girls loved to dance as much as their mother and were

rising stars, or so she said with none of the bias of motherhood. She said they were naturally gifted, the way she'd once been, and was determined to nurture their outsized talent. I'd been warned about the rigors of parenting preprofessional dancers and was wary but excited to see where it might take them.

"What's wrong?"

Iris's question draws me out of the past and back to the present in which my wife and daughters are dead. That call has opened healing wounds, and the pain takes my breath away.

"Gage." Iris sits next to me. "What is it?"

"I got a call from a dance studio in New York asking if the girls were still interested in auditioning for the Radio City Christmas show."

"Oh God. Gage..."

"It's just so hard to believe someone doesn't know, after all this time."

She puts her arms around me and brings my head to rest on her shoulder. "I'm so sorry."

"It's okay. I just wasn't expecting that."

She runs her fingers through my hair, which is oddly soothing. "Of course you weren't."

I seem to have forgotten about my plan to leave while I still could. Her comfort is as necessary to me as my next breath. I'm overwhelmed by memories of my beautiful little girls in tutus and ballet slippers, in full makeup with their hair in buns for recitals. It all comes flooding back to me in wave after wave of nostalgia for a time I failed to fully appreciate in the moment.

I was so busy at work that Nat handled almost everything with the girls, but I never missed a recital or show. We were so proud of them and celebrated their every accomplishment with cake and flowers and lavish praise.

"I've been so far removed from all that. How is it that a single phone call can bring it all back?"

"That's all it takes."

"Yeah, as you know far too well."

"Uh-huh."

"Sorry. This week is about you, not me."

"Don't be silly, Gage. Every week is about all of us and finding a way to get through the days."

I raise my head off her shoulder so I can see her lovely face. "Thanks for being there."

"I'm so glad I was here when you got that call."

"Me, too. I would've drowned my sorrows in bourbon if I was at home alone."

She caresses my face as she gazes into my eyes with affection and concern. "There's no need for that when I'm always right here and happy to listen—and to drink bourbon with you."

I'm leaning in to kiss her before I'm aware of my intention to do so. The pull to her, to the comfort and support and caring that come with her, is too powerful to resist. When her lips connect with mine, the storm raging inside me goes silent, giving way to desire so sweet and intense, it requires my full attention.

When she reclines on the sofa, she takes me with her.

I go willingly, ending up on top of her as the kiss deepens and intensifies into something I can't find the will to resist.

Who am I kidding? I have no willpower at all when it comes to her. We proved that the other night when she slid naked into my bed—totally intentionally, regardless of what she says—and the hard shell I'd put in place to protect myself from further hurt melted like a chocolate bar left out in the sun.

I want her. I need her. I might even love her as more than a friend. With her warm and soft and eager beneath me, I can't recall why I thought it was such a good idea to resist what's happening with her. We get so carried away that we start pulling at clothes with impatience.

"Not here," she whispers against my lips. "Upstairs."

Right. Kids in the house.

I get up, give her a hand and follow her up to her room, where she closes and locks the door. Then she slides her hands up my chest to bring me down to her so we can pick up where we left off. The fire reignites instantly, leaving us straining to get closer. I push her back against the door and lift her into my arms.

Her legs wrap around my hips.

I nearly faint from a surge of desire that makes me light-headed and loopy. I'd forgotten what it was like to want someone this way, how all-consuming it can be when it's the right person. Realizing that Iris is the "right" person is a bit astounding, but I can't take the time to ponder that when she's pulling at my shirt and trying to move things along.

I put her down only long enough to remove clothes. With my jeans pooled around my ankles, I lift her again, press her back against the door and bring her down on my cock. I'm overtaken by a feeling of relief to be joined with her again, like I've been waiting for that every minute since the last time in the wee hours of this morning.

We go at it like we've just been reunited after a long separation.

Worried that we'll disturb the kids, I move us off the door and shuffle carefully to the bed, where I lay her down and hammer into her like a man possessed.

She comes twice before I let myself join her in a release that surges from the deepest part of me. It's more than a physical thing. It's emotional and spiritual, too. It's all the things I had with Nat and then some. Realizing that is devastating.

"Are you all right?" Iris asks.

"Yeah, why?"

"You just went very still for a second there."

"Because you wore me out." I can't very well tell her I'm comparing her to Nat and she's coming out ahead. Why am I even doing that? How fucked up am I?

"I wore you out. Right. You're a wild man."

"I didn't hurt you, did I?"

"The multiple orgasms would say otherwise."

I love the way she's always touching and stroking me, as if she can't help but offer comfort. That's so much a part of who she is, and I knew that about her before we ever slept together. She's a wonderfully demonstrative friend, always hugging, touching, squeezing the people she loves. I'm thankful tonight to be one of them.

"We were supposed to talk about what's going on here," she reminds me.

"Were we?"

"I believe so. I'm up for it if you want to."

I'm so drained by the sex and the grief and the tidal wave of emotions that's come with all of it that I'm not sure I have it in me. Only because three precious kids are involved do I force myself to rally, lifting off her and going in search of a towel to clean up.

I bring it back to her.

"Thanks." She removes the rest of her clothes and gets under the covers, patting the bed next to her to invite me to join her.

Here again is another opportunity to tell her I need to go, but the need for more of her takes precedence over escaping.

I get in next to her.

She curls up to me, her hand on my chest, her leg over mine.

Iris is a world-class snuggler. "Talk to me about how you're feeling."

"I'm conflicted."

"About what?"

"About this." I squeeze her shoulder. Her skin is so soft, it's like silk, and I can't stop touching her.

"Why?"

Here it is. The moment of truth I've tried to avoid for days now. But Iris deserves to know what she's dealing with, so I find the words I need to tell her. "When Nat and the girls died, I made a promise to myself that I'd never again care so much about someone that I'd be devastated to lose them the way I was after they died."

"Oh, Gage... That's an awfully difficult promise to keep."

"So I'm discovering. I was doing a pretty good job of it until a certain someone crawled naked into my bed."

"I'd say I was sorry about that, but I'm really not."

I laugh at that. "You're an evil vixen."

"Sticks and stones."

"Can I ask you something?"

"Anything you want."

"How long had you wanted to crawl into my bed?"

"Like, you want a time frame?"

"Yes, please."

"Well, if I'm being honest… Probably since around the time we met."

"That was like two years ago."

"Sounds about right."

"Iris! Why didn't you say anything?"

"What was I supposed to say? 'Hey, Gage, I want to climb you like a tree'?"

Despite the recent epic release, those words make me hard again even as I laugh. "That might've been a good place to start."

"You weren't ready, and honestly, neither was I."

"What made you decide I was ready last weekend when you 'accidentally' ended up naked in my bed?"

"That was an accident."

"No, it wasn't."

She loses it laughing. "Yes, it was!"

I pinch her ass. "You're such a liar. Why did you decide that was the time to move things along?"

"In order to answer that question, I'd have to implicate myself, so I plead the Fifth."

Amused, I say, "Tell me."

"I don't know exactly. It might've been Roni and Derek getting engaged and being so stupidly happy or being away from the kids and feeling a sense of freedom I rarely experience anymore. Or it was just pure liquid courage."

"Maybe a combination of all those things?"

"Yes, and your jeans."

"What about my jeans?"

"You wear a really nice pair of jeans."

"They're Levi's."

"They're *faded* Levi's, and they look spectacular on you. Very rugged."

"So you were ogling me?"

"I was—and objectifying you—especially when you were tending to the fire. You were bent over, and the jeans were stretched tight and... yum."

"I'm shocked speechless."

"No, you're not," she says, laughing.

"I had no idea my friend Iris was lusting after me for all this time."

"I hope you know... always... that your friendship is more important to me than that ever was."

"I do know that, but thanks for telling me."

"You're one of my essential people in widow-ville."

"Likewise."

"I respect the promise you made to yourself, and I understand better than most people would why you made it."

"But?"

"I'm not trying to change your mind. I swear I'm not. But... I'll just point out that almost three years later, the future and all its many possibilities might look different to you now than they did in those first early days of horrible grief when you probably made the promise to yourself."

"Everything looks different than it did then, when I was quite certain I wouldn't survive losing them."

"I don't know how you did. I really don't."

"The same way you survived losing Mike. One day at a time."

"I guess."

"We're all stronger than we think we are until life tests us and shows us just how strong we can be when needed."

"You're very wise."

I snort out a laugh. "If you say so."

"Everyone says so. Just look at your Instagram followers and what they have to say about you."

"I don't have a million TikTok followers hanging on my every word."

"My stuff is silly compared to what you're doing."

"It's not silly, Iris. It's very cool."

She lifts her head off my chest and looks into my eyes. I love how her hair is a mass of messy curls and her mascara is smudged, but she's still gorgeous. "I want you to know that I have no regrets about what happened last weekend or what's happened since, but if you're not up for it being more than friends with benefits, I'm okay with that."

I curl a strand of her hair around my finger. "I want to be up for it, which is a huge thing for me to admit, but my primary concern is the kids."

Her brows furrow. "What about them?"

"I worry about them becoming invested in us before we're sure it's going to stick."

"Gage..." Her smile makes her lovely eyes dance with amusement. "If I wasn't sure, I never would've ended up naked in your bed."

"Is that a confession that your attack was intentional?"

"Not at all," she says, her grin turning sly. "I'm just saying I never would've taken such a big risk with such an important friend if I wasn't sure about how I felt."

"And how do you feel?"

"That you and I could be epic."

Fourteen

IRIS

What's the point of holding back? Being a widow is a daily reminder to live life to the fullest because you never know when it might end.

"You really think so?"

"I know so, but I don't want you to feel obligated to me or the kids. This isn't about me finding them a new daddy. They have Rob and their grandfathers and other good men in their lives."

"What's it about?"

"You and me, first and foremost. It's about two people who've been to hell and back and found each other along the way and who give each other something new and sweet and wonderful to focus on amid all the heartache."

"That's a lovely idea."

"It's not just an idea. It can be our reality, but only if it's what we both want. Never in a million years would I want you to feel pressured into something you don't want or aren't ready for."

I slide my hand down her back to cup her sexy ass. "I think I've proven repeatedly that I'm interested."

"After the dry spell you had, any naked female body would've sufficed," I say in a teasing tone, echoing our first night together.

"I already told you that's not true at all. I would've turned anyone else away, naked or not."

"Really?"

"Yes, Iris," he says on a sigh. "Really. If I was going to do that for the first time after being widowed, it wasn't going to be with some random person."

"Like I did."

"Still no judgment. I swear. I just couldn't make myself do it."

"I wish I hadn't done it that way, although at the time, it felt necessary to my survival. Imagine that I felt like I was cheating on Mike by doing it with someone else. Ironic, huh?"

"Very."

"I think I want to talk to her."

"Who?"

"The mother of his other child."

"Iris..."

"I know what you're going to say, and I even agree with all the reasons you'll tell me it's a bad idea. But I want to understand what happened between them and how he could've had another family I didn't know about."

"I understand that need to know, but what concerns me is how it might devastate you."

"I'm sure it will, but at least I'll know."

I want so badly to throw myself in front of her doing this, to protect her from being hurt ever again.

"You know how everyone tells us that time heals and how angry that makes us?" she asks.

"I do. I got to the point where I feared I might punch the next person who said that to me."

"Right? Ugh. But here's the thing about the passage of time... I feel oddly disconnected from Mike and our marriage after almost three years without him. What would've been unfathomable to me when he was here feels different after so much time without him. I'm not explaining it well."

"No, you are. I get what you're saying. Enough time has gone by that you don't feel married to him anymore, and as a result, finding out he was unfaithful hits differently than it would have before you lost him."

"*Yes,*" she says on a long exhale. "Don't get me wrong. It still hurts like a motherfucker, but I feel this odd sense of detachment from it, as if it happened to someone else. It's the hardest thing to explain."

"I get it."

"That's why I think I can handle talking to her and finding out more about what went on between them."

"I still wish you wouldn't."

"I know, and I appreciate the concern." After a long pause, she gives me a pointed look. "You know what would devastate me?"

"What's that?"

"If you were to do *this* with someone else while you're doing it with me."

"I'd never do that."

"I already knew that, but then again, I thought Mike never would either."

I take her by the chin and compel her to look at me. "I would never, Iris. I swear to you."

"Thanks."

"You don't have to thank me. Other than the emotional upheaval we've both been through, this has been an amazing few days. I feel better than I have in a long time."

"I'm glad."

"And I want you to know... I'm seriously thinking about whether I can give the dreaded R-word a try."

"You are? Really?"

"Yeah."

"Aw, Gage. Look at you! My little boy is growing up and spreading his wings again."

"Stuff it," I mutter, giving her a light spank on the bum.

Her giggle is the sound of joy, something that's been sorely lacking for me since my world imploded. Along with it comes a hopeful sensation blooming like a flower within me, another reminder that life goes on even when you're sure it won't.

———

AFTER I GET the kids off to school in the morning, I come back to the house to have coffee with Gage, who hid out in my room until the kids and I left. It's far too soon for them to see him in my bedroom or to realize he's spent the night. He moved his car down the street before we finally went to sleep around midnight.

"You're going to work today," I tell him.

"Yes, I am, but only because I have to, not because I want to. I heard Tyler asking about finishing the model. Tell him I'll be back after work."

"You don't have to, Gage."

"Yes, I do, and besides, I want to."

"The least I can do is feed you dinner, then."

"I won't say no to that."

I can see that he doesn't want to leave me, but he's got a company to run, and I have a million things to do after having been distracted the last few days. "Go."

"Can I take Mike's phone with me?"

"No, you can't," I reply, smiling. "It's safe to leave me alone with it. I promise."

He stands and comes to where I'm leaning against the counter, coffee in hand. Taking the mug from me, he puts it on the counter and wraps his arms around me. His lips against my neck send a shiver of desire straight to my core. How does he arouse me so easily?

"Don't do anything to hurt my friend Iris. She means a lot to me."

"I won't."

We hold each other for a long time before he lets go, seeming reluctant.

"I'm fine. I promise."

"If you're not, call me."

"I will.

"And you'd better call Roni before she shows up here to see for herself that you're okay."

"I'll do that."

"All right, then. I'll see you later."

"I'll be here."

He kisses my forehead, the tip of my nose and then my lips. "I'm counting on that."

"You sound an awful lot like a man in a relationship."

"You're such a brat," he says with a grunt of laughter.

I flash him my sauciest smile. "Moi?"

Shaking his head and trying to hide his amusement, he grabs his phone off the table and gives me a wave as he heads for the door.

"Ah, Iris?"

"Yes?"

"Rob is here."

What the hell? He never comes without texting me first, but I've barely glanced at my phone in the rush to get the kids off to school.

Gage opens the door to let Rob in.

The two men give each other the once-over, like dogs circling each other.

"Hey, Rob. Come in. Gage, I'll see you later."

The look he gives me is unreadable, but all hints of amusement are long gone as he walks out the door.

"Did you text?" I ask Rob. "I've hardly looked at my phone this morning."

"No, I didn't. I got in the car to go to work and ended up here."

"Coffee?"

"Yeah, sure." He follows me to the kitchen. "So that guy, Gage... Are you guys like... involved?"

As I pour the coffee, I debate what I should say. I could tell him Gage came over to help me fix something, but he probably wouldn't believe that. I bring coffee for both of us to the table and put his in front of him. "We are."

"Oh. Since when?"

"Not that long, but we've been friends for almost two years."

"I didn't know you were, like, you know, ready for that."

"Neither did I. Until I was."

He looks down at his coffee. "I sort of hoped that we might..."

"Rob. Please. Don't say anything that can't be unsaid."

When he glances up at me, his expression is one of utter devastation. "I don't want to make you uncomfortable."

"Then don't. You're a treasured friend to me and beloved uncle to my kids. I need you to remain both those things. I'm counting on you, Rob, to help me raise my kids into adults Mike would be proud of."

"I'll always be here for you and them." He wipes away a tear. "This news about Mike being responsible for the crash has crushed me."

When I think about what else I need to tell him, I'm crushed for him. "It's hard to believe."

"I read the report. They said he did everything wrong when they hit the weather. How could he have done everything wrong when he trained constantly for stuff like that?"

"He might've been distracted."

"By what?"

"He had another child."

His face goes blank with utter shock. "What?"

"He was born between Tyler and Sophia."

"That can't possibly be true."

"It is true." I tell him how Steve proved it before he brought the info to me.

Rob sits back in his chair, as stunned as I was when I first heard this news, which is sort of a relief as I'd feared he might've known and not told me. However, his shock is genuine. "He had another kid."

"Yes. A son. I don't know anything more than what I've told you."

"How did Steve find out?"

"She's threatening to sue Mike's estate for child support."

"His estate is closed."

"I have a lawyer friend looking into what my liability might be."

"Wait, so she can sue *you*?"

"I was the executor of Mike's estate, so yes, I guess so. But if she thinks she has a case when he didn't name her or her child as a beneficiary, she can also sue the insurance company. I don't know. It's all a big fat mess."

"Where's she been all this time?"

"I guess she reached out to Steve a while ago, but he refused to bring it to me until he had proof that the kid is Mike's."

"Are you pissed that he used Tyler's water bottle to do that?"

"Extremely pissed, but I get that his heart was in the right place. I mean, if it came back that she was full of shit, I never would've needed to know about it."

"Yeah, I guess, but still... That's so invasive."

"It sure is. This whole thing is invasive. I feel like I never really knew the man I was married to."

"You knew him."

"Did I? I'm not so sure, and I wonder if he was so distracted by this situation that he screwed up at the worst possible time. Was she threatening him before the crash? Was that why he made critical mistakes? Was he freaking out about her blowing the lid off their affair and me finding out?"

"Jesus, Iris. Do you think that's what happened?"

"We may never know, but if he had all that weighing on him, who knows what it did to his concentration?"

"I have no idea what to do with this information."

"Welcome to my world."

"I'm sorry. You must be devastated."

"I'm oddly numb, and I'm worried about costly litigation that will chip away at the safety net Mike left for me and the kids."

"That can't happen."

"It could. Her child is his child. She probably has grounds to sue." The thought of that makes my stomach and every other part of me ache with fear and uncertainty. "I'm thinking about contacting her."

"Seriously?"

I shrug. "Why not? I want to know what she's planning, and what better way to find out than to ask her?"

"You should check with a lawyer before you do that."

"I will."

"Jeez, Iris. Just when we think we're coming back from losing him, somehow it gets worse."

"I've decided not to let this cause a setback for me. I've worked too hard for too long to get to where I am today. I can't go back to how I felt when it first happened. I just can't—and I won't."

"You're so strong," he says, his shoulders slumping. "I wish I was half as strong as you are."

"You've been so there for me and the kids. Mike would be very proud of the way you've stepped up for us."

"You really think so?" he asks, brightening.

"I know so."

"If you... end up with him... with Gage... I hope you'll still let me be part of your lives."

I'm shocked he would think I wouldn't allow that. "Of course I will." I cover his hand with mine. "You're my brother-in-law for life and my kids' uncle. You'll always be welcome in our lives, no matter what."

He blinks back tears. "Thank you. I love you guys so much."

"We love you, too."

"You could never love me as anything more than Mike's brother?"

"No, and I'm sorry if that hurts you. There's someone out there waiting for you to find her so you can write your own love story."

"It'd be nice if she'd show up one of these days."

We share a warm laugh that seems to put us back on more solid ground. I'm relieved, because the last thing in the world I want is trouble with him or Mike's family.

"Someone needs to tell your parents about Mike's other son." I put my finger on my nose. "Not it."

"Ugh, seriously? You want me to tell them?"

"Yes, please."

"I don't want to."

"Neither do I."

"They'll be devastated to learn he was unfaithful to you. They love you as much as they loved him."

Mike was adamant that no one know about his earlier indiscretion, so this news will come as a huge shock to his parents. "I know, but there's a blessing to be had in this, too. Another child of Mike's for you all to love. That child is an innocent bystander in this mess."

"True." He closes his eyes and takes a deep breath. "I'll take care of it."

"Thank you. I appreciate you taking one for the team."

"My parents will want to meet him."

"I'll tell her that when I talk to her." At some point, me talking to her has become a matter of when, not if.

"Life's a fucking bitch, isn't it?"

"And then you die."

We laugh again, and he grasps my hand. "Mike was a fool to cheat on you."

"I quite agree. I'm awesome."

"Yes, you are, and he was a lucky man to have you."

"He certainly was." I don't tell him that I'm afraid there might've been more than one other woman. I'm still not sure whether I'm going to try to find that out. Like Gage said, what does it matter now?

Rob stands to leave and takes his mug to the sink to rinse it out. When he turns back to me, he says, "I'm sorry to just show up here unannounced. I won't do that again."

"You can come here any time you want."

"Thank you, but I'll text you first going forward."

I go to him and hug him tightly. "Love you."

"Love you, too."

Fifteen

IRIS

After Rob leaves, I refill my coffee cup and take that and my phone to the sofa to curl up for a bit. I respond to all my Wild Widows, who've texted to check on me, letting them know I'm doing okay and looking forward to our dinner outing on Friday night. Our trip to the beach already feels like a lifetime ago, and it's been only a few days.

I have a text from Joy. *Hey, baby, so this is what I found out doing some digging about estates and stuff. Mike's estate has been closed by the court. The only way they'd reopen it is if some significant asset was uncovered. I doubt the mother of his other child could convince a judge to reopen it when she never came forward right after his passing. The court would've advertised that his estate was in probate, and that would've been the time to come forward. Even if she didn't know he'd died, I can't see them reopening his estate. I consulted with my partners, and none of us believe that she could sue you for something that has nothing to do with you and that you didn't even know about until this week. I hope this info has you breathing a little easier. Do let me know if she follows through on any of these threats, but no attorney with an ounce of sense would pursue a case like this with no chance of winning.*

That's a huge relief, which is what I tell her in my response. *Thanks for taking the time to look into that for me. I feel much better.*

You got it, Joy responds. *Looking forward to Friday night. xo*

I take extra time with my response to Roni. *Thanks for checking on me. I'm okay. Shocked and sad and worried she's going to sue, but Joy says she'd have no chance of prevailing. I was telling Gage last night that I feel oddly detached from Mike, our marriage, who I was when I was married to him. I'm a totally new version of myself, and I'm still getting to know this new woman. But she refuses to be devastated or set back to the early days of terrible grief by this new information. She's tougher than she was then, and I'm thankful for her grit. I think I'm done speaking of myself in the third person now!*

Roni writes back a short time later with laughter emojis. *We're all thankful for our tough-as-nails Iris, who gets us through whatever challenges come our way with the same grit that's going to get her through this situation. And I'm done talking about you in the third person.*

I think I'm going to reach out to her. I want to know...

Ugh, are you sure?

Hell no, but her son is my children's half brother...

God, Iris... I hate that you have to deal with this.

I do, too, but I keep telling myself the child is an innocent party. It's not his fault his father was a cheater.

Do you hate Mike for this? Is that even a fair question?

It's a fair question, and it does change how I feel about him and our marriage. What I thought I had wasn't what I actually had, and that's a bitter pill to swallow.

I can't even imagine.

I also worry she wasn't the only one.

OMG.

Gage told me not to dig any deeper, because what difference will it make now, but it's hard to resist the urge to do a deep dive on his phone.

I agree with Gage. It will only make a difficult situation more so. You know he was unfaithful. You don't need to know to what degree he was unfaithful.

You wouldn't want to know if it was Patrick? (Totally unfair question.)

I don't think I would. It would be enough for me to know it happened once or with one woman. That would change everything.

It does change everything, and yet, it doesn't diminish the grief. How is that fair?

Not fair at all, but grief is a dick that way.

Yes, he is.

Grief is definitely a man, because a woman would never put us through this shit.

I reply with laughter emojis. *Thanks for that. I needed the laugh.*

I want to be here for you the way you've been for me since the day we first connected.

Oh, sweetie, you're always right there for me. And I so appreciate you. I want you to be off celebrating your engagement and your new love and not worrying about me. I'll be fine. I've already survived much worse than this.

I guess that's true for all of us. No matter what happens now, we're like, TOP THAT.

Yep. It's a very, VERY strange thing to find out my marriage wasn't at all what I thought it was. I have all the feels about that, but I refuse to let it take me back to day-one grief. I just cannot go there again.

No, you can't. No matter what.

You must have work to do! Go away and leave me alone. HAHA

Speaking of work, my incredible boss (the first lady... ahem) asked me if I'd like to invite my Wild Widows to the WHITE

HOUSE for tea in the residence. I said I doubt they'd want to do that...

SHUT THE FRONT DOOR. Are you serious?

Yep. She thinks it's awesome that we support each other the way we do, and she wants to meet you guys.

OMG. Everyone is going to DIE.

Don't do that! That's what got us into this mess to begin with.

I cackle with laughter. I love this woman so much. *Thank you for giving me something so exciting to look forward to. She is the coolest first lady ever and meeting her would be a dream come true.* I don't mention my mad crush on her husband, which has only intensified in the months since President Nelson died suddenly and Vice President Nick Cappuano became president overnight.

I'll make it happen. Check in later so I don't worry?

Will do. Xoxo Love you.

Love you, too.

The White House! Holy cow! I send Gage a text to tell him.

That is crazy, he replies. *The wids will go nuts for that field trip!*

Right? How's work?

Crazy as ever. How are you?

Strangely, oddly fine, but taking a few mins to catch my breath, and then I'm going to do all the stuff I haven't done for days around here.

Underwear can be turned inside out for a second wear, if need be.

EWWWW. Stop!

Hahahaha. I knew you'd say that. Go easy on yourself, kid. It's been a rough couple of days.

I will. Don't worry.

And stay away from his phone. I should've brought it with me today.

I'm not looking. I promise.

Good. Looking forward to installing the smokestacks on the Titanic.

He was talking about the model on the way to school, and now he wants to see the movie.

It might be a bit intense for a seven-year-old...

That's what I was thinking, too, but he says he can handle it.

Maybe start with some kids' books that tell the story so he can decide if he wants to see it unfold in real time.

Yes, good idea. Going to see if I can order a few.

See you soon.

I smile as I reply. *Not soon enough.*

Stop.

You stop.

You don't usually tell me to stop. In fact, it's quite the opposite.

Now I'm mortified. I send the red-face emoji and receive laughing ones in response. I send him the eggplant. *What can I say? It's been a while.*

You don't hear me complaining, do you?

Nope.

So is this a RELATIONSHIP?

Go away.

I send more laughter emojis.

He makes me feel like a teenager in the throes of first love, which is silly. I'm so far from the throes of first love, it's not even funny. And what are *the throes* anyway? What does that even mean? I guess it means if the other person makes you feel giddy with excitement at knowing you're going to see him in a few short hours, that might qualify as being in the throes of something. Whether or not it's love, I couldn't say.

I love Gage as a friend, and I have for a while now. But am I "in love" with him? Since it hasn't even been a week since our not-relationship took a turn toward romance, it's far too soon to be asking myself questions like that, especially when he's doing his best to keep it from becoming an actual relationship.

I do know this—I need to be careful. If he can't commit to something more than friends with benefits, I'll have to accept that and not allow myself to be crushed. I'm all about self-preservation these days, which is why I'm not giving in to the temptation to look at Mike's phone.

But I do want to talk to the mother of his other child, and with that in mind, I put through a call to Steve.

"Iris. Hi. I was hoping I might hear from you. How're you doing?"

"I'm just dandy after finding out my husband was leading a double life."

"I don't think he was doing that, per se."

"What, per se, would you call it?"

"He made a mistake and ended up with another child."

"Did you know about it at the time?"

"No. The first I heard of it was when she called me."

"What did she want when she called?"

"To find out if Mike had left anything to her son. She said she'd been waiting to hear something, and when she didn't, she decided to reach out to me."

"He left everything to me."

"That's what I figured."

"Why didn't he request a paternity test?"

"I wish I knew, but she said they never did that. I couldn't believe he gave money to someone without knowing for sure."

This is the first I've heard of him giving her money. "Maybe the boy looks like him."

"I suppose that's possible."

"I want to talk to her."

"You do? Why?"

"Because her son is my children's half sibling, and Mike's family will want to meet him. I told Rob about him today."

"Maybe you should let them talk to her?"

"I want to talk to her. Text me her number, will you?"

"Are you sure that's a good idea, Iris?"

"No, Steve, I'm not, but I'm going to do it anyway."

"I'll send it to you."

"And I want to say this... I understand why you did what you did with the DNA and how you thought you were protecting me by confirming it before you brought it to me. But having my child's DNA tested for anything without my consent is not okay."

"I felt terrible about it. Jenny and I agonized over what to do," he says, referring to his wife. "The last thing I wanted was to make this dreadful situation any worse for you than it already is."

"I understand and appreciate that, but the minute my child's DNA was being used in that way, I should've been told and asked for my consent."

"You're right, and I'm sorry. I truly am."

"Apology accepted. You and Jenny have been wonderful through this nightmare. I don't want any trouble between us, so I had to put that out there."

"Thank you for forgiving me."

"You're not the one who cheated on me and had a child with another woman."

"I was shocked to learn that. I feel like I didn't know him at all. I always saw him as the consummate family man. I used to aspire to be more like him with my own family. And now... I just don't know what to think."

"Trust me, I know. I'm worried about lawsuits, from her and the families of the others on the plane. I've only heard from one of them since the NTSB report landed, and we've all stayed in close touch since the accident."

"If the families sue, they'll sue the company, and we have very good insurance."

"That's a relief."

"If Eleanor sues, well, that's another story."

Eleanor. The other woman in my husband's life is named Eleanor. "She has no grounds to sue me. I had nothing to do with any of this, and Mike's estate is closed. My lawyer friend tells me the court will only reopen the estate if a significant asset is uncovered, not because someone makes a late claim on it."

"I'm glad to hear that. I was worried about how that might affect you and the kids."

"We'll be fine."

"That's what matters. Will you let me know if there's anything I can do?"

"Yeah, I will. Thanks, Steve. I'll talk to you soon."

A minute after we end the call, my phone chimes with a text from him containing Eleanor's contact info.

I stare at it for a long moment before I decide to text her rather than calling out of the blue.

This is Iris, Mike's wife. I've only just heard you and your son exist. I had no idea. I'm not sure what our next steps should be, but now you have my number.

I read and reread it twenty times before I send it.

No taking it back now.

I put down my phone and go upstairs to do four days' worth of the kids' laundry and mine, while wondering whether I'll hear from her or if I did the right thing reaching out.

Time will tell.

Sixteen

GAGE

My concentration at work is nonexistent. All I can think about is Iris, her sweet kids and whether I'm falling into something I won't be able to get out of later if I decide I can't handle it. I love being with her—in bed and out. I've loved being with her since the first time we met when Christy told me about the Wild Widows and convinced me to attend a meeting.

Iris was a ray of light from the beginning, always smiling and propping up others. It took a few months for me to notice that she rarely spoke about her own loss, preferring to focus on what she could do for the rest of the group, particularly those who were just beginning their widow journeys.

Everyone loves her. She's the heartbeat of our group, the sun around which we all orbit as we travel a road none of us would've chosen. That road is far less difficult together than it would've been on our own. When Christy first told me about the group, I wanted nothing to do with it. I didn't think I needed that kind of support.

I was dead wrong. The Wild Widows have done more to get me through this ordeal than anyone else in my life, because they get what I'm going through like no one else ever could. I'm thankful for all of them and have substantial relationships with each of them, but if I'm being honest, my relationship with Iris—and yes, I'm using the dreaded R-word—has been different from the start.

If she's in the room, I'm drawn to her. It's that simple. I want to sit next to her in the sharing circle and at dinners and around bonfires. I want to talk to her about nothing and everything. Her voice is in my head when I'm making decisions for myself in this new, unexpected—and unwanted—life. I love listening to her laugh. I love the way she cares for others and never, ever puts herself first, even though I wish she would occasionally. I love that she still finds joy in every day despite her crushing loss. Even now, after finding out what she has about Mike's deceit, she refuses to let the news undo all the progress she's made since she lost him.

I admire her more than just about anyone I know.

And I love her.

As more than a friend.

"Fucking hell," I mutter as I stare out the window at the colorful autumn leaves swirling in a strong wind.

I love her.

I sit with that realization, letting it bounce around inside me to see where it lands. I wait for it to hit with the dread that comes with caring about people after seeing how quickly and mercilessly loved ones can be snatched away from me. But it doesn't land with dread. Rather, it leaves me with a breathless, light-headed, bubbling feeling of something I haven't felt in so long, I almost don't recognize it for what it is.

Joy.

Loving Iris fills me with joy that can't be denied, even by the low murmur of dread that comes with it now. For there can be no joy in this new life without the undercurrent of dread to remind me of what's at stake.

Everything.

Every freaking thing is at stake. My sanity, my heart, my determination to power through unimaginable losses, to find meaning in my new life without my wife and girls, to survive what shouldn't have been survivable. There's no way I could survive a loss like that twice, which is why I've planned to stay single, even if that means living a lonely life.

Being lonely beats being decimated by grief any day.

But then I recall how fun it was to put the model together with Tyler last night, how excited he was to see it take shape and his endless questions. I'd forgotten about the questions. My girls used to drive me mad with them on the morning rides to school, so much so, I limited them to three each per morning, and they had to take turns. I wish now I recorded those conversations. I had no idea at the time how precious they might one day be or how much I'd miss that time with them. I thought I had years of driving them around still to come, so I didn't appreciate those moments when they were happening. Not the way I should have, anyway.

Mostly, their nonstop questions irritated me when I was eager to drop them off so I could get to the office. I was always so damned excited to get to work. Now I know I should've been more excited to drive my daughters to school. Sometimes that was the only time I got with them all day, and my inclination was to rush through it, to get it over with, to get on with the "important" part of my day.

I regret that so much now. Natasha worked seven to three as a nurse and picked them up after school, so my job was to get them up and dressed, feed them breakfast, make sure they had everything they needed from a list Nat would leave for me every day and drive them to school. After they died, I would stay up as late as I could, hoping to sleep through the hour that had belonged to me and them. On many a morning, I'd startle awake, thinking there was something I was supposed to be doing, only to remember that the thing I was supposed to be doing was gone forever.

If I let this thing happen with Iris—and her kids, for there is no thing with Iris without her kids—I'd be risking all the hard-won progress I've made in the thirty-five months since I lost my wife and daughters. I'd be taking on a new family, one I will love and care for as if they were my own, and that's what scares me the most.

I'll love them so much.

Hell, I already do. I've come to know the kids well. I know that Sophia won't eat a vegetable even if it means sitting at the table until the next morning, which Iris doesn't make her do. We agree that you can't force kids to eat, sleep or go to the bathroom on our schedules.

Laney hates orange juice, and Tyler is fascinated with anything on wheels. They can't stand when their food touches other food on their plates, and they like ketchup on just about everything. Laney is allergic to mosquito bites, and Tyler gets heat rash the minute the temperature goes above seventy-five. Sophia is shy with people when she first meets them, but once she's comfortable, she becomes a chatterbox.

I remember the moment when I realized Sophia was comfortable with me. She told me an elaborate story about one of the kids at school who'd fallen off her bike and ended up in the hospital for a *whole week*. She was so damned cute telling me how the girl had broken her arm and ruptured her spleen falling off her bike.

She said she was afraid to ride her bike now, but I told her how in my whole life, I'd never heard of another person rupturing their spleen falling off their bike. And then I had to explain what a spleen is and how you can live without it.

I love them.

I'd do anything for them—and their mother.

I'm already in deep trouble where they're concerned.

I need to decide if I want to stay that way before this gets any more serious than it already is.

I used to be a very intentional person, meaning nothing

happened in my life unless I wanted it to. I'd see something I wanted—a woman, a job, a house, a car—and I'd direct all my formidable energy toward bringing that person or thing into my life. Nat would tell you I pursued her relentlessly, overwhelming her with flowers and romance and elaborate dates until she had no choice but to fall in love with me.

It hasn't worked that way with Iris. I've sort of backed into this thing with her, and that's why it's come as somewhat of a shock to me that my feelings for her are deeper than I would've thought. I didn't plan this. I didn't execute a campaign to win her over. I didn't set out to take on her or her kids, but now...

"Shit." I take a deep breath and blow it out before glancing at my computer screen to check the time. I've been staring off into space contemplating my non-relationship with Iris for more than half an hour by the time I snap out of it. I've got a ton of emails to answer and meetings to schedule, and everything is more intense than usual after I took the last two days off.

If only I could work up an ounce of enthusiasm for any of it. Standing, I stretch out the kinks in my back with my arms over my head and move to the window to look out on the street below. It's a scene I've looked at so many times since I bought the converted loft in Arlington more than fifteen years ago, hoping to build my business into something more than a big idea.

In the years since, the business has exceeded my wildest dreams. Among the many emails awaiting my attention is the latest in a string of inquiries about whether I might be interested in selling the business. Cybersecurity has become huge in the fifteen years since I started my company, and the need for what we offer has grown exponentially.

I've turned down every offer I've ever received—and there have been a lot of them.

Now, however... I'm open to the idea of selling and seeing what else might be possible, but only if the team that's supported me through the best and worst of times is protected. I experience a little tingle of excitement at the thought of not being tied to the business any longer.

I've enjoyed writing the daily Instagram posts about widowed life and feel like I'm making a real difference for people sharing the journey with me, especially those who are newly widowed and looking for any lifeline they can find. At times, I've wondered if I might have a book in me about navigating deep grief and the lessons I've learned along the way.

Before I can talk myself out of it, I return to my desk and reply to the email inquiry from the industry leader that's interested in my company. *I'd be open to a conversation.* I send the email before I can talk myself out of it. That's nothing that can't be undone. If it's not the right offer, I'll hold out for one that is.

I scroll up to check my new mail and see one from David Lyons, the Assistant Commonwealth's Attorney handling the case against the man who killed my family.

Hey, Gage,
Give me a call when you have a free minute.
Thanks,
Dave

Ugh, what's this now? Dave is a nice enough guy, but every time I talk to him, my gut clenches with anxiety. Wanting to get it over with, I make the call, give Dave's assistant my name and am put on hold to wait for him.

"Hey, Gage," Dave says after a five-minute wait. "Sorry to bother you during your workday."

"It's fine. What's up?"

"I wanted to update you on the status of the plea deal we've been working on with his attorney."

Dave never says the guy's name, for which I'm eternally grateful. "How's that going?"

"We've gone back and forth a hundred times, and we've

landed on three counts of vehicular manslaughter in addition to the DUI charges."

I've been pushing hard for vehicular homicide, which is why the case has been dragged out so long, and the thought of lesser charges doesn't sit well with me. The man had been on a two-day bender when he got behind the wheel of his car and ran head-on into my wife and daughters while driving the wrong way on Interstate 395.

"It's not what we wanted," Dave says, "and I know we'd be asking you to swallow a bitter pill if we accept this deal. But the upside is that it spares you the agony of a trial, where there's always a slim chance he gets off, even though I don't think that would happen in this case. It's just that we can't guarantee the outcome of a trial. A million things can happen."

He told me that before we began plea negotiations ages ago. "What would be the sentence?"

"Twenty-five years with fifteen to serve, ten years' probation after release, lifetime loss of his driver's license, mandatory lifetime drug and alcohol testing and a one-hundred-thousand-dollar fine that would go to the charity of your choice."

I try to process the information, but my brain isn't having it. "Would you put all that into an email for me?"

"Of course."

"How long do I have to decide?"

"Would a few days be good?"

"Yes, that should work. I need to talk to Nat's family."

"Understood. Take the time you need and let me know what you decide."

"Would you take this deal if he'd killed your family?"

"I'd feel the same way you do about wanting more than manslaughter, but more than anything, I'd probably want him locked up for a long time so he couldn't do this to anyone else's family. But as I've said from the beginning, Gage, I can't possibly know what you've been through, and I pray to God I never do. I can't tell you what to do. If you want to go to trial, that's what we'll do."

"I'll let you know."

"Sounds good. I'm here if you have any questions or need me for anything."

"Thank you, Dave. For everything."

"I wish I could say it was a pleasure. Talk soon."

After we end the call, I again sit for a long time staring off into space, thinking about what he said and trying to figure out how I feel about it. Every time the case intrudes to remind me of my terrible loss, I go numb inside when I think of the man who killed my family.

Even though I know it wasn't in my best interest to do so, I did a deep dive on him about six months after the accident, and what I found out infuriated me even more than I already was. Parents, siblings, his girlfriend and other longtime friends knew he had spiraled into full-blown alcoholism and tried their hardest to get help for him. In the meantime, he got behind the wheel and murdered my family.

I'm not sure I can live with a manslaughter conviction when this was homicide. Did he set out to kill Nat and the girls that day? Maybe not, but he was repeatedly told he was going to kill someone if he didn't quit drinking and driving. He was arrested for it twice before, lost his license for long stretches, but always did what he had to do to get it back. Why didn't he just acknowledge that he had no business driving and give up his license for good?

If only he'd done that, none of this would've happened. Which is why I've pushed for the more severe charges. I feel like I owe that to Nat and the girls.

This workday is a bust.

As I stand to leave, my assistant, Tory, appears at my door. "Reminder of your two o'clock conference call with Digi-Tech."

"Can you please ask Luke to take that for me?"

She stares at me for a second, seeming stunned. "Um, sure. Is everything all right? You've been punched out lately."

"Everything is fine. I'll be back in the morning."

"Okay."

I take the stairs rather than wait for the elevator and emerge into chilly fall air that carries the faint hint of woodsmoke. Nat loved this time of year—pumpkin spice everything, hay and jack-o-lanterns on the front porch, chrysanthemums and Halloween costume planning that went on for weeks. I miss her desperately and wish she was here to tell me what I ought to do about this plea deal that would mean justice for her and our girls.

But since she can't help me, I'm forced to do what I've done since I lost her and figure it out for myself.

Somehow.

Seventeen

IRIS

I wait all day to hear back from Eleanor, but she doesn't respond to my text. I wonder if she got it. I've kept busy with laundry, cleaning, changing beds and posting to TikTok, which is how I kept from obsessing about whether I'd hear from her.

Maybe I shouldn't have reached out. I should've listened to Gage and Rob and left that to the lawyers, I suppose.

Ugh. I hate this. I hate that there's another woman out there who was involved with my husband and who gave him a son. Does their son have Mike's last name?

Mike's parents will want to know that. His dad has told me since I first started dating Mike that he needed one of his boys to have a son—or two—to keep the family name going. As an only son, Lou is obsessed with making sure the Levington name lives on. Since Rob shows no sign of settling down or having his own family, they'll be thrilled to know that Mike produced a spare before he left us.

That thought makes me bitter—and it's probably not fair. His mother will be outraged that he was unfaithful to me. Once she got over me being biracial, and that took more time than it should have, she became one of my biggest fans after witnessing how much I loved her son.

And I did love him, from about the first minute I ever laid eyes on him at a college football game at Virginia Commonwealth University. He was rooting for James Madison, and we had a friendly "fight" about why my school was better than his that lasted into the evening. We were pretty much together from that day on, even with more than two hours separating Richmond from Harrisonburg.

We texted nonstop, talked for hours on the phone and made it work with weekends together while we finished college. Mike was already a pilot then. He'd gotten his license when he was eighteen and was training for a career in aviation, but he got a business degree so he could be self-employed. I liked that he had ambition and plans.

My mother forbade me from flying with him, however, even though I was a legal adult and could make my own decisions. Since she was the most important person in my life, I did what she asked me to long after I didn't have to anymore. It took about two years for Mike to convince her that I'd be perfectly safe flying with him. When she finally gave in, she said she only wanted to know about it when it was over. Mom can be a bit clairvoyant at times, and I think she always had a feeling something was going to happen to him in an airplane, although she's never said that to me.

I'm folding clothes an hour before I have to pick up the kids when my doorbell rings. I go to peek out the window and am surprised to see Gage is back hours earlier than expected. I unlock the dead bolt and open the door.

"Hey," he says.

"Hey. Are you okay?"

"I don't know."

"Come in."

"Am I disturbing you?"

"Not at all."

He comes in and hangs his coat on one of the kids' hooks.

"What's wrong?"

"Nothing."

"Don't lie to me. I can tell just by looking at you. Are you stressing out about this? About you and me? Because you don't have to do—"

He encircles my waist with his arm and pulls me in for a kiss.

I'm so surprised that it takes me a minute to react, but once I do, I drop the towel I was folding to the floor and wrap my arms around him to return the kiss. I'm completely dazzled by the time he pulls back to gaze down at me with an intensity that softens as he studies me. "I'm not stressed out about us."

"Oh. You're not?"

"Well, maybe a little."

"Can we talk about that?"

"Yeah, we probably should."

I pick up the towel I dropped, take his hand and lead him to the sofa, moving piles of clothes so he can sit next to me. "Tell me what's on your mind."

"Several things. First, I heard from the prosecutor on the case, and they're proposing a plea deal that would avoid a trial, but he'd be pleading to charges that're less than what I wanted."

"How much time would he do?"

"Twenty-five years with fifteen to serve and ten years of probation. Permanent loss of license, lifetime drug and alcohol testing, hundred-thousand fine."

"That's not nothing."

"No, it isn't, but is it enough? Shouldn't he spend the rest of his life in hell after what he did to us?"

"Yes, he should, and if he's got a heart or a soul, he's probably already there."

"His sister told me at one of the earlier hearings that he's completely broken by what happened."

"He should be." I reach for his hand and link our fingers. "What's your heart telling you?"

"That I don't want to go through a trial. This has already gone on long enough."

"Will you be able to live with lesser charges than what you wanted?"

"That's what I'm trying to decide. I need to talk to Nat's parents about it, too, but they want it over with as well."

"What can I do for you?"

He gives my hand a squeeze. "This is helping. What's new here?" He gives me his stern look, which sure as hell beats his devastated look. "Did you do anything to make your situation worse?"

"I did not," I say with a smile. His stern look doesn't scare me. "I did reach out to *her*, though I haven't heard back."

"What's your plan there?"

"Not sure. I guess that'll depend on whether she responds."

"I give you credit for making the first move. That couldn't have been easy."

"It wasn't, but denial isn't an option, so..." I shrug as if this is no big deal when it's the biggest of deals. "I told Rob about her and the baby. He'll tell his parents. The cat's out of the bag, and there's nothing I can do but try to accept it and go on with my life."

"You're very brave. I'm proud of you."

"Oh, jeez, if you could see the inside of me, you wouldn't be proud. I'm like a giant marshmallow, full of emotions I don't know what to do with."

"Share them with me. I want to help you the way you always help everyone else."

"I'm angry and sad and bitter and betrayed, and the craziest thing is, if he walked in here right now, I'd still be so damned glad to see him. How is that possible?"

"Because the bad stuff doesn't take away the love you had for him."

"Even if I wish it would."

"No, you don't. For all his faults, Mike was still the father of your children, and he'll forever hold a special place in your heart."

"Yes, I suppose he will, even though we're currently in the biggest fight ever."

His low chuckle pleases me because he looked so upset when he first came in. I want him to laugh and smile and be happy, and I like being the one who does that for him. I lean my head against his solid shoulder. "What a pair we are, huh?"

"I've been thinking about that, too."

I lift my head off his shoulder to look at his face. "I meant that as a joke."

"I didn't." He turns to face me, serious again. "It seems that when I wasn't looking, you and I have become a pair."

"You were looking, but you weren't ready to admit it."

"I've been in such a daze these last few years, confused about what I'm supposed to do without them. Some days, I don't even know who I am anymore, and that was never something I questioned before."

"Grief upends everything."

"Yeah, and it clarifies some things."

"Such as?"

He reaches out to caress my face, triggering a shiver of desire I feel everywhere. "I'm not sure when or how it happened—and it happened long before this past weekend—but at some point, in this ridiculously awful journey we're on together, you've become my true north. Yours is the voice in my head telling me what to do when I'm not sure how to handle something. You're the one I want when the prosecutor calls and turns my day upside down."

I don't even try to stop the flood of tears brought on by his sweet words.

"I've been afraid to care about someone else, especially a someone who comes with three precious kids who've suffered their own terrible loss."

"Why are you afraid?"

"I'm afraid of caring too much because I couldn't bear

another loss. It's been easier for me to stay solo, so I didn't have to worry about that. But a funny thing happened on the way to staying single." He leans his forehead against mine as he continues to stroke my cheek. "*You* happened. You're like this ray of light that makes the darkest days more bearable, and not just for me. For all of us."

"You give me way too much credit," I tell him, even though I'm incredibly moved by his sweet words.

"It's not possible to give you enough credit for what you do for everyone in your life."

"You flatter me."

"I speak only the truth."

"Does this mean we're in a dreaded relationship?"

The left side of his mouth lifts into a half smile, but it's the sadness in his eyes that touches my heart. I don't want him to say no.

"I think maybe we are, but..."

I kiss him. "No qualifications allowed. We are or we aren't."

"My concern is about the kids."

My heart and stomach drop like we're on the steepest hill on a roller coaster. "Oh. Well, I'd understand if they're too much for you. They're too much for me most days."

He lays his finger over my lips. "They're not too much for me. I adore them. You know I do."

"I do know that, but it's a lot to ask anyone to take on this shit show."

"You and your children are not a shit show."

"Um, yes, we are."

"No."

"Yes."

"We can fight about that later. My concern with the kids is having them get used to having me around and then having this not work out for whatever reason. I'd want assurances that no matter what happens between us that you'd let me be there for them—always."

"I would, Gage. Unless you cheat. That's a dealbreaker on all fronts."

"Understood, and I don't cheat if I'm committed to someone."

"I didn't think Mike would either."

"All I can do is swear on the memories of Natasha, Hazel and Ivy that I'd never cheat on you. If you know me at all, and you know me as well as anyone does these days, you understand what that means."

"I do," I say softly. "Thank you for that."

"So..."

"So..."

"What now?"

I check my phone. "I have forty minutes until I have to pick up the kids. Do you want to have some noisy sex to celebrate our new relationship?"

"Noisy sex, huh?" he says as he stands and offers me a hand up.

"A rare opportunity around here."

He surprises me when he puts his hands on my backside and lifts me into his arms. I love that he's so much bigger and stronger than me but is only gentle when he touches me. Again, he surprises me when he carries me to the kitchen rather than my bedroom. Pushing aside some mail I tossed on the island, he sets me down, putting me at eye level with him.

"Hi there," he says, curling a lock of my hair around his finger.

"How's it going?"

"Better than it has in a long, long time, and it's all thanks to this petite powerhouse of a woman who has my head turned all around."

"What's her name, and where can I find her?"

His smile is a thing of beauty when he lets it fully happen. It makes his eyes sparkle and reveals deep grooves in his cheeks that

I've rarely seen. I lean forward to kiss them. "I love your dimples. Do you want to know why?"

"Sure."

"Because I only see them when you really, really smile."

"You must be seeing a lot of them lately."

"More than usual, but not as much as I'd like."

"I'll work on that," he says.

"We'll work on it together."

"Do I need to be worried about Rob?"

"I took care of that. He knows the deal."

"Excellent." He kisses me and makes loud love to me right there on the counter with the windows uncovered in the bright light of day. There's no one around to see in, but the open windows heighten the experience, leading to an orgasm that makes me scream—because I can.

Gage laughs as he comes right after me, pressing so deep inside me, he takes my breath away.

"You weren't loud," I tell him as soon as I can speak again.

"You were loud enough for both of us."

"I'd forgotten that this exists."

"What?"

"Spontaneous sex in the middle of the day, in the kitchen, of all places. It's been years since I did anything like this."

"Me, too. We were impaired by having young kids underfoot."

"If you wanted to find someone you could have unimpaired loud daytime sex with on the regular, I wouldn't blame you, Gage."

"There's no one else I'd rather have loud daytime sex in the kitchen with than you."

"You should think about it some more before you commit to anything."

"There's nothing to think about."

"Laney is three. If we stick it out, that's fifteen more years of parenting before we're somewhat free, and then they come home and bring their laundry and their drama, and it'll never end."

"I love Laney. It would be the honor of my lifetime to get to see her and her brother and sister grow up and to help you turn them into the amazing people they're already on their way to being."

"Are you going to freak out about all this the minute you're alone again and realize you're making a huge mistake?"

"I don't think so, but if I do, you'll lure me back into your arms, right?"

I squeeze my arms and legs tight around him. "Yeah, I will."

IRIS

I'd forgotten what it feels like to be happy like this, even with clouds of uncertainty and upset remaining over my head. The day after I sent the text to Eleanor, she still hasn't replied, so I call Joy.

"Hey, honey, can't wait for tonight and some time with my wids. This week has sucked the big one."

"I'm looking forward to it, too."

"What's up with you?"

"I reached out to the woman. The one who had the kid with Mike."

"Baby, what're you thinking doing that?"

"I thought maybe I could talk to her mom to mom and resolve some things, but she hasn't responded."

"Let me reach out as your attorney. You can give me a dollar tonight to retain me, and I'll send you my standard client agreement to sign. I'll handle this for you."

"Are you sure? I know how busy you are."

"Anything for you, my sweet girl."

"I'll only do this if you let me pay you."

"No deal. This is a few phone calls that I'll make on behalf of my dear friend. Please let me help you with this. I would've offered before now, but my week spun out of control."

"You have to let me do something for you in exchange."

"I'll think of something."

"You do that."

"I love your bossy-mom voice. How many hours until martini time?"

I look at the clock on my stove. "Three."

"That is too damned long. Is your mom taking the kids?"

"She is, and they're excited to see the new Pixar movie. Thank God for Grandma and Pop."

"No kidding, right? I'll see you soon. Bring me Miss Thang's info and I'll get this straightened out right quick. Don't you worry. Go take a bubble bath and get ready for our big night out on the town."

I can barely hear her over the screaming from the playroom, where the kids seem to be dismantling the house. My mom will be here in an hour to get them. There may be time for a bubble bath after that. "I'll see what I can do."

"Love you," Joy says, as she always does.

"Love you, too."

We've learned from our losses to never let someone go without letting them know how we feel about them. My relationships with my widow friends are the deepest I've ever had with anyone, even Mike. As much as I loved him, we weren't connected at a spiritual level like I am with my wids. There's just something so bonding about the young-widow experience, which makes me feel guilty at times. I'd never want Mike to die, even knowing what I do now, but losing him has opened me up to a deeper, more meaningful way of living that I might never have experienced without my terrible loss.

And yeah, just thinking that inside my own mind makes me feel terrible. My kids need their dad more than I need the deep connections I've formed since his death.

I'm surprised I haven't heard from Mike's parents, who are back from Italy now, or Rob since I shared the news about Mike's other child with Rob. I shoot him a text. *Did you tell your parents about Mike's other son?*

He replies thirty minutes later when I'm helping the kids pack up for the overnight with their grandparents. *I did.*

And?

They're shocked, of course. They want to meet him. Do you know how we can make that happen?

I'll see what I can find out and let you know. The kids are going to my mom's for the night and will be back tomorrow afternoon if you want to come by.

Not sure I'll make it there this weekend. Will let you know.

I'm disappointed to hear that. He's rarely missed a weekend visit with the kids since Mike died. Is he staying away because of me? Ugh, I hope not. My reply to him is one word: *Ok.*

Hopefully, he just needs a break from us to get past whatever he saw happening between me and him so he can get back to having a close rapport with the kids. I'm counting on him to be there for them, and I hope he doesn't let us down. I don't think he will. He's been amazing since we lost Mike, but was that because he was hoping for something between us?

No, I decide, that's not the case. He's too great with the kids to have it be about that. He loves them, and they love him. He'll be back when he's ready.

Gage worked for hours on the model with Tyler during the week until it was painted with painstaking detail that delighted my little boy. Gage told him he couldn't touch it until the paint dried, and even then, it's not a toy. It's something to look at. Tyler isn't sure how he feels about looking at the model when he was planning to float it in the bathtub.

Gage texts at four, right after the kids leave with my mom. *Be there by 5?*

Sounds good. I'll be ready.

It's okay if you're not.

That puts a smile on my face as I anticipate the night out with him and our friends. *Are you text-flirting by any chance?*

Maybe...

It's working for me.

Excellent. BTW, I'm thinking about selling my company...

Wait. WHAT?

Yep.

Holy out of the blue, Batman.

Not so much. Been getting offers for a while. I think I might take the latest one.

Wow. I want to hear all about this.

See you soon.

I'm stunned to hear him say—so cavalierly—that he might sell his company. He's worked his ass off to build it from nothing. He and a partner started the company in Gage's living room when he and Natasha were newlyweds. Gage told us once how the partner got bored with the grind of business ownership. Gage and Natasha had to get a second mortgage on their house to buy out the partner, which was a huge risk at the time since they had no clue yet if the business would be successful.

The gamble paid off, and now he's thinking about selling it. I'm stunned by this news, and I can't wait to talk to him about it.

I spend the next half hour soaking in the tub, trying to relax and transition from mom mode to girlfriend mode.

Girlfriend... It's been so long since I dated anyone but Mike that I've probably forgotten how to do it.

I can't stop thinking about the things Gage said about how he feels when he's around me or how great he was with Tyler this week. I was brought to tears watching my little boy hang on Gage's every word and soak up the attention like a hungry sponge as they completed the model. He was so good about letting Tyler do most of the work while he supervised, and if I hadn't already been on my way to falling in love with Gage, watching him with Tyler would've certainly put me there.

In a week that should've been a complete disaster, Gage

provided the moments of light that I badly needed. Mike and I became lovers long before we were friends. It's the opposite with Gage. We're starting from a place of deep friendship and common experience, and the difference is remarkable to me. The friendship makes everything between us more intimate than it would've been without it.

I spend more time than I have figuring out what to wear and settle on a black wrap dress with the sexy black velvet boots that my sister gave me for Christmas last year that I've never gotten to wear. For the first time in ages, I put on a bit of makeup and perfume before inspecting myself in the full-length mirror Mike hung for me on the back of the bathroom door.

"Not bad for a gal who's had three kids in the last seven years."

I laugh at my own silliness and head downstairs to wait for Gage.

I can't wait to see him.

GAGE

TODAY HAS BEEN SURREAL. I accepted an offer to sell my company. The deal will ensure that I never have to work another day in my life if I don't wish to. It's enough that I can give life-changing bonuses to my hardworking team on my way out the door, and I've ensured they'll be retained by the new owner.

It's a win-win all around, and I already feel lighter and less burdened than I did before the deal was finalized with remarkable ease. After fifteen years of stressing out about every aspect of the business, now it's going to be someone else's problem.

I pull up to Iris's house, excited to see her, to celebrate my big news, to hold her and love her and sleep with her. I'm looking forward to everything with her, and that's an amazing development when you consider the pits of despair that have marked the last few years.

Iris greets me at the door, looking so sexy that my eyes nearly pop out of my head. "Holy smokes, woman."

"You like?" She does a cute little spin on a high-heeled boot that makes me instantly hard for her.

"Yeah, I like." I reach for her and hold her close enough for her to feel my reaction.

She rubs against me shamelessly. "That's a terrible thing to waste."

"He'll be back later."

Her giggle makes me smile. Everything about her makes me smile.

"I can't believe you dropping that bombshell about the company on me like it's not a huge, big deal."

"It is a huge, big deal." I pull back so she can see me waggle my brows. "Huge-mangous, as Ivy used to say."

"Congratulations, Gage. I'm so happy for you. You've worked so hard."

"I have, and it's exciting to see it pay off this way."

"I thought you loved your job and the company."

"The joy went out of it for me after I lost Nat and the girls. I kept waiting for it to come back, but it never did." I shrug as if losing my joy for the job wasn't another excruciating loss on top of all the others. "The buyers will protect my team, which was critical to me, so it's all good. The timing feels right to move on to something else."

"What's that going to be? Do you know yet?"

"I've been thinking about writing a book about the experience of losing my family and the journey I've been on since. Taking the material from the Insta account and turning it into something more."

"I think that's an amazing idea."

"I'm excited about it." I rub my hard cock against her, wishing we didn't have somewhere to be. "I'm excited about a lot of things lately."

"Excitement looks good on you."

"Thanks for giving me a reason to be optimistic."

She gives me her most innocent look. "All I did was make a terrible mistake and crawl into your bed naked."

"Turns out that was just what I needed." I want to tell her something else, but I struggle to find the words. And then I know exactly how I want to say it. "Before you crawled shamelessly and intentionally into my bed, the call from the prosecutor would've set me back big-time. I got so I couldn't bear to hear from him because of the way I reacted to it every time. The calls would take me right back to the horror of that first day and week and month. But this time when he called, I came to you, and that helped me avoid the setback. So, thanks for that."

"Gage," she says softly, her eyes glittering with tears, "you can come to me any time you need to. Any time at all."

"Same goes, you know."

"I do know, and that's why I've leaned on you this week when my life turned upside down *again*."

I hug her, and she hugs me back, and it occurs to me how perfectly we fit, with my chin on the top of her head thanks to the heels.

Another thought occurs to me. "So, how do we feel about going public with the Wild Widows?"

"I'm up for it if you are," she says. "I'm not the one who's been resisting the R-word."

I give her a playful spank on the rear that makes her laugh.

"I speak the truth, my friend."

"I think I'm done resisting, if you'll have me and all my issues and anxiety and neuroses."

"Since I suffer from many of the same afflictions, how about we have each other?"

Cupping her ass, I press against her. "I'd like to have you right now."

She laughs as she says, "Hold that thought, cowboy. We've got friends to meet."

"Ugh, if I must. Let's go."

We're holding hands in the car on the way to the restaurant to meet our friends when Natasha's mother returns the message I left for her yesterday.

"I'm sorry," I say to Iris. "I need to take this. It's my mother-in-law."

"Of course. Go right ahead."

I take the call on my Bluetooth. "Hey, Mimi."

"Gage, darling. I'm so sorry I missed your call yesterday. I was at a yoga retreat, and we were cell-phone-free."

"No problem. How was it?"

"I still can't find my Zen, but I keep trying."

The loss of Nat and the girls devastated Natasha's devoted parents. "Yoga makes me nauseated."

"I remember that from when you first tried it," she says, laughing. "You turned green."

"Remember how hard Nat laughed at me?"

"I do. She was beside herself that you couldn't hang."

It's amazing how the memories can still lacerate even after all this time. "What'd Stan do when you were at the retreat?"

"He did a golf thing with some of his buddies. They had a good time."

"That sounds fun. Glad you guys are doing well."

"We're doing the best we can. Some days are better than others, but I don't have to tell you."

"No, you don't. So, the reason I called, other than I missed you, is I heard from Dave about the case."

"Oh dear," she says with the same trepidation I experience whenever the prosecutor pops in to remind us that our nightmare isn't over. "What now?"

I give her the details of the deal as explained to me by Dave. "It's not vehicular homicide like we wanted, but Dave thinks it's a very solid offer and we should consider it."

"That's disappointing about the vehicular homicide."

"I agree, but if we decline the plea deal, we're looking at a trial, and I don't know about you, but the thought of that still makes me ill."

"Yes, me, too, and Stan has said he'd do anything to avoid that if possible."

"We've got to be able to live with this, Mimi, so if it's not enough for you and Stan, then so be it. We've gotten through worse than a trial."

"What do you want to do, sweetheart?"

"I think I'm ready for it to be over, but only if you are, too. We're in this together, like we've said from the beginning."

"What a dreadful thing," she says with a sigh, "deciding the fate of the man who killed my daughter and granddaughters."

"It is indeed dreadful. The whole thing is dreadful and sad and so tragic."

"That it is, my friend. Take the deal. Let's be done with this guy once and for all."

"Are you sure?"

"I am. Nat wouldn't want us trapped in this purgatory any longer than we've already been. Enough is enough. He'll do fifteen years in prison. That's not chump change."

"No, it isn't. I'll let Dave know that we'll take the deal. They'll want us to do victim impact statements at the sentencing, but I can do that for all of us."

"Oh, no. I'd never let you do that by yourself. You tell me when and where, and we'll be there."

"I'll find out when it'll be and let you know."

"How're you holding up, love? Dave's calls always set you back."

I glance at Iris in the passenger seat. At some point, I need to tell Mimi and Stan that I'm seeing someone new, but not yet. "I'm all right. It's been kind of a big week on several fronts. I've also decided to sell the business."

"No! Really?"

"Yeah, I think it's time to lighten my load a bit and figure out whether there's more to life than work."

"Good for you, Gage. You've worked so hard to build that business, and now you can enjoy the fruits of your labors. Come visit us! We'd love to have you."

"Can I bring some friends?"

"Anyone you want."

"I might just do that."

"Please do, darling. We'd love it."

"I will. As soon as the deal closes."

"I can't wait to see you. We miss you."

"I miss you, too. I've got to run to meet some friends, but I'll call you next week with the sentencing date, and we'll plan a visit. I could use some vitamin D."

"I've got all the D you need. Talk soon. Love you."

"Love you, too. Give my love to Stan."

"I will."

Nineteen

GAGE

After I press the red button to end the call, I glance over at Iris. "That was Mimi."

"She sounds like a lovely person."

"I adore her. I have from the first minute I met her. We hit it off like two old friends and have been close ever since. Her husband is great, too. They're the nicest people. I don't know what I would've done without them."

"Where do they live?"

"Boca Raton. They moved about a year after the accident. They couldn't bear to be here anymore without Nat and the girls. They were part of our daily lives, helping to run the girls to after-school activities, having them for sleepovers. Like your folks do."

"God bless them. What an awful thing, but I'm glad you guys are taking the deal and that you'll be able to put that part of it behind you."

"Me, too. I feel better about it knowing how she feels. I knew Stan was dreading the possibility of a trial and has been hoping for a deal. Mimi and I both wanted vehicular homicide, and we pushed hard for it. At least I know there was nothing more I could've done that I didn't do, short of going to trial."

"I have no doubt you've been the fiercest of advocates for your ladies."

"I've done what I could, all while dreading having to go to trial. I don't think I could've handled that, so I'm relieved that Mimi said to take the deal."

"I'm glad you don't have to endure that."

Iris's phone chimes with a text that has her sitting up straight and tugging her hand free of mine.

"What is it?"

"Eleanor replied."

"What did she say?"

" 'Hi, Iris, thank you for your text. I wasn't sure how to reply, so I took a minute to think about it. I don't know what to say to you. I'm sorry you were blindsided by this, and I'm sure you have questions. If you want to talk, let's set a time in the next few days. I'm free most evenings after seven. Sincerely, Eleanor.' Is it terrible that I hate how she sounds like a nice person?"

"Nah, I get it. It would be easier if she was a hag."

"Exactly."

"Are you going to reply?"

"I guess so."

I place my hand on top of hers. "You don't have to if you don't want to."

"I know, but I reached out to her, so I'll see it through."

I pull back my hand so she can send the text. When she's finished, she rests her head against the seat and expels a deep breath. "That's something I never thought I'd have to do—reach out to the mother of Mike's other child."

"I can't fathom how hard that is."

"I was proud of our marriage after we survived a massive bump at the beginning. I thought we were the perfect couple. I thought he was as happy as I was. I feel like such a fool now that I know the truth."

"You're not a fool, Iris. You loved the guy. After you put things back together, he never gave you any reason to suspect you couldn't trust him."

"He was so remorseful, so I did trust him. I refused to pry into his life to look for trouble. I remember telling the therapist we saw after he cheated that I couldn't live like that. He said, 'I'll never give you reason to.' I believed him."

"Don't let his mistakes change who you are. I have no doubt whatsoever that you were the most amazing wife to him, and *he's* the one who was a fool for cheating on you." I realize my tone has gotten progressively angrier. "Sorry. Didn't mean to get so hot about it."

"You're hot, all right," she says, smiling at me. "Thank you for that."

"It's all true. You didn't do anything wrong. Tell me you know that."

"I do, but there's this tiny niggling feeling that maybe I didn't do enough."

"Tell that feeling to shut the fuck up. You're enough. More than enough. You give everything you've got to everyone you love, and I know you did that for him, too."

"I tried."

"You absolutely cannot let his massive fuckup derail you. It wasn't you. It was him." I can't bear to hear her sound so defeated. "I don't know what it is about some guys who are just never satisfied no matter how good they have it. Nat and I had some couple friends we hung out with, and one of the guys was a cheater. We all knew it except for his wife."

"Oh God. That must've been horrible."

"It was. Nat and I agonized over it. We wanted so badly to tell her, but we knew it would ruin so much—not just their marriage, but multiple friendships, too. We liked them, but we didn't feel close enough to be the ones to tell her, you know?"

"I do."

"It was an awful position to be in. We got to the point where we started declining invites from that group because we couldn't bear it. The thing that really pissed me off is that his wife is lovely —kind, sweet, sincere, pretty, a wonderful mother and an amazing hostess. Events at their house were always incredible."

"I hate women like her—haha."

I laugh along with her. "Nat used to say she'd love to hate her if she wasn't so damned nice."

"I would've liked your Nat."

"She would've liked you, too."

"So what happened? Did she ever find out?"

"I don't know. After Nat and the girls died, I didn't hear much from those friends. At first, yes, of course, but it tapered off after a while. Nat was the link to them."

"It's strange how that happens, isn't it? People you considered good friends just disappear for whatever reason."

"To be honest, I haven't given them a single thought until now. We had some fun with them, but they weren't my people. They were Nat's. But there've been others who've fallen off that have surprised me, like Nat's cousin Todd, who I was close to. I never hear a word from him."

"I wonder why."

"No clue. I mean, he was close to Nat, too, and it might be too hard for him or whatever. Took me six months to realize he'd disappeared, so I guess we weren't that close after all."

"Grief is the weirdest thing ever."

"Ever." I take her hand and give it a squeeze. "That's why I'm so thankful for people who understand how bizarre it is."

"Same goes. I would've been an even bigger mess this week without you and the others to lean on."

"We can't have you losing it. We need our Iris put together so she can make us all feel like a million bucks."

"Do I do that? Really?"

"God, yes, you do. I don't know what it is about you, but I always feel better when I've been with you, and I know the others feel the same way."

"That's a really nice thing for you to say," she says, sounding tearful.

I pull into the parking lot at the high-end Mexican restaurant Joy told us about and put the SUV in Park before turning to her. "I've told you that you're my true north, and I meant it." I reach over to stroke her soft cheek. "You're always there for everyone. You need to let us be there for you when you need us."

"I'm trying. It's just hard for me to realize I need that kind of help. Just when I think I've come so far from where I was at first, something happens—in this case, two things happened—to set me back to day one."

"You're not back to day one. You're nowhere near there."

"How can you be so sure? You didn't know me then."

"I remember what day one was like for me, and you're far too together and functioning to have gone back that far. It's interesting, isn't it, how we're somehow stronger now than we were before, and that strength gets us through a lot of things that would've flattened us in the past."

"That's true."

"You're stronger than you think, Iris. Don't let this stuff about Mike make you question yourself."

"I'll try not to."

"If talking to Eleanor will wreck you, don't do it. You don't owe her anything."

"Her child is the half sibling to my kids."

"There's no need for them to know about that half sibling right now if you don't want them to. It's up to you and only you."

"Thank you for the reminder. It helps."

"You ready to go in?"

"I am if you are."

"And we don't care if they know we're more than friends these days?"

"I don't care at all."

I lean in to kiss her cheek and then her lips. "I don't care either."

IRIS

EVERYTHING ABOUT GAGE IS DIFFERENT, lighter, since he decided to take the plunge with me—and sell his business. He's even ready to go public with the Wild Widows, which surprises me. He keeps a tight grip on my hand as we walk into the restaurant and ask for Joy's table. We're directed around a corner, where most of our friends are already seated.

They go silent when they see us holding hands.

And then Roni begins to clap. "*Yes!*"

The others join in.

"Stop it," I say as I sit across from Roni and Derek. I'm almost afraid to look at Gage. He's probably mortified.

"Tell us everything," Joy says. "How long have you two been getting busy?"

Remember how I said nothing is off-limits with the widows? Yeah, so... "Not long, and that's all we're going to say about it."

"Well, I think it's *marvelous*," Christy says, raising her margarita in a toast to us.

I'm embarrassed and flustered, neither of which happens very often. "Someone pass me the drink menu, please."

"I recommend the margaritas," Lexi says. "They're to die for."

"I can attest," Christy says.

"They use only the best tequila here," Joy tells me. "None of that rotgut that makes you wish you were dead the next day."

That sounds good to me. "Sign me up."

Gage orders water.

I glance over at him. "We could Uber home and get your car tomorrow."

He thinks about that for a second. "You know, that's not a

bad idea. I'm celebrating tonight. Let's make it champagne for the table."

"*Whoa*," Brielle says. "What's gotten into him, besides you?"

Before I can protest, Wynter says, "Technically, it's *him* getting into *her*, but your point is well taken."

They die laughing.

Leave it to Wynter.

"Knock it off," I say, knowing they never will. To Gage, I say, "Will you please tell them what you're celebrating?"

"Three things, actually," he says. "One, I sold my company this week."

That's met with stunned silence.

"I thought you loved that place," Joy says.

"Not as much as I used to, and I'm ready for a change. Two, we've reached a plea deal with the guy who killed my family. We didn't get everything we wanted, but we got enough, and we'll avoid the trial."

"Aw, Gage," Derek says. "That's a big one."

"Yeah, it feels good to have it settled, even if it doesn't change anything, you know?"

"All too well," Derek says as Roni nods in agreement.

Both their spouses were murdered.

"And the third thing," Gage says, shifting his gaze to me, "is that the lovely Iris here has convinced me that I need to be in a relationship with her, and so I've decided to let her have her wicked way with me."

That sets off another roar of laughter that has my face burning with mortification. "You'll pay for that later," I tell him.

"I can't wait."

Wynter stands suddenly and walks away.

"What's up with her?" I ask Lexi, who was sitting the closest to her.

"No idea. I'll go after her."

"Let me. If it was something I said, I should take care of it."

"It wasn't anything you said," Gage says.

"Still, I'll go. Order me a margarita." I take off in the direction Wynter went and duck into the ladies' room to see if she's in there. I look under the stalls, but don't see the funky sneakers she always wears, so I head outside, wondering if she left.

I find her off to the side of the entrance, having a cigarette as she shivers in the cool autumn air.

"Wynter."

She startles when she sees me there. "What?"

"What's wrong?"

"Nothing. Go back inside. I'll be in after I finish this." She waves the cigarette to make her point.

"Since when do you smoke?"

"I have since I was fifteen. I just don't make a spectacle of it. And don't lecture me about how it causes cancer and tell me I should know better. I've heard it all before."

"I'm not going to lecture you."

"They're right, you know."

"Who is?"

"The people who say I should know better. After what I saw Jaden go through with cancer treatment, I wouldn't wish that on anyone. So why am I smoking something that could give me cancer? I have no clue."

"Did something happen?"

"Other than losing my twenty-year-old husband to cancer?"

Even though I'm freezing, I lean back against a cement planter full of colorful chrysanthemums. "Yeah, other than that."

"It's nothing. You should go back in. You're cold."

"I'm fine. Talk to me, Wynter. Tell me what's wrong."

"Everything is wrong! Every fucking thing! I hate being a widow, and I hate being part of this group even though I love you guys. I hate that I need it. I hate that people are falling in love all around me, and it makes me miss feeling that way so much. And I hate that I'm an asshole who can't be happy for my friends who sure as hell deserve to be happy. Are you glad you asked?"

Before I can overthink whether I should, I hug her.

She stiffens. "What're you doing?"

Rather than respond, I hug her tighter even as she fights to break free. I hold her until she stops fighting and sags against me with the kind of exhaustion only someone else who's been where she is can understand. "You're not alone with any of this, Wynter."

"And yet, which one of us is going home alone tonight?"

"You're a young, beautiful person with so much life ahead of you. I know none of that is what you want or need to hear right now, but it's true. What happened to you and Jaden is awful and wrong and so fucked up as to be beyond fucked up."

Her soft laugh makes me smile. "I love when you're away from your kids."

"Fuckity, fuck, fuck, fuck."

She laughs out loud.

I loosen my hold on her and reach over to wipe the tears off her face.

"I'm an asshole for getting upset about you and Gage. It makes no sense. I love you both, and of course I'm happy for you."

"I know you are, and so does he. And PS, we love you, too."

"I hate being a miserable bitch."

"You're not."

"No, I really am. I don't blame Adrian for not wanting me around Xavier."

"Wait, did he say that?"

"No, but he hasn't exactly jumped on the opportunity to hire me as his nanny. It's probably because I'm such a mess."

"You're not a mess." When she starts to object, I hold up a finger to stop her. "You are not a mess. You're grieving, and that is messy. You need to be kinder to yourself."

"I want my old life back."

"I know, sweetheart. I know."

"Sorry to be a drag."

"You're fine, but will you put that thing out and come back inside with me? I'm freezing."

She takes another deep drag off the cigarette and then squashes the butt under her sneaker.

I'm pleased when she bends to pick up the butt and puts it in the trash before following me inside.

"Hey, Iris?"

"Yes?"

"You're pretty cool for an old person."

I elbow her. "Watch your mouth, kid."

"No, really. Thanks."

"Any time."

"So, is Gage big everywhere?"

"Wynter!"

"Just tell me. You know you want to."

"I do *not* want to."

"Is that because he's huge and hung?"

I want to expire on the spot. She's outrageous.

"He is, isn't he? I knew he would be. He's got those big hands and feet. That's usually a good sign."

"How do you know these things? Are you even twenty yet?"

"I'm twenty-one, and I know things."

I give her a gentle push toward her seat and return to mine next to Gage.

"Everything all right?" he asks.

"It is now. Back to business as usual with Wynter."

"Is that why your face is red?"

"That, and it's freezing outside." I take a sip of the margarita that's waiting for me and try to shake off the melancholy that came with hearing Wynter say she wants her old life back. Two weeks ago, I would've said the same, but now everything's changed, including my feelings for my late husband.

Under the table, I reach over to wrap my hand around Gage's, thankful for him and this thing between us that's sustained me during this difficult time.

Twenty

IRIS

W e eat, we drink, and we laugh—a lot.

I look over at Christy at one point, and she raises her glass to me in a silent toast to this thing we've built together. We marvel all the time about what it's become and how important it is to all of us.

"How are things?" I ask her.

"This has been a good week. The kids haven't had any catastrophes, which means I haven't either." Christy has two young teens who've had a difficult time since their dad, Wes, died of an aortic dissection more than three years ago.

"Glad to hear it. How's the new guy?"

"Eh, I don't think it's going to happen."

"Really? I thought you really liked this one."

"I do, but he's not sure he can take on teenagers on an everyday basis."

"Did he say that?"

"In so many words, and hell, I can't blame him. I'd like to sell them to the circus most days."

"I hate to hear that. I liked him for you, and I haven't even met him."

"I liked him for me, too. We're taking a break before it goes any further. He said he wants to think, and I'm giving him space. I mean, he's never been married or had kids, so we're a lot for him to take on."

"You're amazing, and he'd be lucky to have you."

"I know that, and you know that. We just need to convince him."

"Don't work too hard to convince him of what's right in front of his face, okay?"

"I won't. Enough about me. How are you holding up?"

"Amazingly well, all things considered."

She uses her chin to gesture to Gage, who's talking to Derek. "I'm sure he's been a *big* help."

"You sound like Wynter," I tell her, laughing.

Wynter's eyes light up with delight. "Big hands, big feet, big—"

Christy's hand over Wynter's mouth stops her from finishing that thought.

"I'm just sayin'," Wynter says, her words muffled by Christy's hand.

I shake my head and laugh. "She's incorrigible."

"There's nothing like a big dick to make anything better," Wynter adds.

"I cannot with her," I say to Christy, who's helpless with laughter.

"What did she say?" Gage asks, tuning in to our conversation.

"Don't ask. You do not want to know."

Wynter pushes her tongue against her cheek, which sets Christy off again.

"Don't laugh at her! You'll only encourage her."

"I can't help it," Christy says, wiping tears from her eyes. "She kills me."

I give Wynter a pointed look. "I'm gonna kill her if she doesn't knock it off."

"Truth hurts so good, doesn't it?" Wynter asks.

"Gage, it's time to go home," I say.

"She's horny."

"Wynter!"

Even though I'm mortified by her, I'm also delighted to see her hysterical with laughter at her own jokes.

"What's going on down there?" Roni asks.

"Nothing good," I tell her.

"It's *all* good," Wynter says.

"I need to get going," Roni says. "My boobs are about to burst."

"We can't have that," Derek says. "Let's get you home to that little guy."

Gage has arranged for Derek to drop us at my house, so we walk out with them.

"What's up with Wynter?" Roni asks. "Is she okay?"

"She's more than okay now and having a blast busting my chops about being with Gage. Before that, she had a rough moment over people moving on when her life is a mess. I told her it's not a mess, but I'm not sure she believes me. She really wants to take care of Xavier, but Adrian hasn't said whether he'll hire her."

"Where was he tonight?" Gage asks.

"I don't know. I'll text him to make sure he's okay." I send the text while we wait for Derek's SUV to arrive from the valet. "He says Xavier was having a rough day, so he stayed home."

"How about Hallie?" Roni asks. "Wasn't she supposed to come tonight?"

"Texting." I tell our friend we missed her tonight and hope everything is okay. "She says she got home late from work and had no gas left in her tank. She'll see us at the ALS fundraiser next week."

Our friend Lexi lost her husband to that hideous disease, and his medical bills have left her financially devastated. Kinsley, who lost her husband, Rory, to pancreatic cancer, and Naomi, who lost her fiancé, David, to lymphoma, have organized the event. Half the proceeds will go to ALS research, and the other half will go to Lexi.

"I'm so glad Lexi agreed to let the girls organize something for her," Roni says. "I can't imagine being devastated by loss and left with a mountain of medical bills, too. The loss is bad enough on its own."

"For real," Gage says.

"Has anyone heard anything from Aurora?" Derek asks as he drives us to my house.

"Not recently," I reply.

"I've been following her husband's trial," Gage says. "They've got him totally nailed on rape charges."

We voted to let Aurora into the group after her husband was charged with rape, because we agreed she'd lost the life she'd planned to lead with him the same as the rest of us did when our spouses died. She stopped coming to the meetings after Derek and Roni got together. We suspect it was because she wanted Derek for herself.

"I keep telling Derek he ought to call and check on her," Roni says.

"Not doing that," Derek replies gruffly.

Gage and I laugh at their banter.

"I feel sorry for her," Roni says. "What an awful thing. If I were her, I'd leave the country until the trial was over."

"Maybe she did," I say. "I'm going to text her to tell her we're thinking of her and would love to see her if she wants to come back." I send the text before I can talk myself out of reaching out to her.

"Let us know if she replies," Roni says.

"I will. I feel for her, even if sometimes I didn't like her very much."

"Agreed," Derek said. "No one deserves what she's going through."

"None of us deserve any of the shit we've been dealt," Gage says.

"True," Roni says. "I've been having a rough time of it since the first anniversary of Patrick's death. I keep having these dreams that he's come back, and I have to choose between him and Derek."

My heart breaks for her. "Oh, that's awful, honey."

"It's been pretty awful," Roni says, "but Derek has been a saint."

"I haven't done anything you wouldn't do for me," he says as he brings the SUV to a stop in my driveway.

I lean forward to give Roni's shoulder a squeeze. "Call me if you need to talk. I'm always here for you."

"Likewise, my friend," she says.

"Get those boobs home to Dylan," I call to her as I get out of the vehicle.

I leave her laughing as I close the door and take the hand Gage extends to me. I can't wait to spend this night wrapped up in him.

RONI

"I LOVE THEM TOGETHER," I say the second the door closes behind Iris.

"Me, too."

"I have never seen Gage smile like he did tonight. Between this thing with Iris and selling his company, he's like a new man."

"I thought the same thing."

"It's nice to see people who truly deserve a second chance getting one with each other."

"Like us."

"Just like us."

I'm appalled when my eyes flood with tears that just won't stop this week, no matter what I do. I should be on top of the world after getting engaged to Derek and finally allowing our relationship to become physical during the beach getaway. Everything is great, but the ache I feel for Patrick is unrelenting. I tried to hide it from Derek, but he's too perceptive.

I swipe at the tears, praying they'll stop before we get back to his place, where our wonderful nanny is watching Maeve and Dylan.

"I see you over there," he says softly.

"I wish it would just stop."

"It's never going to stop, Roni. For the rest of your life, you're going to miss Patrick and mourn his loss."

"But does it have to be so intense the same week I agree to marry you?"

"Maybe that's *why* it's so intense. Did you ever consider that?"

"I don't want it to be this way."

"If you find a way to manage the grief on your timetable, I sure as hell hope you'll share that mojo with me."

"I know it's unrealistic to want to be in control of when it rears its ugly head, but why does it have to be now, when things have been so good?"

"If I had to guess, it's because you're taking steps to move on with me when you never wanted to move on from Patrick."

"Why isn't that happening to you, too? You never wanted to move on from Victoria."

"I've had a little longer to process my loss than you have."

I think about that and try to figure out how I feel about it. My emotions are all over the place since I had the first dream two nights ago. I tried so hard to keep the anguish to myself, but Derek wasn't having that.

"It's okay if we slow things down a bit, Roni. You know that, right?"

"I don't want to slow things down. I've had a year to accept that Patrick isn't ever coming back. In that time, you've become my best friend, my new love. Did I expect this to happen between us? Not at all. If you'd asked me a year ago if I'd be engaged, I would've said no way. But we both know how this happened, and why it happened, and how lucky we are to have it."

"That doesn't mean it all has to happen right now. We've got the rest of our lives to get where we're going."

It's no wonder I love this man so much. Was it my intention to find someone new to love so soon after losing my husband? Absolutely not, but our relationship happened so organically and is based on a deep, abiding friendship that is a big part of the reason I survived this last year. If I've learned anything since I lost Patrick, it's that life has a way of laughing in your face when you think you've got all your plans in place.

"I want you to know how much I appreciate you."

"I know you do, Roni, and I appreciate you. We're in this together for the long haul. Please don't put any pressure on yourself thinking you have to meet my expectations. The only expectation I have where you're concerned is that we love each other and each other's children. The rest will sort itself out."

"I hate feeling this way."

"It's all part of the process. The good, the bad, the ugly. We've got to deal with all of it. But there's good news, too."

"What's that?" I ask, wiping my face again.

"We've discovered that there still can be joy and love and great happiness along with the despair."

"The despair seems to be winning the war lately."

"It's winning the battle, not the war. Joy will win the war. It's just going to take a while, but you'll get there. I promise."

"How do you always know what to say to make me feel better?"

"Because I still believe things will get better, even when everything goes to shit."

"Sometimes I wonder if I could've survived losing Patrick if you hadn't come along when you did to provide me with a roadmap through widowhood."

"You would've survived."

"I'm not so sure."

"I am. You're tougher than you think, Roni."

"I never would've described myself as tough before Patrick was killed, although my dad always says I was the toughest kid he ever met."

"I believe it. You never had to be tough like this, but it was always in there, waiting to prop you up when you needed it."

"Still... Thank you for being here and showing me the way through this."

"Being here with you is my pleasure, sweetheart."

IRIS

I WAKE up wondering why the kids haven't woken me before I remember they're at my mom's, and I spent the night having sex with Gage. The memories start my day with a smile that fades when I recall the text exchange with Eleanor. The other woman in my husband's life. And then another thought occurs to me.

"Jesus."

"No, it's Gage, but I do love a good nickname."

"I need to get tested for STDs."

"Um... what?"

"What if Mike brought something home to me?"

"Jeez, Iris."

I turn over and sit up, tucking the sheet under my arms to cover my breasts. "And now I've exposed you."

"Haven't you been to the doctor since Mike died?"

"Yes, but she probably didn't test me for STDs because my husband was dead."

"I'll bet she did, and you didn't even know it. Do you have access to your medical record online?"

"I do."

"Go ahead and check before you panic."

I reach for my phone on the bedside table and open my health chart to scroll through the most recent entries. "She did test me for everything." I expel a sigh of relief. "Sorry for the early-morning freak-out."

"It's okay."

"None of this is okay." My chin quivers as I try to contain emotions that are equal parts embarrassment and outrage. How dare Mike do this to me?

"Come here."

I snuggle up to Gage and make myself comfortable in his embrace. "I'm sorry. That's a heck of a thing to wake up to after having sex with someone."

"I've already forgotten it." His hand moves over my back in slow, caressing strokes that help to ease my tension.

"I'm so angry with him."

"Rightfully so."

"I've been so sad and heartbroken since he died, and now that's morphed into this all-consuming anger."

"I'd be surprised if you weren't furious."

"How could he do this to me? To his kids?"

"I wish I knew. Anyone who has you has it all."

"You really think that?"

"I really do."

I've started to feel a little better when my phone rings. I pull back from Gage to reach for it and sit up when I see my mother-in-law's name on the caller ID. "I have to take this."

"Go ahead."

"Hi, Kathy."

"Iris… Honey, I've been thinking of you nonstop this week since the news came out about the NTSB and then this other situation."

"Thank you." Calling Mike's second family an "other situation" amuses me in a macabre sort of way.

"Mike Senior and I… We don't know what to say."

"There's nothing to say. It happened, and now we must deal with it."

"And you had no idea?"

"None at all."

"Where's she been all this time?"

"I don't know that either."

"I'm so sorry. What in the world could he have been thinking?"

"God only knows."

"Have you… Have you spoken to her?"

"Only by text so far."

"We're so torn between outrage and desire to know this other child he had, but we feel disloyal to you wanting to know the child."

"Of course you want to know him. He's your grandchild. Don't worry about me. Do whatever you need to."

"Iris, we're devastated by this. You were a wonderful, loving wife to Mike, and even though we didn't start off so well, we love you. I hope you know that."

"I do. Thank you."

"If you speak to her, I suppose you can ask if she'd like to connect with us."

"I'll do that."

"And this NTSB thing... How could Mike be at fault?"

"It's possible he was distracted from leading a double life."

"You really think that's possible?"

"We may never know what happened, but that's definitely possible."

"I suppose so," she says, sighing. "How are the kids? We need to get down to see them soon."

It's been months since they've seen anyone but Rob from Mike's family. "They're doing well. Growing like weeds."

"We'll make a date to get together soon."

"They'd like that."

"You take care, Iris."

"You, too." I press the red button to end the call, but the awkwardness of the conversation hangs like a dark cloud over me.

"I take it that was Mike's mother," Gage says.

"Yep."

"And you can't stand her."

"It's not that. She was... How can I say this... Less than thrilled about her precious son marrying a biracial woman and was chilly to me for a long time after we started dating and well into our marriage."

"Ick."

"Exactly."

"I fucking hate racist people, especially the ones clutching their pearls and rosary beads while they actively hate other people for simply being born a different color or nationality or religion or sexual orientation than they are. It's gross."

If I wasn't already madly in love with this man, that outburst might've put me straight over the top. "I agree. I've experienced my share of it, but never with anyone as close to me as his parents were. They've 'come around' over the years, but I don't have much time for them. It was a source of contention with Mike, who told me I needed to be more forgiving toward them."

"I hope you said fuck that."

"Many times, thus the contention."

"It was ballsy of him to ask you to forgive them for being racist."

"I thought so, too, and I told him so. But I also felt for him. They were his parents. He was stuck in a tough position."

"No, he wasn't. You were his wife. He chose you and brought you into his family knowing full well how they were. He should've always taken your side with them."

"You're racking up the points this morning, my friend."

"I hate racists. I fired a guy for making a racist joke at the office. No questions asked. He was gone."

"You're turning me on."

"Stop," he says on a laugh.

"No, really. You are."

"Is that right?"

"Uh-huh."

The next thing I know, he's moved us so he's on top of me, gazing down at me with the intense eyes that see me so clearly.

"I like waking up with you," he says gruffly as he kisses my neck and slides into me for the third—or is it the fourth?—time since we got home last night.

I wouldn't give Wynter the satisfaction of knowing that Gage's big hands and feet are a true indication that he's big all over, but as my sore flesh stretches to accommodate him once again, I can't help but think of her commentary and giggle.

"What's so funny?"

"Wynter was trying to get me to confirm that you're big all over, but I wouldn't. You're just reminding me of that."

He pushes deeper into me, making me gasp from the impact. "Is that right?"

"Mmmm-hmmm."

"Are you complaining?"

"Not at all."

He never breaks eye contact as he makes love to me.

I don't think I blink even once as he gazes into my eyes, making me feel like we're joined body and soul. My heart aches with love for him, a love that's already so deep, it'll wreck me all over again if I lose it.

That can't happen.

We're so perfect together in every way, especially this way, which he proves to me with not one, but two orgasms in the span of five minutes.

"You feel better?" he asks.

"Did I feel bad before? That seems like a long time ago."

His grunt of laughter is just what I wanted to hear. "Let's go pick up the kids and find a fall festival with pumpkins and face painting and apple bobbing."

I look over at him. "You really feel like doing that?"

"I really do."

Twenty-One

IRIS

After dinner at a pizza place the kids love, Gage drives us home in my minivan, keeping up a steady stream of chatter with the kids the way he has all day. They had the best time carving pumpkins, having their faces painted and riding on ponies. We never got to the apple bobbing, which was just as well after the face painting.

Gage insisted on paying for everything and was fully engaged with them the entire time. We even took a group photo, the first of the five of us together. For a while there, it felt like we were a normal family doing normal family things on an autumn Saturday.

In exchange for dinner at their favorite place, Gage got them to agree to baths and pajamas the minute we get home.

He's good with them, and they like him, which is a relief.

"Mr. Gage," Tyler asks when we're nearly home.

"What's up, pal?"

"Are you going to be our new daddy?"

"Tyler!"

"Are you, Mr. Gage?" Sophia asks.

"I'm sorry," I mutter to him.

"I don't know about that," Gage says, "but today was fun, right?"

"So much fun," Tyler says. "That's why I want you to be our new daddy. You're good at models, too."

"That's very sweet of you to say, buddy, but let's not get ahead of ourselves."

"What does that mean? Get ahead of ourselves."

"Your mom and I aren't ready to have those sorts of conversations yet."

"When will you be?"

"Oy," I whisper.

Gage squeezes my thigh. "I don't know, but not for a while."

"Why?"

"That's enough, Ty. We need to be thankful to Gage for a very nice day and not make it into something it's not."

"Shouldn't we get to say who our new daddy is?"

I'm not sure whether to laugh or cry. I turn in my seat to look at my son, who's wearing a defiant look. "Enough." He's heard that tone of voice often enough to know I've reached my limit.

Poor Gage. This is the thanks he gets for giving us a beautiful day—being put on the spot by a daddy-starved seven-year-old.

After we pull into the garage, Gage reminds the kids of their deal.

They take off to do what they agreed to do, while I hang back to apologize to Gage.

"No apology needed, sweetheart. They're adorable and sweet and confused about what I'm doing here."

"Are you? Confused about what you're doing here?"

"Not so much. It feels good to spend the day with you guys and drive the minivan and make deals with kids again."

"Did you make a lot of deals with yours?"

"All the time. Nat called me Monty Hall, who was the host of *Let's Make a Deal* when she watched it with her grandparents, in case that reference is outside your zone."

I laugh. "I love that."

"It was how I got them to do what they were supposed to do without a lot of yelling, which I hate as much as I hate racism. Both my parents were yellers when we were kids."

"I had that teacher who gave me stomachaches. Used to scare me."

"No yelling allowed on my watch. Lots of dealmaking."

"That works for me."

He hooks his arm around me. "It's too much, too soon. I know that and you know that. But today felt good. Maybe we keep doing more of that and see how it fits for all of us?"

I look up at him as I nod. "You've got a deal, Mr. Hall."

MY CALL with Eleanor is scheduled for this morning, and I'm as nervous as I've ever been in my life. Gage offered to be with me when I talk to her, but he's meeting with the people buying his company today and has a full day. Even though I wish he was here, I told him I'd be fine.

I really hope I will be. I'm scared of what she might tell me and how it might make this dreadful situation even worse than it already is.

She's supposed to call me after she drops her son at school.

I should've asked what time that would be. While I wait, I stare at the phone as if it's a bomb that's going to detonate at any second.

By the time the phone rings at nine thirty, I'm a wreck. I nearly drop the phone as I answer the call. "Hello?"

"Hi, it's Eleanor."

"Hi," I say as if it's no big deal that I'm talking to the woman who had a child with my late husband.

For a long moment, neither of us says anything, and then we both speak at once. I don't know what I'm saying and didn't hear what she said.

We laugh.

"How awkward is this?" she asks.

"Mad awkward, as my nieces would say."

"Mine say mad awk."

"That's even better." I don't want to like her, but she doesn't seem terrible.

"I didn't know he was married, Iris, until after I told him about the baby."

"He wore a ring."

"He wasn't wearing it when I met him."

I close my eyes as I absorb that information. He intentionally took off his ring and set out to meet someone.

"I can't begin to know how painful this is for you. Mike... He told me that our son, Carter, would be cared for in his will if anything ever happened to him. He said he'd taken care of that. I waited to reach out. My sister said probate can take up to eighteen months, so I let it ride, hoping I would hear something. When I saw the thing about the NTSB blaming him for the crash, I reached out to Steve to ask him what was going on."

"How did you find out Mike had died?"

"From your social media."

"You follow me?" That shocks me.

"I started to after I found out he had a wife and children. I wanted to know more about his life, since everything he'd told me was a lie."

As I listen to her, I realize we were both victimized by him. "Are there others? Besides you?"

"I don't know that, but then again, I didn't know he had a wife and three kids back in Virginia."

"What did he tell you?"

"That he was divorced and starting over."

Fuck, that hurts. I fight the urge to scream. "After you found out about us, did you ask him why? Because I sure as hell have no idea why he'd do this to me and our kids."

"I did ask, but he didn't have an answer to that. In hindsight,

I think it was maybe the excitement of it all. Long-married guy has a chance to bust loose, and no one will ever know, so why not? That's my theory, anyway."

"If you don't mind my asking, was the baby intentional on your part?"

"God, no. That was the biggest shock of my life. I'm on long-term birth control that didn't work. I wouldn't change a thing, though. I love him so much. I had no idea it was possible to love anyone this much."

"He's my children's half brother."

"Yes."

"What do we do about that?"

"At some point, it might be nice if they could meet. I'm not sure how feasible that would be, but I'd love for him to know his siblings, because he won't have others."

"Mike always loved the name Carter. He wanted to name our son that, but I was hooked on Tyler."

"The name was his suggestion, and I loved it."

"Does he have Mike's last name?"

"It's hyphenated with mine."

His parents will be happy to hear that. "Did you love him? Mike?"

"I thought I did until I found out he'd been lying to me since the second we met. Steve told me the estate is closed, so he also lied about taking care of our son."

"I'm sorry about that."

"None of this is your fault, Iris. He deceived us both."

"He did this to me once before, but I thought we'd gotten past it. I was so proud of the way we put our marriage back together."

"I feel terrible about this. I never would've given him a second glance if I'd known he was married. I was sick to my stomach for weeks after I found out about you and the kids, and that was on top of the pregnancy nausea."

"That must've been a shock for sure."

"It was awful. I was disgusted with him and myself. I only saw him once more after that. He came to see Carter when he was first born. I told him he could see him once a year, but otherwise, we wanted nothing to do with him. He was apologetic, contrite, all the things. Whatever. I was done with him."

"I know it's none of my business..."

"You can ask me whatever you want."

"How many times did you meet up with him? Before you found out about us."

"On and off for about six months."

That information lands like another punch to the gut. This was a full-on affair, not a one-night stand.

"It was all so romantic, you know? The corporate pilot only in town a day here or a day there, and we must make the most of it. To find out it was just sex for him was devastating."

"I'm sorry he did that to you."

"I'm sorry he did this to you. It's horrible."

"Steve said you might sue me for child support."

"I don't want to do that, but I assume there were some assets, life insurance, that kind of thing. Raising a child on my own is expensive. If there's anything left, I wouldn't say no to it."

"There was life insurance, and that's what I'm living on now. It's enough that I don't have to work until my youngest starts school."

"I see."

"I, ah, I'll talk to my financial adviser and see what we can do."

"That's very kind of you."

"Please don't sue me. I don't have the mental energy to deal with that."

"I understand, and I don't want it to come to that, but he made promises to me."

"I know." He made vows to me, I want to remind her, but I don't blame her for any of this. "Let me talk to my guy and get back in touch with you."

"Thank you."

"Mike's parents would like to meet Carter. Is it okay if I give them your number?"

"Yes, that would be fine. What are they like?"

"They're okay. She can be a bit judgmental, but I just ignore her. He's harmless, and Mike's brother, Rob, is great."

"Good to know. Thank you."

"I'll get back in touch after I talk to my financial guy."

"Sounds good. I want you to know... I'm sorry about adding to your grief."

"That's kind of you to say, but you're not the one who added to my grief. In some ways, finding out he wasn't who I thought he was moves things along for me. I'll reach out in the next few days."

"Talk to you then."

I end the call feeling disgusted, furious, heartbroken and surprised by how nice she seems. I'm not sure what I expected, but I'm thankful that she appears to be a decent sort of person.

As I promised I would, I text Gage to tell him I talked to her.

He calls me.

"Hey."

"How'd it go?"

I give him the recap in as few words as possible.

"God, I'm sorry, Iris. Not what you wanted to hear."

"I don't want to hear any of this but finding out he took his ring off and went looking for it was a little tough to take. And that he said he was divorced."

"It's terrible."

"I asked her where she's been all this time, and she said she waited to hear from someone about a settlement for her son. When that never happened, she reached out to Steve through Mike's company, and you know what he did. After the NTSB report was released, she asked Steve for an update and that's when he brought the news about her and Carter to me." I release a deep sigh. "I hate being part of something so sordid, but I keep reminding myself there's an innocent child involved. He didn't ask for any of this either."

"How did you leave it with her?"

"She said she won't sue me for child support if we can come to some sort of agreement that would give her son a piece of the insurance money."

"Can you afford that?"

"I'm going to try to help her out. It's not her fault Mike was a liar."

"True. If I can help, I hope you'll let me know."

"I'm not taking your money, Gage."

"If you need it, I have it, and I'm about to have a whole lot more. Don't suffer in silence, Iris. If I can help, tell me so."

"You're very sweet, but I'm okay. I might have to take some of those endorsement offers I'm getting for my TikTok account. I hear there's lots of money to be made in that space. I've resisted that because it would turn my hobby into a business that would require more energy than I can give it right now, but it's good to know that's an option."

"It's always good to have options, such as very close friends who are willing and able to help with anything you need."

"Stop being so sweet. It's annoying me."

He laughs, as I hoped he would. I love when he laughs. I can picture the gorgeous dimples that appear when he's truly amused. "I can't wait to annoy you more after work."

"Can I ask you something?"

"Anything."

"I've been thinking a lot about what Tyler said last night, and I can see how they're getting attached to you. It's just important to me that they not be hurt any more than they've already been."

"I'd never hurt them. You have my word on that."

"You could hurt them by deciding the insta-family isn't what you really want after all."

"That's not going to happen. I love being with them, and I have since long before things changed between us. They're great kids, and it's not just about me being there for them. They fill some of the gaping void inside me where my girls used to be. I love their silly chatter and their excitement over the simplest things and how fun Saturday was. I've missed that kind of thing more than I realized. Not sure I'm explaining that well."

"You are," I say softly. "That's lovely, but a few days ago, you were still saying you weren't sure you wanted to be in a relationship."

"I know, and I still have misgivings, but those have nothing to do with you or the kids. It's more about my fear of something happening to you guys and having to go through that nightmare again."

"We're not going anywhere."

"I'm counting on that."

Twenty-Two

GAGE

I ris and I settle into a routine that includes dinners and weekends with the kids, outings with our widow friends and an occasional night to ourselves thanks to her parents. I sneak out of her bed at five a.m. every day and leave before the kids are up, so we don't confuse them about where things stand between us before we're ready to make the next move.

That move is coming. I can feel it, and I know she can, too.

After consulting with her accountant and lawyer, Iris made a one-time payment to Eleanor that included a document the other woman signed to ensure she wouldn't be back for more. They've agreed to speak again in a few months about potentially getting the kids together. Iris is relieved to have that taken care of and to know she doesn't have to deal with that situation again for a while.

Iris has also been relieved that Rob has started coming around to see the kids again, after more than a month without visiting. The kids were thrilled to see their beloved uncle, and Iris is glad to have him back.

She's seemed lighter and less burdened lately, which is a relief to me. I'm not sure when exactly it happened, but her happiness—and that of the kids—has become as important to me as my own. As we head toward Christmas, I want to surprise the kids with a trip to Florida for their school vacation week. Before I do that, though, I need to talk to Mimi and Stan about Iris and the kids.

I've been putting this off for weeks, but if I'm going to take them with me, I need to talk to Nat's parents about it first.

It's my last day in the office before we close on the sale. My stuff is in boxes, ready to be taken home, and I feel like I'm already gone. Over the last month, I've sat back and watched everyone move on without me as the new owners held meetings and made plans that don't include me.

I keep waiting for regret to set in, but so far, all I feel is relief. I'm ready to move on and to see what else is out there for me.

The staff is throwing a farewell party for me at two, and before that, I need to get this call over with. I pick up the phone on my desk and dial Mimi's cell number from memory.

"Hi there," she says when she picks up. "I was just telling Stan I needed to call you and see what you're doing for the holidays."

"That's sort of why I called."

"Are you coming down?"

"I'd like to, if that's okay."

"Gage, darling, our home is your home. You know that."

"I do, but there's a wrinkle."

"What kind of wrinkle?"

"The kind where I've sort of been seeing someone who has three young kids, and I'd like to bring them with me." I feel guilty for saying I've "sort of" been seeing Iris when I've spent every night in her bed for months.

Mimi is quiet for long enough that I begin to squirm. "You still there?" I ask her.

"I'm here, honey," she says softly. "I knew this would happen eventually, and I'm so happy for you."

"But still heartbroken, too. I know the feeling."

"Yes, of course, but I'd love to meet them. Please bring them. It'll be wonderful to have children in the house again."

"You'll love Iris, and the kids are great. Very well behaved and funny."

"When are you thinking of coming?"

"Maybe the evening of the twenty-fifth, after we have some time with my family and Iris's?"

"That'd be perfect. Send me their ages and sizes and whatnot so I can have something here for them."

Her kindness nearly brings me to tears. "You don't have to do that, Mimi."

"Yes, I do. I want to. Please let me."

Her gifts to the girls over the years were the things they loved the most. Nat and I used to joke that Santa couldn't compete with Mimi. "You're the best. Have I told you that lately?"

"Not in a while," she says, laughing.

"I need to do better in the new year."

"No, you don't, love. You're perfect just the way you are, and as much as I miss Nat and the girls—and will for the rest of my life—I'm truly happy to see you picking up the pieces and starting over. Stan and I have hoped for that for you."

"I wasn't sure how you'd take this news."

"We're on Team Gage. Always have been, always will be. You made our daughter very, very happy and were a wonderful father to our granddaughters. We want you to be happy. You deserve that."

Damn if she doesn't have me in tears. "You're the best person I know, and I never would've gotten to where I am now without your love and support."

"Sure, you would have. You're a survivor."

"You showed me how it's done."

"Oh Lord," she says, huffing out a laugh. "I don't know about that."

"It's true."

"We got through it together. Somehow. Now we've just got to deal with the sentencing after the first of the year, and we can put that part of it behind us, too."

"I told you I'm willing to handle that if you want to skip it."

"Not happening, my friend. We're in it for the long haul, and we'll see it through to completion right there with you."

"Can't wait to see you and make some new memories."

"Likewise, my love. Keep me posted on your plans and send me the info about the kids. I can't wait to go shopping. It's been too long."

"Will do. Love you forever, Mimi."

"Love you right back. Forever and a day."

After we end the call, I take a minute to absorb the love and devotion I always get from her, and then I suddenly decide I want to write about it. With thirty minutes until my going-away party, I open my laptop and start typing an Insta post about my amazing mother-in-law and how she's made such a difference to me on my grief journey.

Husbands love to disparage their mothers-in-law. Often their MILs give them good reason to by butting into things that are none of their business or criticizing the raising of their grandchildren. My mother-in-law has never been anything but a delight to me since the day I met her. She's been a friend and trusted confidant since long before we suffered the worst loss of our lives. Mimi is a big part of the reason my life didn't completely fall apart when I lost Nat and the girls. She was a rock to me before that awful day, and she's been right there for me every day since. Today, I told her some big news. I'm seeing someone new, and as always, Mimi responded with love and support and the same unwavering devotion she's shown me since the day we first met. Mimi, I love you. Forever and a day.

I find some photos of her with Nat and the girls and one of Mimi and I together, and I add them to the post. After including the usual hashtags, I click the button to make it live. It'll be a big deal to my followers to hear I'm seeing someone new, and I fully expect a flood of comments about that. Maybe I should've told Iris about it beforehand.

I give her a quick call.

"Hey," she says, sounding out of breath.

"What're you up to?"

"I was doing yoga."

"Oh, good, that's better than hearing your boyfriend is there."

"Haha, very funny. What's up?"

"So I did a thing."

"What's that?"

"I told Nat's mom about you and the kids."

"Oh. Wow. That's a big thing. How'd it go?"

"She's very happy for me and can't wait to meet you guys."

"That's great, Gage. I'm glad she was supportive. What brought this on?"

"I told her I was hoping to bring you guys with me for a visit during Christmas break. If you're up for it, that is."

"A trip to Florida in the winter. Hmmm, let me think about that. I'm up for it."

"Ha, I had a feeling you might be."

"Are you sure, though? We're a lot..."

"She can't wait to meet you and wants all the details on the kids so she can go shopping."

"She doesn't have to do that."

"I said the same thing, but when you meet Mimi, you'll understand that she does need to. She said it'll be fun to have kids to shop for again."

"That's so sweet of her."

"She's the best person I know—after you, of course."

"You don't need to qualify it. I know how important she and her husband are to you."

"I'm closer to them than my own parents."

"Funny how that happens."

"Yeah, it is. I also might've mentioned that I'm seeing

someone when I posted about telling my mother-in-law about you."

"Oh, that's big news. Are you ready for that outpouring?"

"I guess I'll find out. So am I allowed to buy tickets to fly south on the evening of the twenty-fifth? That way, we have Christmas Eve with my family and Christmas Day with yours and Mike's?"

"That works for me. Thank you for taking us."

"I can't wait. Mimi and Stan have a gorgeous pool, and they're right by the beach. Maybe we can even take the kids up to Disney for an overnight."

"Whoa, cowboy. You have to plan Disney months in advance these days, so let's not add that to the mix. They'll be perfectly happy with the pool and the beach."

"We'll do Disney another time."

"Gage..."

"Yes, Iris?"

"This is feeling an awful lot like a relationship."

I laugh like I do every time she says that. I laugh more than I have in years around her. "We probably ought to talk about that one of these days, huh?"

"Perhaps."

"I can't wait to surprise the kids with the trip."

"They'll flip out. We haven't been anywhere since before Mike died. Laney doesn't remember flying."

"We'll have a great time."

"When is your work party?"

"Around two."

"Come see me after that?"

"I'll be right there."

IRIS

THE LEAD-UP to Christmas is the usual mayhem for me—shopping, wrapping, cooking, decorating and this year, packing for a trip my kids don't know about yet. It's the first time I've bothered with a big tree since Mike died. And yes, I know I have kids and owe them a magical Christmas, which I've provided sans the tree. I just couldn't bring myself to bother with that without him here to do the heavy lifting.

This year, Gage did it for me, and it felt right that he should be there decorating the tree with us.

On the Friday before Christmas, I host a Wild Widows potluck dinner and gift exchange. We all chose one name from a hat to buy a gift for, and I got Joy. I bought her a gorgeous cashmere sweater and scarf set in a vivid hot pink. I think she'll love it, as everything about Joy is vivid. After Gage hemmed and hawed so much over what to get Roni, I finally picked a pair of sheepskin-lined boots for her. Derek helped me get the size right, and I even wrapped them for Gage. That's the least I could do after he hauled an eight-foot tree home from the lot, put it up and handled the dreaded strings of lights for me.

We're very much in a relationship.

He doesn't even try to deny it anymore, and if I do say so myself, he seems very happy.

My kids adore him. They crawl all over him the way they used to do to Mike. They crave his attention, his approval, his laughter and his love, which he gives them freely and without reservation.

I love him. I am *in* love with him. And one of these days, I need to tell him that.

I've spent days preparing for the Wild Widows get-together, with deluxe appetizers and fancy cocktails. During this holiday season, I haven't seen any of the friends who were so special to me before I lost Mike. They're still out there, still part of my life, but they aren't essential to me anymore, not like my Wild Widows are.

Gage comes early, toting the bags of ice I asked him to pick up for me. The kids are at my mom's for a pre-Christmas sleepover that includes a visit with Santa at the country club they belong to. The kids were super excited to see Santa and couldn't wait for my mom to pick them up. I couldn't wait for a night alone with Gage after the evening's festivities. Everything has been so busy that it's been a few weeks since we had a kid-free night.

He deposits the ice in the cooler I have ready and then wraps his cold self around me, making me shiver from the chill as well as his lips on my neck. "You smell good enough to eat."

"I smell like garlic."

"No, you don't." His hands move over me with a possessiveness that gives me a thrill. "You smell like my Iris."

It's all I can do not to melt right there in my own kitchen with friends due any minute. "Gage..."

"Hmmm?"

"I want to tell you..."

He pulls back to look down at me. "What do you want to tell me, sweetheart?"

I hoped that maybe he might say it first, which is so stupid. Who cares who says it first? Widowhood has taught me to tell the people I love how I feel as often as I can. I need him to know how I feel. The words burn at the tip of my tongue, where they've been sitting for weeks, wanting to be said. "I want to tell you—"

The doorbell rings and ruins the moment.

He kisses me. "Later. I want to hear anything you've got to say."

After he goes to grab the door, I take a couple of deep breaths to get myself together, to put my game face on so I can enjoy this evening with my special friends.

But I can't wait until later.

Twenty-Three

GAGE

E veryone is in high spirits tonight, which is nice to see. Holidays can be a bitch for grieving people, and I'm sure each of us will have our difficulties over the coming days, but tonight, we're able to enjoy each other, to exchange gifts, to eat the delicious food everyone contributed and celebrate getting through the year. We're still here, still capable of joy and love and wonder, which is a surprise to me.

After losing Nat and the girls, I thought those things were gone forever for me. But over time, thanks to many of the people in this room, my family, Nat's family, longtime friends and colleagues and mostly thanks to Iris and her kids, I've found that there's still love and joy and wonder to be found.

With that in mind, I touch a fork against my crystal glass of champagne to get everyone's attention. "Listen up, you Wild Widows."

They stop what they're doing to give me their attention.

"I just wanted to give a quick shout-out to Iris, our lovely hostess, for having us tonight and so many other times during the year. Iris, you've made your home our home, and we're thankful for you and this group that's held us all together through good times and bad."

"Cheers to Iris," Roni says as the others whistle and shout and embarrass Iris.

"Love you all," she says, blowing a kiss.

Joy looks good on her.

I continue my toast. "We've all learned the hard way that life can be an awful bitch. But this group of friends gives me so much hope every day, and I just want to thank you guys for being in my life. I took some big steps forward this year, and you guys are a big part of the reason I felt ready to do that. So, thanks." I hold up my glass to them. "Cheers."

Each of them hugs me or kisses me or fist-bumps.

We eat, we drink, we laugh, and when Iris changes the music on the Bluetooth from Christmas to something faster, we dance like fools. The party rages on until after midnight, when Ubers begin arriving to drive people home.

We put away everything perishable and leave a frightful mess in the kitchen to deal with in the morning.

Joy is asleep on the sofa in the family room, so we throw a blanket over her before locking up, shutting off the lights and heading upstairs.

"So much for our night without kids," I say teasingly.

"Right?"

"That was fun."

"So much fun."

"Play that 'Walk Through Fire' song that came on earlier, will you?"

"Now?"

"Right now."

She reaches for her phone, finds the song and plays it.

I hold out my arms to her. "Dance with me." I love the way she melts into my embrace, her body pressed against mine as we sway to the music. The lyrics really spoke to me when I heard it for the first time earlier. The two of us have walked through fire together, and we've come out on the other side stronger and wiser for the journey.

"It's amazing to me how so many good things have come from the worst thing," I whisper as I kiss her neck.

"I think about that all the time."

"I think about you all the time. Did you know that?"

She pulls back to look up at me, looking as dazzled as I feel. "Really?"

"All. The. Time." I kiss her and then lean my forehead against hers as we dance.

"Remember there was something I wanted to tell you earlier?"

"Uh-huh. Is it the same thing I want to tell you?"

"I don't know. Is it?"

"I think it might be if it goes anything like this: I love you, Iris. I'm in love with you. I want to be with you and the kids all the time, and I love this life we've been leading together these last few months."

"I love it, too. And I love you. So, so much, and my kids do, too. From the minute they get home from school, they're asking when Mr. Gage is coming over."

"I'm going to be retired by the time they go back to school. I can pick them up."

"They'd love that."

"This must be what it feels like to literally rise from the ashes to discover there's still so much living left to do." I swallow the huge lump that's formed in my throat. "I never could've gotten to this with anyone but you. I hope you know that."

"I remember thinking the day we met that you were a remarkable person," she says, "and my first impression of you has never changed."

"Same, sweetheart. I saw right away that you were a fierce warrior and somehow knew you were going to be essential to me surviving something that should've killed me."

"What would you think about living together at some point, or would that be too relationshipish for you?"

I give her the usual light spank on the butt that makes her laugh. "You're never going to let that go, are you?"

"Never, ever." She kisses my chin. "About the question…"

"Since I spend every night here anyway, I might be convinced to make it official. But we'd need to talk to the kids about it. This is their home."

"We could always find a new place together," she says, "and start fresh."

"I wouldn't want to move the kids. They've had enough upheaval."

"Oh, thank you, Jesus. The last thing in the world I want to do is move."

"I get it, babe. That would be too much. It's easier for me to move than all of us."

"How do you feel about leaving your place?"

"I'm okay with it. I moved there after the accident. I couldn't live in the place where I lived with them, so I don't have a deep emotional attachment to it. I could rent it."

"You should have a backup plan in case we drive you crazy."

"I don't need a backup plan," I tell her, smiling. "I have a good feeling about this fivesome. We're gonna make a go of it."

"You really think so?"

"I really do." After that, I set out to show her how completely she's captivated me. When I first lost Nat, I honestly couldn't conceive of having this sort of physical relationship with someone else. I figured I'd eventually go through the motions out of sheer need. I never expected the intense, intimate connection I've found with Iris.

"This feels so good," I whisper against her lips.

"So good."

We move together like we've been doing this forever, in perfect harmony. Every time I'm with her this way, I experience a profound feeling of homecoming. She's become home to me.

That's another thing I never thought I'd have again. There are houses that provide shelter, and then there are houses that are homes. This house began to feel like home to me long before our relationship—and that's what it is—became more.

She slides her hands down my back to pull me deeper inside her when she comes.

God help me, but she renders me powerless to resist her, not that I want to. Not when I've seen what's possible since I surrendered to the inevitable with her. I wanted to hold on to give her another orgasm, but I can't wait any longer.

Afterward, we snuggle together, our bodies still intertwined, her head on my chest.

"Do you want more kids?" she asks, surprising me with the question.

"Do you?"

"Not particularly, but I'd have more for you."

"I think I'd be good with your three, if they'll have me."

"They will, Gage. They adore you."

"And I adore them."

"I can't believe we're really talking about this," she says.

"I know. There was a time, not that long ago, when it would've been inconceivable for me to be in this place with you. I guess that's what people mean when they say that healing happens when you're not looking. Not that I'll ever be completely healed, but at least I'm capable of more than misery."

"You're capable of so much more than that, and so am I. But do you worry we're rushing into things? Our timeline would've freaked me out in my old life. I dated Mike for four years before we got engaged, and we didn't live together before we were married."

"I was with Nat for six before we got married, three of them living together."

"And here we are talking about moving in together two months after we started this part of the program." She uses her hand to gesture to the bed.

"But we've been friends for a lot longer, and that time counts. Besides, if this widow journey has taught us anything, it's that we have to grab on to happiness where we can and not worry about what anyone else thinks."

"I don't care what anyone thinks, except my kids, and I already know how they feel about you."

"Let's see how the trip goes. We can talk to them after that if you think the timing is appropriate."

"That works for me. I still need to figure out what to do about Eleanor and Carter."

"I thought that was resolved."

"The financial part is, but she's asked if I'm interested in getting the kids together in the next few months."

"Ah, you didn't tell me that. How do you feel about that?"

"I don't know. At first, I thought I should wait until they're older, but when I talked to my mom about it, she said it might be easier to introduce him now when they're too young to understand the finer details of how they happen to have another brother. If we wait until they're older, it might be more traumatic for them."

"I think your mom has a good point."

"The craziest part for me is that I still feel this need to protect their memories of Mike. I don't want them to hate him for this."

"Which is way more than he deserves from you."

"I'm trying to keep the two things separate. Their relationship with him can and should be separate from mine with him."

"That's awfully magnanimous of you, Iris."

"Losing their father when they were so young is going to affect the rest of their lives. If they hate him, that'll make it worse. I don't want them to hate him. When they're old enough to understand, I'll tell them that Daddy made a mistake that hurt me very deeply, but it shouldn't change how they feel about him or how they feel about Carter."

"It's all so bloody complicated, but I agree that it's better to introduce Carter to them when they're all too young to understand the deeper meaning. By the time they're older, he'll just be Carter, their half brother. No biggie."

"You're right. Mom's right. It's just the thought of seeing her and the child she had with my husband that's so overwhelming."

"I'll go with you. Whenever it happens, we'll face it together."

"You'd do that?"

"I'd never want you to do that without all the support I could give you."

"Thank you for that. The kids have another school break in February. Maybe we can do something then." She sighs deeply. "Add this to the list of things I never thought I'd have to do."

"It's outrageous that you have to deal with this. I'll never stop saying that."

"More than anything, I hate how it's changed how I feel about Mike. I loved him so much. I loved him unconditionally, and now I feel like it was all a big illusion. I find myself picking over so many things that didn't make sense at the time, wondering if I was missing what was right in front of me."

"You were busy having babies and taking care of your family."

"Was I too busy taking care of the kids that I didn't give him what he needed?"

"I hate to hear you ask that kind of question. You give so much to everyone in your life. There's no way you weren't giving him enough, even with three babies to care for."

"That's nice of you to say, but things did change between us after we had Tyler. We were both exhausted. We'd go weeks without having sex. We never had time to ourselves, even with my parents close by and helping where they could. We stopped dating."

"Nat and I didn't have sex for almost a year after the twins were born. We were so overwhelmed taking care of two infants while trying to work, too, we could barely function. I never once thought about going looking for it somewhere else."

"I bet Eleanor wasn't the only one."

"Why do you say that?"

"Because like you said, men either cheat, or they don't."

"You may never know one way or the other, and there's no point in tormenting yourself with those thoughts. It's enough to know it happened more than once."

"I suppose so. I'm sorry to be talking about him when I'm in bed with you."

"Don't be. He has nothing to do with me or us."

She surprises me when she moves so she's on top of me, gazing down at me with love in her eyes. "You have no idea how much I've come to rely on your input into everything that happens, since way before we got naked together."

"You mean since you crawled naked into my bed."

"That was such an accident."

I poke her sides, making her jolt and then laugh. "You're such a liar."

As she kisses her way down the front of me, I'm incredibly thankful that she crawled into my bed and changed both our lives for the better.

Twenty-Four

IRIS

Christmas is the usual mess and madness, but the kids have a blast, which is all that matters. This year is different because Gage is with us for Christmas morning. We were supposed to spend Christmas Eve with his family, but both his parents came down with the flu, so we've postponed that visit until after our trip. He FaceTimed with them earlier and introduced me and the kids to them.

They seem like nice people, and I'm looking forward to getting to know them. If I'm a tiny bit relieved that I don't have to meet all the important parents in Gage's life in the same twenty-four-hour period, well, I won't admit that to anyone.

"Guys, Mr. Gage has a special surprise for you," I tell the kids after breakfast.

Laney bounces in her booster seat. "Surprise!"

"That's right, pumpkin," I tell her. "Tyler and Sophia, sit back down so Mr. Gage can give you his present."

When the older two have returned to the table, Gage gets up to retrieve the backpacks he bought them with their names embroidered on them. He hands them out to the kids.

"Mine says Laney! Does yours?"

"You're silly," Tyler replies. "Mine says Tyler, and Sophia's says Sophia."

"They're really nice, Mr. Gage," Sophia says. "Thank you."

"Look inside," he says, smiling.

We told the kids he slept in the guest room so he could spend Christmas morning with us. He's wearing a navy T-shirt and flannel pajama pants and looks right at home at my kitchen table.

The kids unzip the bags and pull out the sun hats, sunscreen bottles, floaties, flip-flops and bathing suits he got them, in consultation with me.

Tyler is the first to pull out the folded paper that has the plane ticket printed on it. "Are we going to Florida?" he asks, eyes big.

"We are," Gage says.

"When?"

"Tonight."

Tyler lets out a shriek of excitement as he throws himself into Gage's arms. Fortunately, Gage sees him coming and catches him in a big hug. "You guys!" Tyler says to his sisters. "We're going to Florida *tonight*!"

Laney is so excited she nearly falls out of her seat. I grab her and unbuckle the clip to release her. She goes right to hug Gage with Sophia following. I love that his big surprise has gone over so well.

"You guys know how my wife and little girls died in the accident, right?"

Sophia's nod answers for all of them.

"We're going to see my friends Mimi and Stan, who were my wife's mom and dad and my girls' grandparents. They're so excited to meet you guys. Mimi has made all kinds of plans for swimming in the pool and going to the beach. We'll have so much fun."

The kids are so excited about the trip, they barely give their new toys another look as we make final preparations to depart.

My parents are going to drive us to the airport in the minivan and are due to arrive at four.

"You ready for this?" I ask Gage after he's showered and changed into shorts and a long-sleeved T-shirt. He told me he always wears shorts when heading to Florida, regardless of the temperature in Virginia.

"I think so."

"They're apt to be a lot to manage on the trip."

"It'll be fine. I'll take Tyler and Sophia. You focus on Laney."

While I have the chance, I give him a tight hug. "Thank you so much for this. It's just what I need right now."

"I always want to be just what you need."

"So far, you're doing a brilliant job of that."

"Did I tell you Mimi asked if we wanted one bedroom or two?"

"What did you tell her?"

"One was fine."

I wince. "Maybe we should sleep separately when we're there. They were Nat's parents, after all."

"It's fine. You'll see. Mimi is the best. You'll love her."

"This is just another one of those crazy widow things that no one can prepare you for, isn't it? Spending time with the parents of your boyfriend's late wife."

"Life is crazy, strange, devastating and wonderful all at the same time."

"It certainly is."

"Mimi and Stan will always be family to me, and I promise you they'll love you and the kids because I do. That's all they need to know."

I take him at his word, because I want so badly for this trip to be a huge success for his sake. It'll be the most time he's ever spent with my kids, and we'll be with Nat's parents, too. I'm trying not to feel stress about that, because Gage has assured me that I'll love them and vice versa. I sure hope so, or this is going to be a very long week.

Three hours later, we have the kids buckled into seats on the airplane. Gage is across the aisle with Tyler, and I'm between the girls. He gives me a thumbs-up and that big grin that comes with the dimples I love so much. He looks so happy that I can't help but note the change in him over the last few months. When I first knew him, he rarely smiled, and now he does it so often that it's become routine. I like knowing I had something to do with that.

It's been so long since we traveled that Tyler and Sophia have no memory of trips to Arizona to see Mike's parents, who winter there. The flight is a source of endless questions and excitement and a tiny bit of fear when we hit a few bumps of turbulence. Gage patiently explains that it's just like hitting a pothole on the road.

"But we're in the sky," Tyler says. "There's nowhere to pull over."

Gage laughs. "Right you are, my friend, but the plane is built to withstand much worse than a few little bumps. Don't worry."

The direct flight to Fort Lauderdale is just over two hours, and we land at seven o'clock, which is perfect to get the kids fed and to bed at a decent hour since they were up at the crack of dawn this morning.

Mimi and Stan are waiting for us at baggage claim. She's petite, with short gray hair and blue eyes. He's tall and thin with white hair and a tanned face. They're both smiling widely as they welcome us. After they both hug Gage, they greet me and the kids like we've always known them.

Mimi hugs me tightly. "We're so thrilled to have you visit and to see our dear Gage smiling like he used to."

"Thank you for having us."

"We couldn't wait for you to get here."

Gage introduces us to them, and Mimi tells the kids to call them Mimi and Stan.

They look to me, to ask if that's okay, and I nod to give them permission.

Mimi takes Laney by the hand while Stan helps Gage with

the luggage. They have us loaded in their silver Cadillac Escalade in no time for the thirty-minute ride to their home in Boca Raton. The kids love the palm trees, which are lit up for the holidays.

"These days, the palms stay lit all year," Mimi tells them.

"I love palm trees!" Laney says.

"I do, too, sweetheart," Mimi replies. "Palm trees equal vacation, even when I see them every day."

"Remember how Nat used to say that?" Gage asks.

"I sure do. She loved them, too."

Their single-story home is spacious, comfortable and welcoming. Mimi shows us to two guestrooms, one for me and Gage and the other for the kids. "Tyler, I thought you'd like to sleep on the air mattress so your sisters can have the bed. Is that okay?"

"Sure, thanks." He drops his backpack by the air mattress on the floor. "When can we swim?"

"In the morning," I tell him.

"Why can't we swim now?" Tyler asks on a whine. "We're in *Florida*, Mom."

Mimi looks at me as if to say it's fine with her if it is with me.

"Oh, all right. Get your suits on."

The three of them let out shrieks of excitement and tear into their suitcases to find their bathing suits.

"I'm sorry," Mimi says with a sheepish grin while the kids get changed. "You're going to have to let me spoil them."

"You're more than welcome to. You'll be their best friend for letting them swim tonight."

"I'd love to be their best friend."

She's so sweet and kind that I can't help but hug her. "I'm so, so sorry for your loss."

"I'm sorry for yours, but I'm so glad you and Gage have found each other."

"I am, too. I told my friends I was worried it would be

awkward to be with his late wife's parents, but he told me it wouldn't be. I should've listened to him."

Laughing, she says, "My home is your home."

The kids swim for an hour, with Gage supervising while I help Mimi and Stan grill burgers and toss a salad. I already know that Mimi is going to be my friend, too, after this week together. She's delightful, sweet, funny, thoughtful and wonderful with the kids, who gravitate to her the same way they do to my mom and Mike's.

"Are you doing okay?" Gage asks when we get a quiet moment alone while Mimi and Stan supervise the kids at the table. The older couple is clearly delighted to have young children in their home again. A photo of Nat and the girls sits on a side table in the living room, but that's the only photo of them I've seen so far. My heart goes out to Nat's poor, sweet parents who had to endure such a tragic loss.

"They're incredible," I tell him. "Just like you said they'd be."

"The kids have gotten themselves a new set of grandparents."

"How lucky they are." I look up at him. "How lucky we all are."

He kisses and hugs me, and I feel calmer in that moment than I have in almost three years. That there can be such joy amid the grief still amazes me.

Mimi serves ice cream for dessert, and Stan appears with a huge bag of Christmas presents for each of the kids.

"Oh my goodness, you guys! What do you say to Mimi and Stan?"

"Thank you so much," Sophia says, eyeing the stack of presents Mimi has put in front of each of them.

"Go to it, kiddos," Mimi says, clapping her hands joyfully.

With her permission, the children tear into the festively wrapped presents to find toys and games and books and a new outfit for each of them.

I'm in tears as they're showered with love by a woman who'd

never met them before today and never would've known them if it hadn't been for multiple tragedies.

"You're amazing," I tell her. "Thank you so much."

"Shopping for them was the most fun I've had in years," Mimi says softly.

GAGE

SEEING Iris and the kids fit right in with Mimi and Stan has me battling my emotions throughout our first evening together. It's all so familiar and yet unfamiliar, too. Nat and the girls were never in this house, but it still feels odd to be with Nat's parents without her and our daughters there, too.

I knew Iris and Mimi would hit it off and be great friends in a matter of hours. They're very similar in that they give everything they've got to the people they love. But watching them laugh and talk and even tear up a little has my heart doing all sorts of crazy gymnastics.

Life is so fucked up and crazy and wonderful and terrible all at the same time.

My gaze shifts to the photo of Nat and the girls in the living room. I took that photo on a trip to California, and it was one of Nat's favorites of her and the twins. In my mind, I'm already writing about introducing my new girlfriend and her children to my beloved in-laws. I refuse to refer to them as my former in-laws. They will never be that.

I'll post about this strange and beautiful gathering at some point this week. So many of my widowed followers will relate to the struggle to carry on in the aftermath of enormous loss, to do justice to the people we've lost while living every minute we have left to the fullest with the people who remain.

I help Iris corral the excited kids into the shower and pajamas. I supervise Tyler while she handles the girls.

"How do you like my friends Mimi and Stan?" I ask Tyler as I hand him his pajama shirt.

"They're awesome!"

"Yes, they are."

"How do you know them again?"

"They were my wife's parents and my daughters' grand-parents."

"Oh. Right. You must've been so sad when they died."

"So, so sad."

"I'm not going to die, am I?"

"Oh, no, buddy. Not until you're an old man."

"How do you know? Your little girls died."

"That was a tragic accident that never should've happened. You don't need to worry about that happening to you."

"My daddy died, too."

"I know."

"I'm still sad about that."

"You probably always will be."

"My mom isn't going to die, is she?"

"No, Tyler. She's not going to die."

"Okay."

He skips off to bed like he hasn't a care in the world when he's completely rocked mine. The poor kid has had way too much exposure to death and dying. Getting the kids settled is a bit of a project since they're hopped up on Christmas, excitement and sugar and all sleeping in the same room, which Sophia says is a slumber party. Thankfully, they're tired from a long day, so their shenanigans don't last for long.

"Phew," Iris says after we leave their room and head for ours. "I thought that was going to take longer."

Mimi and Stan said good night and retired to their room on the other side of the house with orders to text if we need anything.

"The last time I was here, I stayed in this room alone." I hook an arm around her waist and bring her in for a kiss. "This is so much better."

"This was such a lovely evening. I adore them."

"I knew you would—and vice versa. I haven't seen them smile and laugh like they did tonight since before."

"I was thinking all night how crazy it all is, how we never would've met them without two epic tragedies."

"While I'd never wish the losses we've suffered on anyone, sometimes I feel sorry for people who don't know how lucky they are every minute of every day they get with the people they love."

"That's so true," she says. "I like to think I was grateful for all my many blessings before I lost Mike, but my gratitude is different now. It's sharper and more immediate. I see it as it's happening rather than realizing later that something was rather wonderful."

"Yes, that's it exactly."

"How lucky we are to have found each other in all the madness."

I pull the floral blouse over her head and reach behind her to free her bra. "So very, very lucky."

"I need a shower," she says.

"Let's take one together."

"It's okay for us to do that here? You're okay with that?"

"I was thinking earlier that Nat and the girls were never here. This wasn't one of our places, even if Mimi and Stan were our people. Does that make any sense?"

"It does. Nat's parents live here, but Nat and the girls don't."

"Yes."

"You'll tell me if anything feels off to you?"

"I will. I promise."

"It's very important to me that I be respectful of her and the girls always, but especially when we're with her parents."

"You're nothing but respectful. I want you to just relax and enjoy every minute of this time away from it all."

"I can do that," she says with the sexy smile I love as she turns to lead the way into the adjoining bathroom that has a big, tiled, walk-in shower. "This house is gorgeous."

"It really is. They wanted plenty of room for friends and family to visit any time we wanted."

"I'm going to want to come back here—often."

"They'd love that."

We step into the shower and stand under the warm water, wrapped up in each other and this new life we're creating for ourselves and her kids, one small step at a time. Today was a big step, and I'm relieved that it went so well.

"Thank you for introducing me to your special people."

"Thank you for coming. I know it's a big deal to ask you to meet Nat's parents."

"They made it easy."

She washes my back and then I return the favor, my hands moving over her until she shivers from the sensations that bring goose bumps to her skin.

"It's so nice to see you happy like you were today," she says.

"This was a good day, even if it's the strangest of scenarios. Bringing my new girlfriend and her kids to meet my late wife's parents. Never thought I'd say that sentence."

"I know, but here we are in the 'after,' where life is never the same, but still beautiful in so many startling ways."

I wrap my arms around her and lifts her against the tile wall, making her shiver again. "It's beautiful again thanks to you," I say, kissing her as I push my cock into her.

"Ah, that's so good," she whispers. "So, so good."

I'm completely overwhelmed by love for this beautiful woman as I take us on a wild ride that ends in gasps and pleasure so powerful, it brings us to tears. She clings to me as I pulse into her, aftershocks rocking us both.

"Wow," I whisper against her neck.

"Mmm, vacation Gage is even hotter than everyday Gage."

I laugh and kiss her before I withdraw, setting her down carefully. "You good?"

"I'm great. You?"

"Haven't been this good in a long time." I kiss her again. "Love you."

"Love you, too."

After a stressful couple of months for both of us, I'm more than ready to relax and enjoy this time away with her and the kids.

Twenty-Five

IRIS

The next afternoon, while Gage golfs with Stan, Mimi and I supervise the kids in the pool. We sit on the stairs at the shallow end while the kids splash and play with the floats and noodles Mimi bought for them.

"They're good little swimmers," she says.

"Their father insisted on swimming lessons from the time they were very young." Laney is the only one still wearing arm floaties as a precaution. By this time next year, she won't need them.

"That's a good thing to give them. Nat took the girls to swim lessons when they were two. We thought they were too young, but she was insistent."

"I've read that people are now teaching infants as young as six months to save themselves if they fall into water."

"Wow."

"I saw a video of a baby completely underwater managing to turn himself and float on his back. It was amazing. If I was having babies now, I'd get them in the water even sooner."

"Do you want more children?" Mimi asks.

"Ah, well, not particularly. I've got my hands full with these guys."

"I wondered if Gage would have more children if he found the right person."

"He said he'd be happy with these three."

"It's wonderful to see him smiling and happy again. There was a time when I worried he'd never recover. Not that you can recover from such a thing, but you know what I mean."

"I do, and I've seen the same change in him. We're very happy together."

"I can see that."

"Is it terribly hard for you? I'd understand if it was."

"Not like I thought it would be, but that's mostly thanks to you and the kids. I can see how perfect you all are for him. He was quite determined to never fall in love again or risk more than he could afford to lose."

"I know."

"I hated that plan, and so did his family. His sister, Heather, and I have had so many conversations about how we wished we could change his mind about that. Turns out, all we needed was you."

"That's very sweet of you to say."

"It's true, Iris. I know Gage as well as I knew my daughter, and I don't think he ever would've taken such a chance again if it hadn't been with you and your kids."

I'm not sure that's true, but she probably knows him even better than I do. She knew the "before" Gage. I've only known the "after" Gage. "He's very special to all of us."

"I love to see him with the kids. Cutting their food and separating it the way they like and answering all their questions. He was like that with the girls, too. Attentive and loving."

"He has regrets about how much time he spent at work when they were alive."

"I know, and I hate that for him. He was building his business, which allowed Nat to work part time while the girls were young. She'd never want him to feel guilty about that. The girls *adored* him."

"What happened to them, to all of you, was so cruel. I encourage him not to compound the tragedy by being harsh on himself. We all do the best we can on any given day, and I have no doubt that Gage was an excellent husband and father."

"He was. We loved him for our Natasha from the first day she brought him home."

"He said you had an instantaneous friendship."

"We did, and that's gotten us through the losses."

"It's very special to be here with you and Stan."

"We're so glad to have you, honey."

GAGE

THE WEEK in Florida is nothing short of magical. We spend long days at the beach, take the kids for ice cream, watch amazing fireworks and celebrate the sale of my business on New Year's Eve, swim in the pool until long after the kids' usual bedtime and spend hours at the firepit with Mimi and Stan after the kids are in bed. I knew they would love Iris and vice versa, and it's been a thrill to see them talking and laughing like old friends after the week together. Mimi took several photos of the five of us together to add to the collection we started at the harvest festival.

"I can't believe how fast the week flew by," Stan says on our last night as we linger at the firepit with drinks after the kids are in bed. "You'll have to come back again soon."

"We'd love to," I tell him.

"And you should come visit us, too," Iris says. "I have a lovely guest room at my house that you're welcome to any time."

"That's very nice of you," Mimi says. "We'd love to visit."

"I should mention that Iris and I are talking about moving in together."

"That's wonderful," Mimi says, her eyes sparkling with tears. "We're so happy for you two. Are you moving to Iris's house?"

"We thought that would be easier on the kids than starting over somewhere else."

"I agree," Mimi says. "They've had enough upheaval losing their dad."

"That's how we feel, too," Iris says.

"I spend so much time there, it's like I already live there anyway," Gage says. "Her home felt like a home away from home for me long before our friendship turned romantic."

Iris smiles at me and gives my hand a squeeze.

"Life goes on, doesn't it?" Stan says. "Even when you think it can't possibly."

"Yes, it does," I reply, mindful that while I can start a new relationship, they can never have another daughter. "But it's important to us to honor the past while we plan the future. I hope you know that."

"We do," Mimi says. "Of course we do." She stands and leans in to hug Gage. "Let's go to bed, Stan, and give these young people some time alone."

"Good night," Iris says. "And thank you again for a lovely week."

"It was entirely our pleasure, sweetheart," Mimi says. "We'll see you in the morning."

"I'll put the fire out," I tell Stan.

"Thank you. Good night."

"Night," Iris says.

"Alone at last," I whisper as I give her hand a tug to bring her from her chair onto my lap. "I have to remind myself all day every day not to pat you on the ass in front of the kids or anything that would start a scandal."

She laughs. "They're getting used to us holding hands and being gross, as Tyler put it."

"It's weird to be in this new relationship with little ones watching our every move."

"I know! And PS, you said the R-word."

"No, I didn't."

"Yes, you did!" In a singsong voice, she says, "Gage is in a *relationship*."

I kiss her. "Only because you made it impossible for him to resist you."

She shrugs. "What can I say? I'm irresistible."

"You certainly are. Let me put this fire out and get to bed. I've been dying for you all day."

"You had me this morning."

"That was a long-ass time ago." I'd forgotten the heady feeling of new love, the excitement of knowing you've found someone who brings you joy and the overwhelming desire to be alone together as often as possible. That last one is a challenge with three kids underfoot, and we've had some late nights this week that we paid for the next day. But every second with her is worth going without sleep.

With the fire out and the doors locked, we head to bed, laughing softly as we pull at clothes as we go. We're both so primed that we fall onto the bed, and I'm inside her in a matter of seconds. "Yes," I whisper. "That's what I've wanted every second since the last time."

"Me, too," she says. "Every second."

We go at it like we haven't done it in ages, when we've done it more times than I can count this week. I cup her breast and tease her nipple with my thumb. Wait. What the hell was that? I move my thumb over the spot again and go cold all over when I realize there's a lump under her skin.

"Gage?"

"What's this?"

"What's what?"

"This." I bring her hand to the spot in question and show her what I'm talking about. "Do you feel that?"

"I get weird bumps around my time of the month sometimes. They usually go away afterward. That's probably all it is."

"Are you sure?"

"Well, no, but there's nothing we can do about it now, so don't worry."

With the moment lost, I withdraw from her and hold myself over her, staring at the spot on her breast.

"Gage... It's nothing. I'm sure of it."

"Okay." I get up to use the bathroom and splash water on my face, trying to shake off the dread that's overtaken every cell in my body. I should've known something like this would happen. She says it's nothing, but what if it's something? And how long will we have to wait to find out?

I can't bear this.

IRIS

HE'S COMPLETELY different since he found the lump in my breast last night—quiet, withdrawn and unsmiling, like he was when I first knew him. I messaged my doctor's office first thing this morning and made an appointment for tomorrow.

I'm sure it's nothing to worry about, my awesome doctor said, *but let's take a look to be sure.*

I text my mom to ask if she can watch the kids for an hour in the morning, and she says she'd love to because she's missed them while we were gone. Thankfully, they have one more day off before they go back to school.

I do get weird, lumpy breasts during my time of the month, but this one feels different to me. Not that I'd ever tell Gage that. He's already a wreck over it—and just when I had him convinced it was safe to take a chance with me. This is the last thing we need.

Mimi and Stan drive us to the airport and drop us and all our bags at the curb with warm hugs for each of us.

"What do you guys say to Mimi and Stan?" I ask the kids.

"Thank you," they say in unison.

"You're very welcome. Come see us again soon, okay?"

"Mom, can we come back soon?" Tyler asks.

"We'll see what we can do."

"That means yes," Tyler tells Mimi, who laughs as she hugs him again.

Gage is so quiet that I worry I may never see these delightful people again. "Thank you so much for everything," I tell Mimi when I hug her a second time. "It was such a special week."

"For us, too, honey. Please do come back. Any time."

"We will."

"I told you that was a yes," Tyler says.

We leave them with smiles and blown kisses and follow Gage inside. He's pushing a huge luggage cart with all our bags on it. That he's barely made eye contact with me since last night's discovery is only because he's scared, or so I try to tell myself, because I can't bear to think it might've ruined everything by reminding him how quickly things can change.

My stomach is a ball of stress as we check in, navigate security with the kids and head for our gate to fly home. The kids are tired and cranky, and that only adds to my distress. Five long hours later, Gage pulls the minivan into the garage at home and helps me unload kids and bags. Before he says the words, I know what's coming.

"I'm going to head home. I've got some stuff to do there."

Since the kids are upstairs, I say what I really want to rather than just nodding in acceptance of his statement. "Do you really, or are you running from what happened last night?"

"I'm not running."

"Aren't you? If it turns out to be something, it's game over for us? Is that who you really are?"

"No, it's not. I just need a little break. That's all."

"A break. I see. Well, go take your break." I turn to walk away, disgusted by him and myself for wanting to fall apart on the spot.

"Iris."

I stop, but I don't look back at him. "What?"

"I'm sorry. I just need a second to think."

"Do what you've got to do." I walk away while I still can, even as tears slide down my cheeks. I wipe them away, determined to get it together so the kids won't see I'm upset. Baths and bedtime take longer than ever tonight, and I'm thankful for one more vacation day before we get back to our usual routine. I'm going to need that day to do laundry, grocery shop and get our collective act together—not to mention have my breast checked while I nurse a broken heart.

I'm disappointed in him, even if I understand why he's acting this way. This was exactly what he was afraid of—something happening to me or the kids after he took a risk and fell in love with us. It just never occurred to me that if something *did* happen, he'd walk away.

I should've seen that coming, and I'm sick to my stomach that I didn't.

I tuck Tyler in and kiss him good night.

"What was wrong with Mr. Gage today?" he asks, too observant for his own good—and mine.

"I think he was tired after the busy week."

"He was acting weird."

"I'm sure he's fine. We all need some sleep."

"Is he going to be our new daddy?"

Dear Lord, child. Hit me when I'm low. "I don't know, sweetheart, but he loves you and your sisters very much."

"I love him, too. I want him to be my new daddy."

I simply can't handle this right now. I kiss my son again and tuck the covers in around his little body. "I'll see you in the morning, buddy. Love you."

"Love you, too. Thanks for a fun trip."

I want to tell him that all the thanks go to Gage, but I'm suddenly uncertain if we'll ever see him again. "You got it."

I go into my own room, close the door and slide down to the floor as I dissolve into sobs that remind me far too much of the early days after Mike's death. I resent Gage for that, too. How can he do this to me? To himself? To the kids? All over something that may be nothing.

But what if it isn't? He didn't sign on to nurse me through a serious illness after he's already been to hell and back losing his wife and daughters.

I'm devastated and scared. As a single mom, any threat to me or my health is a very big deal.

I pull my phone from my back pocket and text Christy. *Can you talk?*

My phone rings with a call from her. "Hey."

"What's up? I thought you guys were in Florida."

"We just got back."

"How was it? I was thinking of you all week."

"Wonderful. Nat's parents are delightful. We had the best time."

"Then what's wrong?"

"On the last night we were there, Gage and I were, you know, fooling around, and he found a lump in my breast."

"Oh, Iris. Oh my goodness."

"Gage brought us home and then left. He said he needs a break so he can think."

"Oh no."

"He's in a total tailspin over this, and it may turn out to be nothing."

"He's scared, Iris. That's all it is."

"But he left! How could he just leave? Doesn't he think I'm scared? I'm a single parent to three young children. Is this what's going to happen any time something scary or worrisome happens?"

"It might," she says softly. "He's preconditioned to fear history repeating itself."

"But what are the odds of that?"

"Astronomically high in your favor, but you can't tell him that when he's learned how brutal life can be."

"Haven't we all learned that?"

"I don't like to compare one person's grief to another, but I'm not sure I could've survived losing Wes and my kids, too. His loss was massive compared to mine—and yours."

"I know," I say with a sigh. "And I agree, but we were making a go of this. We just went on vacation like a little family in the making. I visited his late wife's parents and loved every minute of it. Doesn't that count for anything?"

"It counts for nothing when stacked against his fear of it happening again."

"I don't know what to do."

"Give him the space he asked for. That's all you can do. If he comes back to you and the kids, it must be his choice."

"I can't believe we're even having this conversation. Everything between us was perfect until last night."

"You had to expect there'd be some difficulties along the way."

"Absolutely, but I also expected we'd get through them together."

"It's important to manage your expectations where he's concerned. He was adamant that he'd never again be with anyone. He preferred that plan to having to worry about losing someone else he loved. You're the exception to his rule. You're still the exception."

"Not if I have breast cancer."

"Don't even say that."

"Why not? It's possible. I mean, anything is possible. I could get hit by a bus tomorrow when I'm out getting my mail. Living in fear of what *might* happen is no way to live."

"I agree, but that doesn't stop us from being afraid. I want to ask every man I date whether he's had a full cardiac workup recently, but I can't exactly do that without them thinking there's something wrong with me."

That makes me laugh for the first time all day.

"It's not easy to come back from what we've been through, and it's not easy to take a second chance on love. I've seen you two together, and I'm sure he loves you as much as you love him."

"So what do I do while he tries to decide if he can handle the possibility of losing me?"

"You wait and you be patient and you show him the same grace you'd want others to show you if you were wrestling with something."

"How has the lump in my breast become about him?"

"It's about all of you, isn't it?"

"Yes, I suppose it is. God, Christy, what am I going to do if this turns out to be cancer?"

"Take it one step at a time. When are you seeing the doctor?"

"Tomorrow."

"Then just keep breathing until there's something to worry about. It could be nothing."

"But what if it's something? My kids…"

"Breathe, Iris. Are you breathing?"

"I'm trying to, but it's not easy."

"There's no sense going to the worst-case scenario until you know for sure that it's something bad."

"What would you do if you found a lump?"

"Freak the fuck out like you are for the same reasons. We're single moms. We have no time for illness. But I still think you need to try to stay calm until you know more. Making yourself sick over it isn't going to change the outcome."

"You're right. It's so hard not to go to worst-case when I've been living it for almost three years."

"Believe me, I understand. It's easy for me to say calm down, but I'd be just as worked up. Do you want me to come over?"

"No, thank you. I'm okay. I'll know more tomorrow."

"Keep me posted?'

"Yes, I will. Thanks for listening to me go on and on."

"That's what I'm here for. And try not to worry about Gage. He'll be there if you need him. You know he will."

I know no such thing, but I keep that thought to myself. "Thanks, Christy. Love you."

"Love you, too. Call me tomorrow."

"I will."

Twenty-Six

IRIS

After I end the call, I strip off my clothes and head for the shower. Standing under the warm water, I check my breast to see if the lump is still there. It is. I'm terrified of what it might turn out to be. I'm so anxious, I barely sleep and am up before my alarm. The kids are still asleep when I go downstairs to make enough coffee for me and my mom.

She comes in through the door to the garage shortly after eight and hugs me. "I'm so glad you guys are home. We missed you."

"We missed you, too." I make her a cup of coffee and add half a teaspoon of sugar to it.

"Thanks, love. So how was it? The pictures were great."

"We had a wonderful time. Gage's in-laws are lovely people. They were so happy to have us visit."

"Was it awkward at all?"

"Not really. They're super supportive of him and glad to see him doing well and moving on."

"Still... I can't imagine how hard that must be for them."

"Everything's hard after a loss like theirs, but they're making the most of it. They were very welcoming and so sweet to the kids. She had bags of gifts for each of them. She said it was so fun to shop for kids again."

"That is sweet. One grandma to another, I feel so sorry for her losses."

I glance at the clock. "I need to go get dressed for my appointment. The kids are sleeping in. They were extra tired after the trip."

"Go ahead. I'm going to watch the *Today* show."

After I get dressed, Laney comes in looking for me. I scoop her up and take her downstairs and deliver her to my mom, who'll oversee breakfast for them. "I shouldn't be too long, Mom."

"Take your time," she says, snuggling with Laney. "We're fine."

I drive the short distance to my doctor's office, trying not to think about any of the worries that kept me awake most of the night. I thought maybe I might hear from Gage this morning, but so far, nothing, which makes me sad and angry. How can he do this to me? To himself? Things were so good, and now he's just gone? All because of a lump that may or may not be anything to worry about?

I just can't wrap my head around this development.

The doctor is already running late, and I'm forced to wait nearly thirty minutes alone in an exam room wearing one of those stupid gowns.

A knock on the door precedes her entrance. She's pretty, with light brown hair, brown eyes and flawless skin. "I'm so sorry to keep you waiting." She washes her hands. "I had a baby arrive at six a.m., and that little darling has thrown off my entire day."

"No problem." What's thirty extra minutes when you're waiting to hear if you have a dreaded disease?

"Let's see what's going on, shall we?"

I lie back and bare the breast in question. As she gives it and the other one a very thorough examination, her expression never changes until she returns to the first one and zeros in on the area where the lump is.

"There's definitely something there that shouldn't be."

My insides fold in on each other in a cascading tower of fear and panic.

"That's not to say it's something sinister, so don't go there. I'll send you for a mammography and, if warranted, an ultrasound."

"I'm trying not to have a full-blown panic attack here."

"Don't do that. It won't help anything." She types the orders for the tests into the computer and tells me where to go. "They'll be expecting you."

I try not to make a thing out of her saying they'll be expecting me, but it's hard not to. Did she put some sort of flag on the orders that says *urgent/possible breast cancer* or something like that? I'm so scared and rattled, I can barely unbutton my shirt at the mammogram place, so I pull it over my head without unbuttoning it. I put on the smock and meet the technician in the freezing-cold room where she smashes breasts for a living.

As this is my first mammogram, the tech takes a little extra time to explain what will happen, to tell me it'll be uncomfortable, but only for a few minutes, and that I should tell her if it's too painful.

Lovely. Now I'm even more stressed out than I was before.

She positions me where she needs me and manhandles my breast like it's a side of beef. I suppose she does this a hundred times a day, and one breast is the same as another to her. The smashing hurts. Badly. I have tears in my eyes by the time it's over, and then I find out she wants a side view, too.

We repeat the entire ordeal on the other side, and then she asks me to wait in the room until she's sure she got what she needed. I wait for a long time, shivering from the cold as much as the fear. Will those images change my life?

I've never experienced fear quite like this, even in the dark days after I lost Mike. Somehow, I knew I could handle raising our kids on my own if I had to, but this... I can't handle this.

She returns with another woman, who gives me a kind smile that sets my nerves further on edge. "If you'll come with me, we're going to do an ultrasound."

That means they saw something worrisome on the mammogram.

"I, uh..." I'm paralyzed. I couldn't move if I had to.

"Let's see it through before we jump to any conclusions, okay?" the second woman says, her tone kind and reassuring.

I nod and manage to rise to my feet and follow her to another freezing-cold room. "Why is it so cold in here?" I ask when she settles me on an exam table.

"It's for the equipment."

"Freeze the patients and save the equipment. I see how it is."

She laughs. "We get complaints about it every day." She puts a blanket over me that I'm immediately thankful for.

The ultrasound is painless but seems to take forever as both breasts are thoroughly examined. When she's finished, she says, "I see two areas I'm concerned about. One in each breast."

Dear God, just when I thought this couldn't get any worse. "Wh-what does that mean?"

"I'd recommend we biopsy both areas."

"Do... Is... Is it cancer?"

"We can't know for certain either way without the biopsies. Do we have your consent to proceed?"

I want to say no. Hell no. I do not consent to any of this. I'm a single mom to three young children. There's no way I can have cancer. The universe wouldn't be that cruel to me, would it?

"Iris?"

"Yes, you have my consent."

She summons other people to the room, and they get busy prepping me for the procedure.

"We'll numb you up, so it shouldn't be painful, but you're apt to experience a pinch or two, all right?"

"Um, okay." I'm shaking so hard I wonder how they'll be able to do anything to me without tying me down.

Everyone is very efficient, like this is no big deal to them when it's the biggest of big deals to me. My whole life is riding on the results of these tests, and I can barely hold it together as they do the needle biopsies. The "pinch" is slightly more than that, but it's not unbearable.

"We're all done," the woman in charge says after they've done both sides. "We've included markers to identify the sites so we're able to get right back to them if need be."

"When will I know?"

"A few days."

"Ugh." How will I survive waiting to hear that kind of news? How will I function? I can't tell my parents because I don't want them to be as upset as I am. As I put my bra and top back on, I try to summon some inner calm, but there's none to be found, and there won't be until I get those results.

I'm completely numb with fear, anxiety and despair, and I feel desperately alone without Gage to tell me everything is going to be okay.

GAGE

AFTER THE ACCIDENT, I couldn't stop crying. Tears for days and days, until my eyes ached as much as my heart did. There were times during that early darkness when I wondered if I was destined to cry for the rest of my life. Eventually, the tears dried up as I was forced to confront the fact that I had a lot of living left to do without my girls.

Since I left Iris's last night, the tears have come back with the same intensity I experienced right after the accident. I miss Iris so much, I ache from wanting her, which is ridiculous because I chose to leave. And I feel like the biggest asshole for leaving when she's stressed out and panicked over what that lump might turn out to be.

What the fuck is wrong with me? Right when I was putting my life back together and moving in such a positive direction with Iris and her kids, I lose my shit over a lump? I hate that I left. I hate that the stupid lump triggered such an enormous backslide. I hate that I'm so terrified of losing her that I ran from her. I hate everything about grief and the way it can bitch-slap you in the face right when you're making a comeback from the lowest point in your life.

I hate everything about this situation, but more than anything, I hate myself for leaving when she needed me most.

My phone rings with a call from Christy. I stare at the screen, riddled with uncertainty, until I find the wherewithal to take the call.

"Hey."

"Hey yourself."

I can tell with those two words that she's spoken to Iris and knows what a fucking coward I am.

"Are you okay?" she asks.

"Nope."

"What can I do?"

"Tell me that Iris is fine and that she'll forgive me for bailing when she needed me most?"

"I can't do either of those things. Not yet anyway."

"Have you heard anything from her today?"

"No, but she was scheduled to see her doctor this morning. I'm sure we'll hear something soon."

"I won't hear from her. She's probably done with me."

"No, she isn't."

"I wouldn't blame her if she was. All I could think about on that flight home was how I'd ever survive losing her, too."

"Was it easier to walk away than to face whatever might be coming for her?"

"At the time, yes. Now, not so much."

"Nothing you've done can't be undone, Gage."

"I don't know if I can do it. I thought I could. Iris made me believe I could, but this has shown me just how fucked up I still am. It wouldn't be fair to subject her or the kids to that."

"You're not fucked up. You're too close to it to see the progress, but I see it. When I first met you, you were nothing like you are now. You hardly said a word. Your sadness was the first thing anyone saw when they met you. But over time, you've come so far from who you were then. These days, you laugh, you smile, you love, you write, you contribute, you support other widows on their journeys. You're being incredibly unfair to my dear friend Gage by saying you're still too fucked up to make a go of this thing with Iris."

She'll never know what her words mean to me. "What does it say about me that the second things went a tiny bit sideways, I cut and run?"

"It says you're scared for her and yourself. It says you're human. It says that after what you've been through, your first impulse is to hide from anything that can ever hurt you like that again. It says that you care so much for Iris that the thought of anything happening to her can set you back on your grief journey. It says all those things and so many others."

"I do care for her that much. I love her. And the kids."

"I know you do, which is why this health scare has sent you reeling."

"I can't handle it, Christy, but I also can't handle losing her."

"You have to decide which you can't handle more—the possibility of losing her tragically, which we both know all too well can happen thousands of different ways when we least expect it, or losing the chance to love her and her kids, to build a life with them. The way I see it, you're choosing to lose her preemptively because that's easier than loving her."

Her stark words bring the issue into stunning clarity. I can either be so afraid of losing Iris to some sort of tragedy that I lose her anyway, or I can love her and build a life with her and the kids. Christy is right, though. I can't have both those things at the same time.

"This has helped. Thank you."

"You're welcome. Can I say one more thing?"

"Sure."

"I've enjoyed the way happiness looks on you, my friend. It's given me hope that I might someday find what you have with Iris. I'd hate to see you lose her and all the hard-won progress that made it possible for you to love her in the first place."

"I'd hate that, too."

"We're all going to die, Gage. Some of us sooner than we should. We've had an up-close-and-personal view of what that's like, and it's only natural to want to avoid it in the future. But you can't be so afraid of loss that you forget to live what's left of your life, you know?"

"Yeah, I do. And you're right. It does come down to a choice, and I'd choose her every day, no matter what."

"Then you need to tell her that and make her understand that you ran because you love her too much to bear the thought of anything ever happening to her. She'll understand. How could she not? She's been there, too. She knows."

"I'll tell her. Thank you so much for this. It was just what I needed to hear." At some point during my conversation with Christy, the tears have dried up, and new resolve has set in. I need Iris and her kids in my life. I need the hope, joy and happiness they've brought me to survive whatever comes next, even if that's a battle for Iris's life. I'm here for it, and I need to tell her that.

As soon as possible.

Twenty-Seven

IRIS

I'm not quite sure how I managed to fake my way through a breezy chat with my mom when I got home with groceries or how I managed to deal with the kids for the remainder of that very long day when every minute felt like an hour.

With them in bed, I pour a huge glass of wine that I drink most of before refilling my glass. I wish I had something stronger in the house, but we drank all the good stuff at the Wild Widows Christmas party. So I'm stuck with wine. I stand at the island in my kitchen, staring out in the darkness in the backyard, and drink my wine while trying not to think about anything other than getting through this minute and the next one until I hear from my doctor.

I'll be certifiably insane if the wait is more than a day or two.

Thank God the kids go back to school tomorrow. Then I can roll up into the fetal position until I get the call.

I think about Kinsley and how her husband, Rory, died of pancreatic cancer at forty-two, Naomi, who lost her fiancé, David, after a brutal two-year battle with lymphoma, and Wynter, who lost her young husband, Jaden, to bone cancer.

They've been right where I am now, waiting to hear news that might change their lives forever. I could reach out to any of them for advice on how to cope with waiting for test results, but it feels selfish to ask them to relive their trauma to help me through mine.

Any of them would do it for me. I'm sure of that, but I can't bring myself to ask them. It's sobering to realize that every day, thousands of people around the world are stuck in this hellish purgatory of waiting to hear if they have cancer or some other horrible disease.

How'd it go today? Christy asks by text.

Mammo, ultrasound, biopsies on two places, one on each side. Now I wait.

Ugh, the waiting is the worst. I won't send platitudes or tell you everything will be fine. I'll only say I love you, and I'm praying for the best possible news.

Thanks. I may go insane before I find out either way.

I know how hard it is to not think the worst but try not to go there until you have to, which you may not.

Trying. Harder than it seems.

You want me to come over?

Nah, that's okay, but thanks for asking. Love you.

Love you, too. Call if you need anything, even in the middle of the night.

Xoxo

I'm about to put my phone down and go back to the fetal position when it chimes with a group text from Adrian that includes me, Gage, Roni, Derek, Christy and Joy.

I'm reaching out to a small sector of the brain trust because I need to decide about letting Wynter take care of Xavier when I'm at work. She really wants to do it, and you guys know I love her. We all do—and she's great with him. It's just that there's something giving me hesitation that I can't put my finger on, which is why I need your opinions as the wisest people I know. I also fear a huge setback for her if I decide to go in another direc-

tion, and I'd hate to be responsible for that. Help! What should I do?

Joy responds first. *I have a few things to say about this. First, it's not your responsibility to prevent a setback for her, so don't take that on. Your only consideration should be what's best for your son. With that said, I've seen her with him and agree she adores him, is good with him, and he loves her right back. Your hesitation is most likely rooted in the fact that Wynter can be a bit unpredictable at times, but I have no doubt whatsoever that Xavier would be safe with her. I hope that helps a little.*

Derek chimes in next. *I agree with Joy on all points. Maybe you could do it on a one- or two-month trial basis, so you have an out if it's not working for you? I'd also suggest some sort of written employment agreement that spells out all the expectations on paper. Hopefully, that would protect your friendship with her if the nannying doesn't work out.*

Lawyer Joy should've suggested that. I agree with Derek.

It's such a big decision to leave your child with someone, Roni says. *You should do whatever you feel is right for Xavier and for you with no regard whatsoever to hurting anyone's feelings. That said, I love Wynter and think she'd be a great nanny to Xavier. But what matters is if YOU think that.*

I read and reread their replies before I type mine. *Not sure what I can add to the great suggestions above other than that you're a wonderful father to Xavier, Adrian, and just by asking our opinions, it shows you're doing your due diligence. You could hire a professional nanny who'd probably know all the important stuff about babies and their milestones, etc. But that nanny wouldn't love Xavier like Wynter already does. So, there is that...*

I keep waiting—and hoping—Gage will chime in, but he doesn't.

I knew y'all would have the answers, Adrian says. *I love the idea of a trial period and the employment agreement, and you're right—Wynter already loves my guy, which is a huge plus in her column. This stuff is so hard! You parents out there need to tell me it gets easier!*

Christy responds with *Hahahahahahahahahaha. Believe it or not, the infant/toddler/little kid years are the easiest, so enjoy them before shit gets real.*

What she said, I reply, using the up-arrow emoji to point to Christy's response.

Damn, that's not what I wanted to hear, Adrian says. *LOL. Thanks for the heads-up that it gets harder from here.*

It also gets easier, I add, just so we won't totally freak him out. *When they can feed and bathe themselves, get themselves dressed, etc. Of course they're also talking at that point, which brings its own challenges. HAHA*

LOL, Adrian says. *Good to know. I'm so, so thankful to have you guys in my life to help me with this stuff. Sadie would know just what to do about all this, but I'm like a deer in headlights trying to figure it out.*

You're doing great, bro, Derek says. *Just keep doing what you're doing. You've got this.*

Thanks again, guys. I'm going to ask Wynter if we can meet for coffee tomorrow. I'll keep you posted.

I find myself rooting for both of you, Joy says. *Love you both.*

Love you, too, Adrian replies. *All of you. Talk soon.*

Between my conversation with Christy and the group chat with Adrian, I've managed to kill an hour I would've spent rocking in the corner. Wild Widows to the rescue once again. Since I'm already feeling emotionally fragile and desperately need something to do to get me through what promises to be an endless night, I decide to venture into Mike's office to begin cleaning it out so I can use it going forward.

We donated his clothes a long time ago, keeping something special for each of the kids, but I've stayed out of this room for the most part, knowing it would be the toughest thing to conquer. He called it his man cave-slash-office and kept most of the treasures that meant the most to him in here. From the airplane models on the shelves to the framed certificates on the wall that document his career as a pilot to the faint scent of the cologne he wore all his life, Mike is very much alive in here, which is why I've avoided it until now.

I've been tossing empty boxes in here for a while now, knowing I'd have to deal with it eventually. Tonight feels like a good time since my emotions are all directed elsewhere. I start with the file cabinet and fill black plastic trash bags with tons of stuff to be shredded. Why did he keep every bill he ever paid? I throw that shit out the minute it's taken care of. I toss notebooks from college and pilot training, old textbooks and outdated FAA directives.

When I have the file cabinet cleaned out, I move on to his desk, going through each drawer, making piles of things to keep while filling more trash bags. Mike was a pack rat. I knew that about him before this, but my trip through his office only confirms it.

I find a card with a flower on it and open it.

Mike, I'll never be able to tell you what our time together meant to me. I'm sorry that it has to end, but I understand why. If you ever get back to Boise, you know where to find me. Love you. Kelly.

What the actual fuck? Who is Kelly? I know the names of all his significant exes, and there was no Kelly. If I wanted proof that Eleanor wasn't the only affair he had, here it is.

"How could you do this to me?" I ask him. "You son of a bitch." I tear the card into tiny pieces and toss it in the trash.

When I first lost him, I never imagined the day would come when I could say I'd grown to actively hate him. But here we are. He was a lying, cheating asshole who played the role of devoted husband and father when he was home. The minute he left the house, though, he became someone else altogether. Staring at the framed photo of the five of us on the corner of the desk, I speak my truth to him. "I hate you for this. I hate you for the mess you left behind and how someday I'm going to have to tell our children how you came to have another son. You unfaithful, cheating, lying mother*fucker*."

Hey, at least I'm not crying my eyes out over the demise of my so-called relationship with Gage or the possibility that I might have breast cancer. That makes me laugh until I cry.

My phone chimes with a text from Gage. *I'm outside. Can we talk?*

I want to tell him to fuck off and leave me alone, but I'm aware enough to know that directing my Mike-fueled rage at Gage wouldn't be fair.

Come in. I'm in the office.

I gave him the code to my house weeks ago, back when I thought we were on our way to something lasting. Now, I have no idea what we are. All I know is when shit got real, he left, and that can't happen again. Especially when I could be facing something serious.

He comes in a few minutes later and stops in the doorway to take in the chaos I've unleashed in the once-orderly room.

"It was time," I tell him, shrugging as if none of this is a big deal when it all is. Everything is a BFD these days, and I yearn for a time when the BFD of the day was what to have for dinner. How funny that seems now. "I found proof of yet another woman. He was a busy guy, my husband."

"Should you be doing this now?"

"It beats rocking in the corner waiting to hear biopsy results."

"You had a biopsy?"

"Two of them. One on each side." As I say that, I sift through another pile of papers that I move to a third trash bag.

Gage crosses the room to me and stands awkwardly next to the desk. "Did they give you any idea what to expect?"

"Just a long couple of days waiting to hear. Thus, the office project. It's something to do while I wait." I absolutely refuse to look at him out of fear of losing what's left of my composure.

"Do you think you could take a break from that so we could talk?"

"If I stop, I'll think, and I don't want to think." The large bottom desk drawer is stuffed with more file folders. I pull out a chunk of them that I put on the desktop.

"Please, Iris. I need to talk to you."

"Too bad." I look up at him for the first time, and I'm sure my eyes are blazing with fury. "I wanted to talk to you last night, but you left, and today, I went through the scariest thing of my life completely alone. So, I'm sorry if I don't want to talk to you right now. I want to keep moving so I won't lose my mind worrying about what'll become of my kids if I die of cancer."

"I'll take care of your kids."

That gets a bitter-sounding laugh from me. "You say that now, but can I trust you to be there for them and me if shit gets real? I don't know anymore."

"I freaked out. I'm sorry. I worked it out."

"Good for you. I'm happy for you."

"I'm sorry I left. I shouldn't have done that."

"No, you really shouldn't have. What if we'd found the lump on one of your testicles? Where do you think I would've been while you were getting that checked? And PS, I lost my husband, so don't tell me I don't get the fear."

"You're one hundred percent right, and I totally fucked up. I own that, and I'm so sorry I left when you needed me. I hate myself for that."

"I hate you enough for both of us."

"Ouch."

"Well, what did you think I'd say? 'Oh, thank you *so much* for coming back, Gage. I appreciate that more than you'll ever know.' Is that how you thought this would go? Let me tell you one thing widowhood has taught me. I have *zero* tolerance for bullshit."

"I understand, and I deserve all of that and more. Five minutes after I left, I regretted it."

"And yet, it took you more than twenty-four hours that I spent in hell to come back? I'm finding it difficult to feel sorry for you."

"I don't want to lose you. I love you."

"I know you do. I also know that the thought of losing me terrifies you, but that doesn't give you the right to bail on me when I needed you most."

"I had no right to do that to you. I have no defense other than grief, which picked the worst possible time to rear its ugly head."

I can't help but soften a bit as he takes total ownership of his colossal fuckup.

He comes around the desk to lean against it, facing me.

"You look like hell."

"I haven't slept since Florida." He extends his hand to me.

I stare at it for a long moment before I reach out to wrap my hand around his. I can't deny the profound feeling of relief that comes with being with him again.

"I want to be here for you and the kids, no matter what comes next."

"I need to know I can count on you. If that's too much to ask, go away and don't come back."

"It's not too much to ask."

I look up at him again, this time with tears in my eyes. "I'm scared."

He reaches for me, and I stand to let him wrap his strong arms around me. "I am, too."

I appreciate that he doesn't offer platitudes or blow smoke up my skirt, even though I thought I'd welcome that earlier. I vastly prefer that he's as frightened as I am.

"What am I going to do if it's cancer?"

He holds me even tighter. "We'll fight it with everything we've got until you're completely well again."

"*We'll* fight it?"

"Yes, we will, you and me."

"What if it goes bad?"

"I'll be here for all of it. No matter what, and if the worst thing happens, I'll finish raising your children. I promise."

"If you make that promise to me, Gage, if I let you back in, you have to keep it."

"I'll keep it. I swear to God on the memories of Nat and the girls. I'll be here for you and the kids."

Since I can't ask for anything more than that, I decide to take him at his word.

GAGE HOLDS me close all night, which is the only reason I get any sleep at all. I'm awake ahead of my alarm and wiggle out of his embrace to shower before the kids get up. I'm standing under the warm water when Gage appears with a mug of coffee. When I turn toward the glass door to take a sip of coffee, his gaze shifts to the bruises on my breasts.

"Do they hurt?"

"No."

"Did it hurt when they did it?"

"A little. It wasn't bad, though." I take a sip of the coffee and hand it back to him. "Thanks."

"You want some company in there?"

"Sure."

When he steps into the shower and puts his arms around me from behind, I'm reminded of the last shower we took together in Florida. That already seems like a long time ago. Nothing about last night or this morning is sexual. It's all about comfort, which I need more than anything while I wait to hear if a bomb is about to detonate in my cobbled-together single mom/widow life.

I've gotten used to that life. I know what's expected of me every day. I've learned to cope with being the sole source of parenting for my kids and know how to meet their many needs. That was the most daunting part at first, being responsible for three little beings on my own. But I've never been completely on my own with my parents nearby and a strong network of friends who were more than willing to help where they could.

I can handle all that, but could I handle a cancer battle on top of it? I just don't know. I suppose, like widowhood, I'd have no choice but to step up to the moment, but I really, really, *really* hope I don't have to.

"How're you feeling this morning?"

"Unsettled, terrified, stressed. Other than that, fine."

I can feel his lips curve into a smile against my neck. "You're the toughest person I know, Iris. If anyone can get through whatever is coming, you can."

"I wish I felt so certain."

"Whenever you're not sure, just ask me. I'll remind you that you can handle anything that comes your way."

"You're really in for the long haul here?"

"If you'll have me."

I squeeze the hand he's rested on my belly. "I'll have you."

"Mom! It's time to get up!" Tyler comes into the bathroom and skids to a stop when he sees us in the shower.

"Shit," Gage mutters.

"Hurry up," Tyler says as he turns to leave the room, probably to go poke out his mind's eye.

"At least we weren't having sex," I say to Gage, who laughs.

"Is he going to be upset?"

"I don't think so. They're used to having you around by now, but I suppose it's time we talk to them about you moving in and see how they feel about it. You still want to do that, right?"

"Very much so."

"All right, then. Let's take it to the kids."

Twenty-Eight

GAGE

I'm nervous about what the kids will say, especially now that Tyler has caught us in the shower. When I'm dressed, I go to find him in his room. He's dressed for school and sitting on the floor among some of his favorite trucks and cars.

"Hey, pal, you ready for some breakfast?"

He nods but doesn't look at me. I squat down to his level. "I want you to know that I love your mom very much, and I love you and your sisters, too." I thought about what I should say to him and decided that was the most important thing.

"Are you going to marry my mom?"

"Maybe someday. We're not talking about that right now, but we are talking about the five of us being a family. What would you say about that?"

He gives it some careful thought, which I can see from his serious expression. "That'd be cool," he says after a full minute of consideration. "Would you sleep in my mom's room with her?"

"Yeah, I would."

"That's where my dad used to sleep."

"I know, and it's important to me that you know I'd never

want to take his place with you or your sisters. He's your dad. But I'd love to be your friend, if you'll have me."

"You're already my friend. You have been for a long time."

"And you're my friend, too." I reach out my hand to him. "You wanna shake on it?"

Smiling, he takes my hand and shakes it.

"Always make eye contact with the person as you shake their hand. That way, they know you really mean it."

He looks me dead in the eyes, and my heart does a somersault at the love and trust I see in his. "Please don't ever hurt my mommy. She's the best mommy ever."

"I won't, buddy. I promise I'll take the best care of her and you guys."

"Okay, then. I want pancakes."

He gets up and runs off, leaving me gutted from the sweetness and the sadness and the wonder of it all. His dad and my wife and kids had to die for us to have the relationship we do now. These moments of joy amid the grief are simply astonishing.

I go downstairs to join breakfast already in progress.

Iris glances at me, as if to ask how it went with Tyler.

I give her a thumbs-up.

Her smile is full of relief.

"So, guys," Iris says, "what would you think if Mr. Gage lived here with us?"

"Yes!" Laney punctuates her reply with a fist in the air.

"That would be nice," Sophia says with a sweet smile for me.

"I'm cool with it," Tyler says.

"Thanks, guys," I say, choked up by how much I care for them. "I really love being here with you."

"Are you going to be our new daddy?" Sophia asks.

Her shyness slays me. "I can never replace your daddy, sweetheart, but I'm here for you in any way you'd like me to be."

"Okay."

I notice Iris wiping a tear from the corner of her eye.

Each of the kids hugs me before they leave with Iris for the ride to school. I'm relieved at how well that went, and I'm sure Iris is, too. I stay back to clean up the kitchen and do the breakfast dishes. When she comes back in, the kitchen is standing tall, and I've made another pot of coffee.

"Um, wow," she says when she takes in the clean, orderly kitchen. "Are you available for hire?"

"I'm jobless at the moment, so make me an offer."

"I'm not sure I can afford you."

"There's lots of different ways you can pay me."

"Are we talking money?"

"Nope." I crook my finger at her. "Come here."

When she's right in front of me, I tip her chin up for a kiss. "There. That pays for dishes." I kiss her again. "That covers wiping the counters and table." After another kiss, I say, "That's good for cleaning up the Legos in the living room."

"You're a cheap maid."

"The big things are far more expensive. Like, snow shoveling is a blow job. Nonnegotiable."

That has her laughing like she did while we were on vacation when everything was fun and funny.

"Good to know. I'll be ready for snow days."

"Pool maintenance is also a blow job, whereas vacuuming is covered by a kiss."

"Is this written down somewhere so I can be prepared for future obligations?"

"I'll make you a spreadsheet."

"Don't put it in writing!"

Her eyes are sparkling with happiness that immediately dims when her phone rings. "Oh God, that's my doctor."

"Take the call. Find out what it is, and we'll figure it out. I love you."

She nods and nearly drops the phone as she presses the green button and puts the call on speaker so I can hear, too. "Hello?"

"Hi, Iris, it's Dr. Jenkins."

It freaks me out that the doctor herself is calling, but I keep that thought to myself.

"I've got your results, and there's good news along with a tiny bit of bad news. We did find a small precancerous spot on the right side that's been caught at the earliest stage, which is the best possible timing. The second biopsy was negative, which is great news."

"So... What do we do about the precancerous spot?"

"The oncologist will probably recommend a lumpectomy to remove it, most likely with a short course of radiation therapy to reduce the likelihood of recurrence. After the spot is removed, it's sent to pathology. Those results determine any future treatment. You'll be on a regular schedule of mammograms and ultrasounds going forward. Finding that lump when you did most likely saved you from a much bigger deal down the road."

The doctor goes on to tell her that an appointment has been made with the oncologist for two days from now and that we'll know more after that meeting.

"I know this is a lot to take in, Iris, but please don't panic. Try to think of it the same way you would having a suspicious mole removed before it can turn into something more, with a little added treatment to reduce the odds that it comes back."

"Thank you," she says tearfully. "I appreciate you getting back to me so quickly and explaining it the way you did."

"I'm here for you. We'll get you through this. I'll talk to you again after you meet with the oncologist."

"Okay. Thanks again."

"You got it."

I take the phone from Iris, put it on the counter and then place my hands on her shoulders. "If it was going to be anything, it sounds like a best-case scenario, don't you think?"

She nods. "I suppose so."

"We'll take this a step at a time. We'll see the oncologist on Thursday and see what they recommend and then do whatever it takes to get this thing out of you so you can move on."

"You saved my life when you found that lump. With my busy life, who knows how long it would've taken for me to find it on my own?"

"Your life is very important to me. I'm so glad we found it early." When I realize she's shaking, I hug her. "It's going to be okay."

I'll do whatever it takes to make sure of that.

IRIS

As expected, the oncologist recommended a lumpectomy with a five-week daily course of radiation afterward as a precaution. Two weeks after the appointment, I've reported to the hospital at the crack of dawn for the procedure. Gage is with me, and my parents stayed at my house last night so they can be there when the kids wake up. Telling my parents and close friends about what's going on has been the hardest part, because I don't want them to worry.

My mom was a wreck over it for two days before I told her she had to pull herself together because I didn't have the bandwidth to prop us both up. To her credit, she did as I asked and has calmed the hell down. I keep telling her that every doctor I've spoken with believes the surgery will solve the problem, and it's highly unlikely I'll need further treatment after the radiation. I've clung to those assurances as I counted down to this day.

Gage and I decided not to tell the kids about the surgery, because it would only scare them unnecessarily. Afterward, we'll tell them I have a boo-boo, and they need to be gentle with me. That was his idea, and it's a good one. I can't bear to have them worry about losing the only parent they have left. Tyler and Sophia have had friends whose parents had cancer, so they know that's something to be feared.

Hopefully, the entire ordeal will be over in seven weeks, so there's no point in putting those fears in their minds when they're still dealing with the loss of their father.

When Mimi and Stan heard what was going on, they offered to come up and stay with the kids if I wanted to recover for a few days at Gage's place before going home. As much as the kind offer tempted me, I thanked her, but said I would prefer to be home with them afterward.

I don't want to give the kids any reason to worry, and having me home, even with a boo-boo, is what's best for them.

Gage has been amazing through all this. He's left my side only for the time it takes to run home and grab more clothes and to hit the grocery store. He's taken on the laundry and far more of his share of the homework-helping, toy-picking-up and bath-supervising. He's fit right into our family like he's always been there, and his ability to spot a need before it happens has given me respite from my worries, along with his solid presence and the regular reminders that I'm going to be okay.

He's standing by my bed when the anesthesiologist comes in to go over his plan. "You've already got the IV, so you won't feel a thing in the OR. The next time I see you after that, you'll be in recovery. Have you had general anesthesia before?"

"Once, when I had my appendix out."

"Did you feel sick afterward?"

"I was throwing up."

He produces a small patch that he places behind my ear. "That'll prevent nausea after the fact. I'll see you in the OR."

I get a text from Roni. *Derek and I are thinking of you and praying for the quickest, easiest procedure ever and that you'll be past this in no time at all. Love you so much! Xoxo*

That's followed by good wishes and prayers from all the Wild Widows, which means someone sent a reminder to the group that my surgery is today.

Wynter's note makes us laugh. *You better not turn this into a big deal, because if you do, I'll never forgive you. Love you.*

"Leave it to our Wynter," Gage says, smiling.

"She's the best." She's in her second week of nannying for Xavier, and Adrian has done nothing but sing her praises. We're so happy it's working out well for them.

"They're ready for you in the OR," my nurse says when she returns to the room.

Gage leans over to kiss me. "You've got this, you hear me?"

"I do. I've got this."

"Love you."

"Love you, too."

"I'll be right here waiting for you."

I nod because I'm too choked up to speak. As I'm wheeled to the operating room, I say every prayer I remember from childhood that this is truly a quick and simple thing and not the start of a terrible ordeal.

GAGE

IRIS'S NURSE directs me to the surgical waiting room, where the doctor will find me after the procedure is complete. She signed paperwork to make me her contact person. I have the numbers of everyone who needs to be updated after the fact. Her mom wanted to be here, but Iris pleaded with her to stay with the kids, to keep things as normal as possible for them.

I've promised to call her the second I hear anything from the doctor.

A few minutes after I settle in with my iPad, planning to scan the morning headlines, Roni and Derek appear with a tray of coffee and a white bag.

"We brought refreshments," she says as they sit on either side of me.

"What're you guys doing here? It's a workday. The White House won't be able to function without you."

"We took the day off to hang with you and help with the kids or anything else that's needed," Derek says.

"You guys…"

"We couldn't let you sit here alone, Gage." Roni puts her hand on my arm. "Now drink your coffee and eat your scone."

"You got me a scone?"

"Dude, we know what you love."

"I love you two." Their kindness nearly breaks me. My composure has been wavering all morning as I struggled to not show Iris how worried I am for her. "I hope you know that."

"We do. And we love you and Iris right back. That's why we're here."

"Now eat your scone," Derek says. "That'll make everything better."

He no sooner says that than Joy comes around the corner with another tray of coffee and a white bag.

"Damn, you had the same idea," she says when she sees Roni and Derek on either side of me. "Let me guess. Scones?"

"You know it, girlfriend," Roni says. "Our guy is a bit predictable that way."

"Thanks for coming, Joy."

"Where else would I be when our girl is in surgery?"

She sits with us, and I eat a second scone because I can't resist them, and it gives me something to do.

Adrian comes in next, followed by Lexi and Brielle and then Kinsley and Naomi, who seemingly came together. I'm not at all surprised when Christy shows up a few minutes later, bearing yet another bag of scones. Wait until Iris hears they all took the day off to be here for her—and me.

"In case I forget to tell you, the Wild Widows are the best."

"We know," Joy says. "Through thick and thin, right?"

"Yeah." I'm choked up all over again. "For sure."

They told me to expect the surgery to take an hour, so when the clock goes past that mark, I start to worry. Before I can work myself up, Wynter comes into the waiting room with Xavier strapped to her chest.

"I thought you said you weren't coming?" Adrian says to her.

"I lied."

"Nothing like a nanny who lies," he says as the rest of us laugh.

"I wasn't sure I could handle being here, to be honest," Wynter says. "The smell brings it all back."

"Girl..." Kinsley nods knowingly. "The fucking smell."

"I hate that smell more than baby poop," Wynter says, making us laugh, as she does so effortlessly.

When the surgeon appears, he seems taken aback by the gathering. "Am I missing a party?"

"These are Iris's people," I tell him. "You can give us all the report." I have no doubt she would approve.

"She did great. It was very routine, as expected. We did sentinel node biopsies on the lymph nodes to check for spread, and we should have those results in a week or so. She'll be in recovery for about an hour to an hour and a half, and then you should be able to take her home. The nurse will come find you when you can see her."

"Thanks, Doc." I'm overwhelmed with gratitude that it's over and she did so well. Not that there was any doubt. My Iris is a trouper.

"Well, that's a fucking relief," Wynter says, summing it up for all of us.

Indeed, it is.

IRIS

I'm loopy from the anesthesia, but other than an ache in my breast, I feel surprisingly fine after the surgery. More than anything, I'm relieved to hear it went so well. I've spent some time online in recent weeks, reading breast cancer forums, and from what I've seen, the radiation is worse than the surgery. I'm not looking forward to that, but I've got two weeks before that starts, and I'm determined not to obsess about it.

The kids are downstairs doing homework, with my parents supervising. They gave me gentle hugs and kisses when I got home and had lots of questions about my boo-boo, which I answered with as little information as possible.

I couldn't believe it when Gage told me the Wild Widows took the day off to be with him in the waiting room. They asked if they could bring dinner over, and we gratefully accepted.

I'm in my room, trying to nap before they come, but my mind is racing with so many thoughts. Chief among them is an overabundance of gratitude.

Gage tiptoes in to check on me, and when he sees I'm awake, he sits on the edge of the bed. "Why aren't you sleeping?"

"My brain won't shut down." I hold out a hand to him. "Come lie with me."

He moves carefully to stretch out on the bed, keeping my hand tucked into his. "What're you thinking about?"

"How funny life can be."

"How so?"

"If I hadn't crawled naked into bed with you—accidentally, of course..."

"Of course," he says with a chuckle.

"You might never have found that lump in time to stop it from turning into something far more serious. I'd like to say I was diligent about the breast self-exams but being the single mom to three kids means a lot of things get overlooked. That's one of them."

"I'm so thankful it was found early."

"I'm thankful to *you* for finding it."

"I'm thankful to *you* for crawling accidentally naked into my bed."

"The naked part wasn't accidental."

"Whatever you say, love. I'm thankful for all of it."

"How about the Wild Widows showing up in force today?"

"And they say it wasn't even planned."

"They're the best friends I've ever had in my entire life."

"Same."

"They know how fragile life can be, so they show up for the people they love. They show up, and they bring all the love and comfort you need to get through anything."

"And the scones. I couldn't believe when they came in one after the other, as if it was no big deal to rearrange their schedules to be with us."

"When I first lost Mike, all I could see was the darkness. The years ahead stretched before me like a barren wasteland. I couldn't imagine then the blessings that would come from the grief."

"Same. I wouldn't wish Nat and the girls gone for anything,

but I've been surprised to find that the journey from loss hasn't been all bleak terribleness. There's also been startling joy and new love and incredible friends who've held me up during the tough times and made me laugh during the good times."

"Life goes on."

"I'm very thankful my new life includes you," he says, leaning in to kiss me.

"Same." I wrap my hand around his. "When are you officially moving in?"

"That's up to you."

"Today would be good."

"Then today it is."

TODAY IS my last day of radiation and hopefully my last day ever of treatment for any kind of breast cancer. Radiation has sucked every bit as badly as I was told it would. I have seeping blisters on heat-ravaged skin. Gage and I have jokingly equated my radiated breast to boiled chicken. If you don't laugh, you cry. So, we've done a lot of laughing.

He's waiting for me when I come out of the treatment area, bearing my certificate of completion. "Let me see."

I hand him the certificate.

"We're gonna frame that bad boy."

"I'd rather burn it and never think of it again."

"That works, too."

After I say goodbye and good luck to the people I've seen here every day for the last five weeks, Gage puts his arm around me and leads me out of there for the last time.

"Thank you, Jesus," I say when we step into the cold winter air. "Me and my boiled chicken have had more than enough of that place."

Gage holds the door to the passenger side of his SUV for me and leans in to carefully buckle me.

Seat belts have been a problem for my sore breast lately.

Then he kisses me. "This is a full-fledged kidnapping, my love."

"What is?"

"The rest of today, tonight and all day tomorrow until kid-pickup time."

"Seriously?"

"Yep. It's all arranged. Your parents are staying at the house tonight while we celebrate the end of treatment and the first day of the rest of our lives."

I respond with a giddy laugh. "Have I told you yet today that you are the awesomest?"

"I don't think you have."

"Well, you are, and I love you so, so much."

"I love you, too."

"I don't have any clothes!"

"I packed for you."

I shoot him a skeptical look. "You packed for me?"

"Yep, and I expect I totally fucked it up, but we'll see."

"Eh, who cares? All I need is you and a bed to be happy."

"I was sort of counting on that when I packed for you."

"This might be the best day ever."

"And it's only going to get better before it's over." He kisses me one more time and then closes my door to go around to the driver's side.

"Where are we going?"

"You'll see."

I love this mysterious, excited version of him and marvel at the changes in him, as I do daily, since he decided to go all in with me and the kids. He's been incredible during my treatments, which left me fatigued and sore and out of sorts. He was right there to step in as needed with the kids and did almost everything around the house to keep things running smoothly while I was focused on the treatments.

The kids absolutely adore him. Last week, Tyler told him he

wants to call him Daddy Gage instead of Mr. Gage and asked if that would be all right.

Gage blinked away tears as he told my son he'd be honored to be his Daddy Gage.

"I want to call you that, too," Sophia said. "And so does Laney."

"You guys can call me whatever you want," Gage said while looking at me with wonder in his gorgeous eyes.

"Why are you so quiet over there?" he asks as he exits onto Route 1, heading toward Pentagon City.

"I'm thinking about the kids asking if they could call you Daddy Gage."

"One of the single best moments of my entire life."

"You earned it, you know."

"I love them."

"And they love you."

"Look at us becoming a sweet little family." He glances over at me. "I never thought I'd have that again, so thanks for sharing your kids with me."

"My kids and I are happy to have you. So, so happy to have you."

"You're gonna have me, all right."

Laughing, I say, "Thanks for the warning, stud."

A few minutes later, he pulls up to the Ritz-Carlton in Pentagon City. "Here we are!"

"Oh my goodness. The Ritz!"

"Nothing but the best for my baby."

I can recall few times in my life that I've felt as elated as I do right now, knowing the dreaded treatment is behind me and I have twenty-four hours to spend completely alone with my love. I release the seat belt and wince when it brushes against my sore breast. Not even that, however, can dull the joy today.

Gage has two bags hooked over his shoulder when he comes to help me down from the SUV. He knows that some movements can be painful, so he's always there to make things as easy for me as possible.

I'm surprised when we go straight to the elevator. "We don't have to do the check-in?"

"I took care of that earlier. I didn't want to waste one minute of our time alone."

"You thought of everything. Thank you so much for this."

"This day required celebration."

"There are celebrations, and then there's the Ritz!"

When we get to our suite on the top floor, I discover the surprises are only just beginning. There's champagne chilling, and lunch is delivered about five minutes after we arrive. I'm starving, so I devour the chicken Caesar wrap that Gage knows I love and pick at his fries as he eats a burger.

"Next, you need to change into the robe in the closet," he says.

"How come?"

"You'll see."

"Those are becoming my two favorite words after 'love you.'"

His smile lights up his face. "You ain't seen nothing yet, love."

Because he's put so much thought into this getaway, I do what I'm told and change into the robe. Then he does the same, which further surprises me. A minute later, there's a knock on the door. Gage admits two women carrying massage tables.

I let out a squeak of excitement that makes him laugh. "Good surprise?"

"Yessssss. The best."

"They brought a special device that they use for people who've been through treatment, so you can lie face down."

I'm brought nearly to tears by his thoughtfulness. "I can't believe you thought of everything."

"We can't have the boiled chicken ruining a perfectly good massage."

"No," I say, laughing. "We can't have that." I look around

him at the two attractive women who are erecting side-by-side tables for us. "You'd better not enjoy having her hands on you."

"I'll hate every minute of it just for you."

"Excellent."

The massage is heavenly. I haven't been this relaxed in years, since before I lost Mike and had my life turned upside down. The recent health scare gives me even more perspective than I already had about how precious life can be, and I'm determined to live every minute I have left to the fullest.

That's my last thought before my therapist is gently shaking me awake. I can't believe I fell asleep!

"Wow, you're a magician," I tell her. Every part of my body feels loose and limber. For the first time in weeks, the tight knot of stress I've carried at the base of my neck is gone. "Thank you so much."

"Our pleasure."

Gage tips them and walks them to the door, adding his thanks.

"That robe is super sexy on you," I say with a giggle.

"Not as sexy as that robe is on you."

I hook a finger through the belt on his and bring him closer to me. "That was wonderful. Thank you."

"You're welcome. I wanted you nice and relaxed for the next phase of our program."

"What phase is that?"

"The naked one."

"Oh, I like that one."

The massage therapists had drawn the blinds in the suite, but there's just enough light peeking through to cast a warm glow over the space as Gage walks me backward toward the bedroom.

"Should we shower off the oil, so we don't end up buying the Ritz new sheets?"

"We'll keep the robes under us."

"Oh, good plan."

He unties my belt and removes the robe, spreading it out behind me. "Have a seat, love," he says as he kneels before me.

I like where this is going, especially when he guides my legs onto his shoulders and moves in for the kill. Dear God, the man is gifted in the oral department. Hell, he's gifted in all the departments. I'm so relaxed from the massage that he's able to coax a quick, powerful orgasm from me with only a few strategic strokes of his talented tongue.

"You got another one for me?"

I hold out my arms to him. "Only if you come with me."

He stands, wipes his face on the sleeve of the robe and then removes it.

I enjoy watching the way his muscles flex as he moves, coming down on top of me.

"Hi there." He smiles down at me as he holds himself up, so he doesn't touch my sore breast.

"How're you doing?"

"Much better than I have for the last seven weeks, when my best girl was going through some shit. But she's gonna to be fine now, and that's the only thing that matters."

"Not the only thing…"

"The most important thing, because I love her so, so much, and I can't bear to see her suffer."

I reach up to frame his one-in-a-million face and bring him down for a kiss.

As he has been throughout my recovery and treatment, he's super gentle with me and touches me only with the utmost reverence. "Thank you for being my rock through it all."

After his initial freak-out, he's never wavered in his devotion to me and the kids.

"There's nowhere I want to be but wherever you are—and the kids."

"That makes us very, very lucky."

"I'm the lucky one."

"We all are, and we're going to stay that way."

As he makes sweet love to me, I'm more content than I've been in years, with the future stretching before us with so much hope, love and joy, all things that have been in short supply for both of us since we lost our loved ones.

We shiver as we come together, straining to eke out every ounce of pleasure we can get before the moment passes and we're left in the cozy aftermath with nothing to do and nowhere to be.

Gage withdraws from me, slides his arms under me, settles me under the covers and then gets in next to me, putting his arm around me. "How're you feeling?"

"Tired, sore, blissful, relaxed, happy, optimistic." I look over at him. "Madly in love."

"I like that last one."

"I thought you might."

"I like it the best because I'm right there with you, sweetheart. You and your sweet kids have given me a second chance I never could've imagined for myself until you crawled into my bed —deliberately, I might add—and showed me how much living I still had left to do."

"Are you accusing me of deception?"

"I am. You're a bald-faced liar, and your pants are on fire."

"That is just not true!"

We'll "argue" about this for the rest of our lives, and I'm here for that. I'm here for all of it.

"I was thinking about something else," he says, his expression serious.

"What's that?"

"I might be up for another kid or maybe two, if you are."

"Really? I thought you said that ship has sailed for you."

"I thought so until it occurred to me that Tyler, Sophia and Laney would be such incredible older siblings. I'd sort of like to see that."

"Wow."

"But only if you want it, too."

"I'd need to consult with my doctors because pregnancy can be troublesome for certain kinds of breast cancer."

"It's completely off the table if there's any risk of that."

"We'll see what they say and go from there, but I'm not opposed." I give a little laugh. "A year ago, the thought of more kids would've been a huge nope, but now... Anything seems possible, doesn't it?"

"Anything and everything."

"I want you to write that book."

"I'm already working on it."

"You are? When can I see it?"

"Soon."

"Are you writing about me and us?"

"Some. Is that okay?"

"Sure, that's fine with me."

"Don't worry. I won't write about how you shamelessly seduced me into this whole new life."

I smack his shoulder. "It wasn't shameless, and you love your new life."

"Yes," he says with a sigh. "I sure do."

Epilogue

GAGE

"My name is Gage Collier, and my wife, Natasha, and twin eight-year-old daughters, Ivy and Hazel, were killed when Mr. Previn chose to get behind the wheel of a car after he'd been drinking 'all day,' by his own admission." I've been dreading this day for weeks, but now that it's upon me, I feel only determination to see it through and to speak for Natasha, Ivy and Hazel.

"His friends tried to stop him from leaving, but he wouldn't be stopped or talked out of driving a three-thousand-pound vehicle while impaired. A few weeks prior, Mr. Previn's wife of twelve years had left him and taken their children with her because, in her words, 'his drinking had gotten out of control.' I saw that on a social media post she made after the accident in which she talked about how she'd tried desperately to convince him to enter rehab and get his life in order before it was too late. Mr. Previn is the lucky one here. His wife and children were able to leave before his alcoholism cost them everything.

"My wife and daughters weren't so fortunate. They were coming from the dress rehearsal for their holiday dance recital.

283

The girls were in high spirts and excited for the big show that was to be the next night. My wife, Natasha, sent me photos and videos from the dress rehearsal. When I received them, I had no idea they'd be the last photos or videos I'd ever have of my beautiful, talented, sweet, loving girls. I've looked at them a thousand times since that dreadful night when the police came to my door to tell me my wife and children had been killed in a wrong-way crash.

"It's hard to describe what happens to a person when they receive news like that. The best way I can put it is, everything stops. Everything just stops. Life as you know it is over forever. Nothing is ever the same. The three most important people in your world are gone, and they're never coming back."

Behind me, I hear Mimi's sniffles, even as I struggle to maintain my own composure. I'm determined to get through this without breaking down.

"Ivy was brilliant. She was reading before she was four and knew her multiplication tables through twelve by the time she was six. She loved to read and learn and ask questions about anything and everything. We called her the sponge. She was always acquiring new knowledge. Hazel was our artist. She could draw or paint anything and was usually lost in her own world, creating her latest masterpiece. She had a beautiful singing voice and had been asked to sing in the choir at our church on Christmas Eve. She'd practiced 'O Holy Night' so many times that Nat and I were hearing it in our dreams, but her rendition was glorious. Both girls were exceptional dancers and had attracted attention from talent scouts. Who knows how far their many talents could've taken them?"

I'm gratified to realize the defendant is weeping. He ought to be.

"Natasha was a dedicated nurse, a loving wife, mother and daughter, her parents' only child. She was a friend to more people than most of us meet in a lifetime. She regularly heard from patients she'd had years ago who wanted to check in with her and let her know they were doing well. I received two thousand cards after she died, many from people whose names I didn't recognize, but they were all in the contacts on her phone with notes about her dealings with them. That was my Nat, the girl of my dreams who became the most incredible nurse and mother. Our girls adored her. She was the sun around which we all orbited as she took care of everyone in her life.

He looked directly at Previn. "These are the people you took from me, my family, Natasha's family, their friends, coworkers and fellow dancers. The Christmas recital was canceled because the other girls were too heartbroken to go on without Hazel and Ivy. So many hearts were broken because of your actions, Mr. Previn.

"Natasha's parents and I spent hours talking about what sort of punishment would be 'enough' for us. We talked about what charges would be enough, and for many months, we fought for vehicular homicide charges because we felt that most accurately reflected the crime. You got into that car knowing you had no business driving that night, and you did it anyway. You ended up driving the wrong way on the interstate, plowing into my wife's car at full speed and instantly killing her and our girls. If that isn't the very definition of vehicular homicide, I don't know what is.

"We've accepted the deal in which you've pleaded guilty to the lesser charge of vehicular manslaughter, but please know, we did that only to avoid a trial, not because we don't think you're guilty of homicide. You killed my family, and I hope you think of them and what you took from them, from me, from everyone who loved them every second for the rest of your life.

"Thank you, Your Honor, for the opportunity to address the court."

"Thank you, Mr. Collier, and please accept the court's condolences for your tragic loss."

I leave the podium and go to sit between Iris and Mimi, taking a hand from each of them and holding on as the judge announces the sentence and sends Previn off with the sheriff's deputies.

"I thought I'd feel some closure after that," I say after he's been escorted from the room.

"Is there any such thing?" Mimi asks.

"Your words were powerful, Gage, and your girls would be proud of you," Iris says.

"I suppose that's what matters, right?"

"That's all that matters," Mimi says. "That we make them proud of us every day."

"I have no doubt they are," Iris says. "No doubt at all."

IRIS

"CAN you believe where we're going?" I ask Gage the Sunday after his victim impact statement. He's been quiet and withdrawn since that day, and I'm hoping that today's outing might help to give him something else to think about. I'm still trying to bounce back from radiation-induced exhaustion, which has been kicking my ass, but I wouldn't have missed today's outing.

"It's surreal that we have friends who work at the White House," he says, "and that their friend the first lady invited us over for tea."

"I'm so excited to tour the White House and meet her. I think she's the coolest person ever. That she chases murderers, too, is amazing."

"She does seem pretty cool."

My parents took the kids to the movies and dinner, so they're having a fun outing while we hobnob with the first lady. "I wonder if the president will be there, too."

"Roni only promised her, so don't get your hopes up."

"I'll try not to."

"And don't embarrass me by drooling on him or something if you do meet him."

As I laugh, I'm relieved to hear him crack a joke. I've been so worried about him the last few days. "I'll try to maintain some decorum, but that may be difficult. Our president looks like a movie star."

"Whatever," he says, rolling his eyes as he and the other guys have done every time the Wild Widows have discussed this day and how we hope we might get to meet the "ridiculously hot" president.

"When was the last time we had a guy roughly our age in the White House?" I ask him.

"Like, the sixties?"

"Exactly. So let us have our fun."

"Just remember that his wife carries a gun, and she's probably not afraid to use it when a band of wild widows is ogling her husband."

"That's true. She is rather possessive of him."

"And you know that how?"

"I've been a fan of theirs for years. I had a party for all my mom friends on the day of their wedding. We watched it with more excitement than we did the royal wedding."

"Are you serious?"

"Very serious. My friends and I are in love with the two of them. When he became president... We lost our minds. We *love* them."

"Wow. I had no idea."

"It's funny because I'd kind of lost track of my mom friends for a while after everything happened, but him becoming president brought us back together, which is nice. Our group text was on fire for days after Nelson died."

"You're like a bunch of teenage girls."

I can't deny that, so I don't try. "Yes, we are."

"Now, I'm scared to take you to the White House."

"Ha! I promise to be on my very best behavior if I happen to see *him*, but we love her just as much. A few of my mom friends have said they'd switch teams for her."

"You think you know a girl..."

"And then you find out she's secretly in love with the president."

"Yes. This is deeply disturbing."

"Aw, baby, you know I love you the very bestest."

"Do I, though?"

"Yes!" I love to laugh and tease with him, and it's a relief to be doing that again after a quiet few days. "Of course I love you the most, even more than the president, which should make you feel honored."

"I'm *so* honored."

His tone drips with sarcasm. "As well you should be."

Roni and Derek are waiting for us at the gate when we arrive at the White House. The freaking White House. My mom friends are so jealous, they may never speak to me again. I told them widowhood has its privileges, which is rarely true. Today, however, it's very true.

After we park and join the others, who have gathered outside until everyone arrives, Roni and Derek bring us visitor badges and lead us into a reception area, where we're greeted by the first lady and the chief usher, Gideon Lawson.

Dressed in black dress pants, boots and a plum-colored turtleneck sweater, Samantha Holland Cappuano shakes hands with each of us as Roni introduces us and is incredibly warm and welcoming. I can't believe I'm three feet from her and that she's even prettier than she appears in the media. "Please, call me Sam," she says.

"Breathe," Gage whispers to me, nearly making me giggle.

"Gideon gives a much better tour than I do," Sam says. "So let's follow him, and he'll show you around the public spaces before we go upstairs to the residence."

We visit so many rooms, the names of them run together—China, Vermeil, Roosevelt, East, State, Map. We pop into the East Wing offices of the first lady before crossing over to check out the West Wing and the Oval Office.

Sam knocks on the door to the Oval and ducks her head in. "Ready for some visitors?" She waves for us to follow her inside, where the president himself stands and comes around the Resolute desk to greet us.

It's all I can do to hold back my squeal of excitement.

"Remember your decorum," Gage whispers.

I'm dying. He's *right there*, and oh my Lord, he's handsome in a navy-blue sweater and well-worn jeans. When he shakes my hand, I nearly faint.

The first couple poses for photos with our group, taken by the official White House photographer.

"This is amazing," Joy says. "Thank you so much for having us."

"Any friends of Derek's and Roni's are friends of ours," the president says.

Did you hear that? I'm a *friend* of the president and first lady!

They point out the Rose Garden as we cut through the West Colonnade to the residence. I can't believe I'm seeing things I've only ever seen on TV. We go up a flight of red-carpeted stairs to the second floor to tour the Lincoln Bedroom and the first family's private quarters.

As we head up to the third floor, a yellow dog comes flying up the stairs, sprinting ahead of us and nearly taking out Lexi.

"Scotty!" The president's bellow echoes through the stairway. "Get Skippy!"

"Sorry about that." The first couple's handsome, dark-haired son chases after the dog. "She's out of control."

We're delighted to meet the first dog and the first son, both of whom are nearly as famous as the president and first lady. In the conservatory, which we learn is the family's favorite gathering spot in the White House, a table full of refreshments has been set out by the staff.

"Please help yourselves to some treats," the first lady says. "The White House bake shop is incredible, and I have five new pounds to prove it."

I love that she's so *real*.

After we help ourselves to the little sandwiches and baked goods, we sit together on sofas and the extra chairs that were brought in to accommodate our group. The White House staff takes drink orders and delivers tea, coffee, soda and water.

"I'm so happy you all could come to visit today," Sam says. "Roni has told me about your group, and I think it's wonderful the way you support each other."

"Iris and Christy were the founders along with another woman, but the two of them have kept it going," Gage said. "We have them to thank for it."

"Well done, ladies," the president says, smiling.

It's all I can do not to swoon from the power of that smile directed at me.

"We'd love to hear more about all of you and your stories," Sam says. "If you'd like to share, that is."

"We're good at sharing," Joy says in her typically blunt fashion.

Each of us gives a one-sentence summary of the incident that brought us together. The first couple's compassion nearly brings me to tears more than once. An hour has never gone by so quickly as we talk and laugh with them like old friends. Scotty brings Alden and Aubrey, the twins the Cappuanos took in last fall, up to meet us, and it strikes me that they, too, have experienced incredible tragedy, losing their parents in a home invasion and fire.

As we make our way downstairs to leave, I'm more in love with the first couple than I was before. "How will I ever summarize this experience for my friends?" I ask Gage when we're back in the car headed home.

"They were great," he says. "I feel like I could be friends with both of them."

"Yes! Exactly. I loved them even more than I expected to. I like that they didn't get all dressed up for us and were so down-to-earth."

"They're ordinary people living an extraordinary life."

"Indeed. This was such a perfect day. I'll never forget it."

ONE OF THE greatest surprises to come out of my recent health woes has been the friendship extended to me by Eleanor, the mother of Mike's son Carter. After my surgery, she checked on me daily, sent a lovely basket of food and treats for me and the kids and has—remarkably—become a new friend.

Just when I think life can't get any stranger...

Eleanor and Carter are coming to visit, and they're going to stay with us.

Before they get here, I need to talk to the kids and tell them who Carter is to them. I've gone round and round about this decision, talked for hours with their therapist and every friend who has young children and have concluded that telling them about Carter now would be less traumatic for them than introducing him later as their half brother.

As I've worked my way through this dilemma, my resentment for Mike has grown exponentially. How dare he leave me to clean up his gigantic mess on my own? Although, the more I get to know Eleanor and care about Carter, who is adorable, the less it becomes about Mike and his mess and the more it becomes about me, my kids and new friends/family.

Bizarre, right? Sometimes I have to laugh because I couldn't have made this up if I tried, me becoming friends with my late husband's mistress as we navigate the thorny path of bringing our children together.

Eleanor is a lovely person. Her son, who I've "met" through pictures and videos and the occasional FaceTime call, is delightful. There's no downside to having them in our lives, and that's why I've invited her to come to our home, to stay with us and give our kids a chance to get to know one another.

"You ready for this?" Gage asks as he joins me at the kitchen table for early-morning coffee.

The kids will be up soon, and I told him I needed caffeine to face this conversation. We decided to do it in the morning when they're well rested. They tend to get crankier as the day goes on, as do I, so doing it now presents our best chance before Eleanor and Carter arrive this afternoon.

Tyler comes down first, followed shortly after by his sisters. I serve the pancakes I made earlier and join them at the table with Gage.

"So, guys, I wanted to tell you something exciting."

"What?" Tyler asks around a mouthful of pancake.

"It turns out that you have another brother, and his name is Carter." I pause to let that settle with them.

"We have another brother?" Sophia asks, glancing at Tyler as she often does to gauge his reaction.

"Where did he come from?" Tyler asks.

"He's Daddy's son, so that makes him your half brother."

"Why did Daddy have another son?" Tyler asks, his chin quivering. "He had me."

"Oh, sweetie, it had nothing to do with you. Sometimes these things just happen, but Daddy loved you so much. You were his pride and joy." I wish I could stab Mike through the heart for doing this to us. Over these recent months, I've managed to compartmentalize what Mike did and keep it separate from Eleanor and Carter. I don't blame them for his transgressions.

"Where is our brother?" Sophia asks.

"He's on his way to see us right now. He and his mom, Eleanor, are coming to visit for a few days so you guys can get to know each other."

"I don't want to know him," Tyler says, his chin still quivering.

"You should give him a chance," Gage says. "He might turn out to be your best friend."

"He won't," Tyler says. "I don't want a brother."

"I want a brother," Laney says. "Will he play with me?"

"I'm sure he will," I tell her, thankful for her sweet innocence. "I know this is a lot to understand, but all you need to know is that you and Carter had the same daddy, and he's a very nice boy. I think you'll like him a lot."

"Have you met him?" Sophia asks.

"Only through FaceTime and photos his mom has sent me. He's very sweet and funny, and he loves to play baseball, just like you do, Ty."

At that, Tyler perks up ever so slightly. I'm hoping that once Carter arrives, Tyler will see only someone new to play with and not a potential rival.

The girls finish their breakfast, clear their plates and run off to watch Dora while Tyler sits staring out the window, looking as if he has the weight of the world on his little shoulders.

"I want to know how Daddy had another son," he says, his gaze shifting to me. "Mommies and daddies are supposed to have children with each other. Not other people."

"You're right," I tell him, following the therapist's advice to give the smallest amount of information necessary to bring Carter into their lives. "They are."

"Are you mad with Daddy because he had another son?"

"I was, but after I got to know Eleanor and Carter, I don't blame them for mistakes that Daddy made, and you shouldn't either."

"Was Daddy a bad man?"

"No, honey. He was human, and human beings make mistakes. Sometimes they make big mistakes that hurt other people, but Daddy loved you and your sisters, and he loved Carter. He would want you two to be friends."

"He would?"

"Yeah, I really think he would. Maybe you can try to be friends with Carter?"

He shrugs. "I guess." He gets up and takes his plate to the sink before leaving the room.

I drop my head into my hands.

Gage massages my shoulder. "You did good, Mama."

"Then why do I feel like my insides have been lacerated?"

"Because Tyler is old enough to understand the implications of this news, and it hurt him to find out his daddy wasn't perfect."

"I suppose that's it." I cover his hand on the table with mine. "Thank you for stepping in to help."

"I wish there was more I could do."

"Just having you here helps."

"Nowhere else I'd rather be."

HOURS LATER, Gage, Eleanor and I supervise the kids in the backyard as they run around and play on the gigantic play set Mike and Rob built years ago. After some initial reluctance, Tyler has been trying to be friendly to his brother.

"This is such a wonderful yard," Eleanor says. "It must be fun when the pool is open."

"It is. The kids love to swim."

"Carter does, too. It's his favorite thing."

She is tall, blonde and willowy—everything I'm not. She's the kind of woman you'd love to hate if she wasn't so damned nice. When they arrived, she greeted me with a warm hug and said it was so great to finally meet me in person. Right away, she felt like an old friend who'd come to visit after years apart.

After dinner, Gage lights the firepit, and even though it's cold, we make s'mores for the kids before sending them inside to start taking showers.

"I'll show you where things are," Tyler says to Carter, who follows Tyler around with interest bordering on hero worship.

"I'll supervise," Gage says as he follows them in.

"Tyler and the girls have been great with Carter," Eleanor says when we're left alone by the fire. "I wasn't sure what to expect, but today has been lovely. Thank you for having us."

"Thanks for coming and for making what should be the most awkward thing in my life so easy."

"It's not our fault we're in this boat. All we can do is make the best of it. At least that's what my therapist tells me."

"Same, girl," I tell her as we share a laugh. "Life is such a fucked-up mess of awful, wonderful, tragic, joyful. I get whiplash sometimes from feeling all those things in the same five-minute period."

"Right there with you, although I can't begin to know what it was like to lose my husband and the father of my children and then find out the things you have about him. I hate that for you."

"I hate it for me, too, and for my kids, who will one day wake up to the realization of what had to happen to bring Carter into their lives. Widowhood has taught me that all we can do is play the hand we were dealt, and that's what I'm trying to do."

"You're doing it beautifully, and your Gage is such a lovely guy. I'm happy for you both."

"Thanks. He's the best, and we're enjoying our chapter two."

"Chapter two. I like that."

"That's widow-speak for a second chance at love."

"It's wonderful, and I couldn't be happier for you."

"What about you? Are you seeing anyone?"

"Not really. Trust has become a big issue for me, as you might imagine, and it seems that every guy I meet is hiding something or just generally full of shit. I'd rather be alone than put up with that crap."

"I'm sorry Mike did that to you."

"I'm sorry for what he did to you."

"Eh, fuck him," I say with a laugh that gets her laughing, too.

"For sure, but let's be thankful for the wonderful kids he left us with."

"I can drink to that."

She touches her glass to mine. "Cheers to great kids."

GAGE

THE KIDS ARE CHARGED up after an exciting day, but they manage to get their showers done and change into pajamas. Carter is sleeping on the trundle bed we pulled out from under Tyler's bed, and Tyler has been great about showing him where everything is and asking if he needs another pillow. He's gone from rejecting Carter to accepting him in the span of a few hours, which doesn't surprise me. Tyler has a great big loving heart, and I had a feeling he'd soften once he met his brother. Although, I can't pretend to know what it would be like to find out you have a half brother a year and a half younger than you when you're seven.

Iris was right to take care of this now when the kids are innocent enough not to ask too many questions. I have no doubt there'll be questions later when they put the pieces together, but for now, Carter is someone new for them to love, and the three of them have made me proud today.

My phone rings with a call from Adrian. Since the kids are all in their rooms, I take the call. "Hey, what's up?"

"Gage... I can't find Wynter and Xavier. I got home an hour ago, and they weren't here. She's not answering her phone. I checked the park and all their usual places, but she's nowhere to be found. I don't know what to do. If I call the cops, this becomes a big deal, and I don't know..."

He's on the verge of hysteria. "Try to stay calm. I'll be right there."

"Thank you."

―――――

THANK you for reading Iris and Gage's Wild Widows story! I'm having the best time with this wonderful new cast of characters. They make me want to know what happens next! Watch for

Adrian's story in 2023, which may or may not include Wynter. We shall see!

Join the Someone to Hold Reader Group at *www.facebook.com/groups/someonetohold/* and the Wild Widows Series Group at *www.facebook.com/groups/thewildwidowsseries/*. After Roni and Derek's story, SOMEONE LIKE YOU, was released earlier this year, it became clear we also needed a place where readers could share their own grief journeys. You can find that group here: *www.facebook.com/groups/wwsupportgroup1*. Everyone is welcome to join this group, regardless of what type of loss you're coping with. Thank you to everyone who has written to me to share their widow journeys since SOMEONE LIKE YOU released. It means a lot to me that you share your personal stories with me.

A huge shout out to my team, who makes everything possible: Julie Cupp, Lisa Cafferty, Jean Mello, Nikki Haley and Ashley Lopez. Thank you to Dani Sanchez and Wildfire Marketing, my editors, Linda Ingmanson and Joyce Lamb, as well as my front-line beta readers Anne Woodall, Kara Conrad and Tracey Suppo, and continuity assistant, Gwen Neff.

Thank you to the Wild Widows Beta Readers: Jennifer, Mona, Jennifer and Gina.

Finally, thank you to all the readers who come with me anywhere the muse sends us, and who've welcomed this new series with such open arms and generous hearts. Love you all!

Xoxo

Marie

Also by Marie Force

Romantic Suspense Novels Available from Marie Force

The Fatal Series

One Night With You, *A Fatal Series Prequel Novella*

Book 1: Fatal Affair

Book 2: Fatal Justice

Book 3: Fatal Consequences

Book 3.5: Fatal Destiny, *the Wedding Novella*

Book 4: Fatal Flaw

Book 5: Fatal Deception

Book 6: Fatal Mistake

Book 7: Fatal Jeopardy

Book 8: Fatal Scandal

Book 9: Fatal Frenzy

Book 10: Fatal Identity

Book 11: Fatal Threat

Book 12: Fatal Chaos

Book 13: Fatal Invasion

Book 14: Fatal Reckoning

Book 15: Fatal Accusation

Book 16: Fatal Fraud

Sam and Nick's Story Continues....

Book 1: State of Affairs

Book 2: State of Grace

Book 3: State of the Union

Book 4: State of Shock

Contemporary Romances Available from Marie Force

The Wild Widows Series—a Fatal Series Spin-Off

Book 1: Someone Like You

Book 2: Someone to Hold

Contemporary Romances Available from Marie Force

The Gansett Island Series

Book 1: Maid for Love *(Mac & Maddie)*

Book 2: Fool for Love *(Joe & Janey)*

Book 3: Ready for Love *(Luke & Sydney)*

Book 4: Falling for Love *(Grant & Stephanie)*

Book 5: Hoping for Love *(Evan & Grace)*

Book 6: Season for Love *(Owen & Laura)*

Book 7: Longing for Love *(Blaine & Tiffany)*

Book 8: Waiting for Love *(Adam & Abby)*

Book 9: Time for Love *(David & Daisy)*

Book 10: Meant for Love *(Jenny & Alex)*

Book 10.5: Chance for Love, *A Gansett Island Novella (Jared & Lizzie)*

Book 11: Gansett After Dark *(Owen & Laura)*

Book 12: Kisses After Dark *(Shane & Katie)*

Book 13: Love After Dark *(Paul & Hope)*

Book 14: Celebration After Dark *(Big Mac & Linda)*

Book 15: Desire After Dark *(Slim & Erin)*

Book 16: Light After Dark *(Mallory & Quinn)*

Book 17: Victoria & Shannon (Episode 1)

Book 18: Kevin & Chelsea (Episode 2)
A Gansett Island Christmas Novella
Book 19: Mine After Dark *(Riley & Nikki)*
Book 20: Yours After Dark *(Finn & Chloe)*
Book 21: Trouble After Dark *(Deacon & Julia)*
Book 22: Rescue After Dark *(Mason & Jordan)*
Book 23: Blackout After Dark *(Full Cast)*
Book 24: Temptation After Dark *(Gigi & Cooper)*
Book 25: Resilience After Dark *(Jace & Cindy)*
Book 26: Hurricane After Dark *(Full Cast)*

The Green Mountain Series
Book 1: All You Need Is Love *(Will & Cameron)*
Book 2: I Want to Hold Your Hand *(Nolan & Hannah)*
Book 3: I Saw Her Standing There *(Colton & Lucy)*
Book 4: And I Love Her *(Hunter & Megan)*
Novella: You'll Be Mine *(Will & Cam's Wedding)*
Book 5: It's Only Love *(Gavin & Ella)*
Book 6: Ain't She Sweet *(Tyler & Charlotte)*

The Butler, Vermont Series
(Continuation of Green Mountain)
Book 1: Every Little Thing *(Grayson & Emma)*
Book 2: Can't Buy Me Love *(Mary & Patrick)*
Book 3: Here Comes the Sun (*Wade & Mia)*
Book 4: Till There Was You *(Lucas & Dani)*
Book 5: All My Loving *(Landon & Amanda)*
Book 6: Let It Be *(Lincoln & Molly)*
Book 7: Come Together *(Noah & Brianna)*
Book 8: Here, There & Everywhere *(Izzy & Cabot)*

Book 9: The Long and Winding Road *(Max & Lexi)*

The Miami Nights Series

Book 1: How Much I Feel *(Carmen & Jason)*

Book 2: How Much I Care *(Maria & Austin)*

Book 3: How Much I Love *(Dee's story)*

Nochebuena, A Miami Nights Novella

Book 4: How Much I Want *(Nico & Sofia)*

Book 5: How Much I Need *(Milo and Gianna)*

The Quantum Series

Book 1: Virtuous *(Flynn & Natalie)*

Book 2: Valorous *(Flynn & Natalie)*

Book 3: Victorious *(Flynn & Natalie)*

Book 4: Rapturous *(Addie & Hayden)*

Book 5: Ravenous *(Jasper & Ellie)*

Book 6: Delirious *(Kristian & Aileen)*

Book 7: Outrageous *(Emmett & Leah)*

Book 8: Famous *(Marlowe & Sebastian)*

The Treading Water Series

Book 1: Treading Water

Book 2: Marking Time

Book 3: Starting Over

Book 4: Coming Home

Book 5: Finding Forever

Single Titles

Five Years Gone

One Year Home

Sex Machine

Sex God

Georgia on My Mind

True North

The Fall

The Wreck

Love at First Flight

Everyone Loves a Hero

Line of Scrimmage

Historical Romance Available from Marie Force

The Gilded Series

Book 1: Duchess by Deception

Book 2: Deceived by Desire

About the Author

Marie Force is the *New York Times* best-selling author of contemporary romance, romantic suspense and erotic romance. Her series include Fatal, First Family, Gansett Island, Butler Vermont, Quantum, Treading Water, Miami Nights and Wild Widows.

Her books have sold more than 12 million copies worldwide, have been translated into more than a dozen languages and have appeared on the *New York Times* bestseller list more than 30 times. She is also a *USA Today* and #1 *Wall Street Journal* bestseller, as well as a Spiegel bestseller in Germany.

Her goals in life are simple—to finish raising two happy, healthy, productive young adults, to keep writing books for as long as she possibly can and to never be on a flight that makes the news.

Join Marie's mailing list on her website at *marieforce.com* for news about new books and upcoming appearances in your area. Follow her on Facebook at *www.Facebook.com/MarieForceAuthor*, Instagram at *www.instagram.com/marieforceauthor/* and TikTok at *https://www.tiktok.com/@marieforceauthor?*. Contact Marie at *marie@marieforce.com*.

Made in United States
North Haven, CT
16 September 2022

24133536R00186